Feyland

The Bright Court

BOOK 2 IN THE FEYLAND TRILOGY

D0873216

ANTHEA SHARP

Feyland: The Bright Court - Copyright 2012 by Anthea Lawrence. To obtain permission to excerpt portions of the text, other than for review purposes, contact antheasharp@hotmail.com or visit the author at www.antheasharp.com.

QUALITY CONTROL: This work has been professionally edited. Still, if you encounter any typos or formatting problems, please contact antheasharp@hotmail.com so they may be corrected.

COVER:
Design – Kimberly Killion, hotdamndesigns.com

ISBN-13: 978-1470182656

ISBN-10: 1470182653

DEDICATION:
For all the gamers in my family – but most especially, for Lawson.

PROLOGUE

The eerie call of a hunting horn floated over the drowsing city, sending sleepers' dreams spiraling into nightmare—or jolting them awake, hearts pounding in sudden terror.

Tam Linn sat upright in the hushed dimness of his hospital room. His breath rasped in his throat, the echo of that fey and terrible noise shuddering through him. Forcing his breathing to slow, he listened intently. Nothing. He slid out of the bed and padded to the window, then slowly pushed aside the curtain.

The dark gray sky arched over the city, the lights of Crestview washing out any stars that might be hovering there. No spectral hounds or horned riders galloped across the night. No faerie magic breaking through into the mortal world.

Yet.

Tam watched a single car navigate the streets beyond the medical center. Soon the city would wake, and he'd finally go home. After three weeks in the hospital, the need to be out of there was severe—jangling his thoughts, burning his nerves. He clenched his hands into weak fists. He was still shaky, but he'd hidden it well enough that the docs had agreed to release him. There wasn't any more time to lose.

Dangerous magic was about to be turned loose in the human world—and he was one of the only people who had a chance of stopping it.

CHAPTER ONE

Tam walked the crowded halls of Crestview High, feeling like an imposter in his own skin. Everything was different, but it was an invisible change—like his brain had been taken out and refolded into a new shape, then stuck back inside the same old packaging.

Being in a coma would do that.

Not to mention being held as a sacrifice by the faeries of the Dark Court, an experience so outside of normal that it still seemed like a fever-dream. But it had happened.

After that, going back to school was so ordinary it was surreal. Other students brushed past, bits of their conversation floating like mist in the air. Nothing felt solid—until he caught sight of a girl with pale blond hair moving toward him against the tide. Jennet Carter. The one person who knew everything he'd been through.

His world clicked into place.

"Tam," she said, giving him a warm smile. "It's great to see you back on your feet."

She reached out like she was going to hug him, and he did a quick side-step. Not that he didn't want her to touch him—a part of him did. But they were friends, against all odds, and that was enough. It had to be.

He tried not to notice her high-end clothing, the perfect sheen of her hair, the expensive tablet peeking out of her bag. Especially tried to ignore the wrist-chip implant that proved she was one of the elite. Jennet had everything going for her, while he…

He glanced down at his worn jeans with the frayed knee, his battered shoes with cracks in the sole. He had a falling-apart family, in a falling-apart house, in the most falling-apart neighborhood in Crestview.

They had nothing in common, except a love of sim gaming—and nearly dying in the Realm of Faerie.

He took a quick look around to make sure no one was listening. "We need to talk, soon. About Feyland."

She nodded, her smile fading. The bell blared, the harsh, metallic sound startling through him. Welcome back to the real world.

"Let's talk at lunch." She stepped forward. "Come on—we don't want to be late to World History. Ms. Lewis might frown at you."

"Oh yeah, scary." The teacher was notoriously soft.

He followed her down the hall, stumbling briefly as a wave of dizziness washed over him.

"Are you sure you're ready to be back in school?" She slowed, her eyes concerned.

"The med techs said I was in decent shape," he said, evading her question. "Besides, I've been gone too many weeks already. If I miss any more school, I'll have to repeat the year."

No way did he want to do extra time at Crestview High. Though maybe it didn't matter—not with the dark creatures of Feyland trying to break through into the mortal world. Who knew if there would even *be* a next year?

"If you say so." Her voice softened. "I was worried about you."

He shot her a sideways glance. "You visited me practically every day in the hospital."

And, weirdly, visited his dreams as well. Did she share those hyper-real visions? Tam felt his cheeks heating, and dipped his head, his hair falling over his eyes. So, he'd imagined kissing Jennet. In dreams. Not real, and he'd better not start thinking they were.

"Seeing you in the hospital…" Jennet's voice was unsteady. She cleared her throat. "Anyway, you're up and walking and, well, you're you again."

He wasn't so sure, but there didn't seem to be words to explain. And even if there were, Ms. Lewis's classroom wasn't the place to go all emo.

"Mr. Linn!" The teacher clasped her hands together and smiled at him as he took his seat. "How wonderful to see you."

He mumbled a greeting, then pulled out his battered school tablet. Luckily, Ms. Lewis's attention was diverted today. She kept glancing at a tall, unfamiliar boy seated in the front row. As soon as the second bell rang, she held up one hand.

"Class—attention, class! I'm pleased to announce we

have a new student here at Crestview High. Mr. Royal Lassiter—oh, do stand up, Roy." She beamed at the new boy. "Tell us a bit about yourself."

An introduction speech. Really? Tam shot a look at Jennet, who raised her eyebrows. Crestview never bothered with things like that. At least, they never had in the past.

The new student stood and turned to face the class. All the girls drew in their breaths, and Tam squinted, trying to see the appeal. Despite his expensively rumpled clothes, Roy Lassiter didn't seem all that special. Reddish-brown hair, angular nose, chin a bit on the weak side. An easy grin lay on his face, but his dark eyes were calculating.

Something glinted at his wrist—a chip implant. He was one of the company kids who lived up at The View. One of the privileged ones, like Jennet.

"Hey, everybody," Roy said. His voice had an odd, hollow timbre. "I know I'm happy to be here, and that I'll make a lot of new friends. Crestview seems pretty sparked. So come up and say hi after class, alright?"

He sat down, and the class applauded. Applauded? Tam shook his head. That was the weakest speech he had ever heard—plus Roy hadn't said anything real about himself. But for some reason everyone was smiling and nodding.

Everyone but Jennet. She had her head down and was scribbling something on her tablet. A second later, the corner of his screen lit up with a private message. He glanced at the front of the classroom, to make sure Ms. Lewis wasn't watching, then clicked the message open.

Roy Lassiter = son of VirtuMax CEO.

Great. Unease shivered down his spine. The new student was hooked into VirtuMax, the company Jennet's dad worked for. The company that was developing the immersive sim game of Feyland. The game that had nearly killed him.

"Sorry I'm late." Jennet slid her lunch tray onto the table across from Tam. She glanced at the front of the cafeteria, where Roy Lassiter was holding court. "Our *dear* new student is in my Lit class, and it took forever to get out of there. You'd think the world revolved around him."

Tam shook his head, his brown hair, as usual, falling over his eyes. Just once, she wished she could brush it back for him—but she could feel him prickle any time she got too close. She let out a soundless sigh. Maybe he just needed time to re-adapt to the real world.

"Well, look who's finally in school again," their friend Marny said, walking up with her lunch. "Welcome back, Tam. Not that Crestview High is anything to celebrate."

He nodded. "It's still better than a hospital bed. And the food here is marginally more edible."

"Hey, Marny," Jennet said, scooting over to make

room.

Marny sat beside her, and Jennet noticed that she shifted until she had a clear view of Crestview's newest student.

"At least there's something interesting going on," Marny said. "Roy Lassiter is in two of my classes. Isn't that great?"

Tam laughed, then stopped when Marny didn't join him. "Wait. You're joking, right?"

"No." She sounded distinctly unamused.

Jennet looked at her. "You're *glad* that he's in two of your classes?"

"I wish it were more." Marny rested her chin in her hand. "Roy Lassiter is flawless."

"What?" Surprise made Jennet's voice higher than usual. She glanced at Tam, to see the same confusion on his face.

Marny wasn't one to follow the crowd. She was unapologetic about who she was—big and smart and completely blunt in expressing her thoughts. The kind of person who would deliberately turn around to swim against the tide, rather than be carried along by the current.

"Roy Lassiter. Have you ever seen hair that color?" Marny's voice was dreamy—shockingly different from her usual no-nonsense tone.

"You mean, brown?" Tam asked. He waved his hand in front of her eyes. "Wake up, Marny. He's just average-looking. What's wrong with you?"

"It's ok to be jealous," Marny said. "I'm sure all the guys are—how could you not be?"

Jennet traded a worried look with Tam. The bite of roll she'd taken was suddenly too dry, and she washed it down with a long swallow of water.

"So," Tam said, turning to her, "the new student is a Viewer? Have you seen him up there at the company compound?"

"No, but I've been," —*mad with worry for you*— "a little busy, you know." She'd spent every hour she could with Tam in the hospital, whether he was conscious or not. "My dad said the CEO had finally moved in, and her son was my age. I didn't think much about it." Clearly, she should have.

"Ask your dad more," Tam said, an edge in his voice.

"Oh, yes." Marny turned her usually sharp brown eyes on Jennet. The lack of focus in her expression was unsettling. "I want to know everything about Mister Royal Lassiter." She said his name like it was made of candy.

"You and the rest of the school," Jennet said. "Maybe I could sell his personal info and make a fortune."

"Maybe." Tam folded his arms. "I won't be buying."

"You don't look good in jealousy, Tam," Marny said. Then her expression sharpened. "In fact, you don't look good, period. Go home and get some rest."

"What are you, my manager?" Despite the sharp

words, there was warmth in his voice.

"She's right," Jennet said. From what she could see of his green eyes behind the scrim of his hair, he looked exhausted. He'd lost weight in the hospital, and with a lean build to begin with, he was on the edge of gaunt. "I can get George to drive you home after school, if you want."

The chauffeur wouldn't mind—he'd taken Tam into the Exe before, even at night, when it was most dangerous. But as she knew he would, Tam shook his head.

"Nah, I'm good."

"I'll walk partway with him," Marny said, glancing at Jennet.

"Girls." Tam rolled his eyes.

"Your job is to get completely better," Jennet said. "I'll find out... whatever."

She looked again to the front of the cafeteria. It was weird, how quickly Roy had made friends—especially with that wrist-chip. In her experience, Viewers were treated with wary suspicion. She still got the cold shoulder most of the time.

So why was the whole school in love with Roy Lassiter?

CHAPTER TWO

After school, Tam again shrugged away Jennet's offer of a ride home. He'd made Marny get on the bus instead of going blocks out of her way just to walk him to the outskirts of the Exe. No way he'd let her go with him into the decaying core of the city. Though Marny was quick and smart, it was a lot easier for one person to navigate the dangers of his neighborhood.

Jennet waved to him as her car pulled away. While he appreciated their concern, he didn't need babysitters. When the grav-car turned the corner, he shoved his hands in his pockets and trudged off toward the Exe.

Weariness blurred his vision, but he forced himself to stay alert. One careless step and he could end up a pile of bones in a dark alley. He kept to the shadows of the graffiti-etched walls, breathing lightly of the rot-flavored air.

Strange noises echoed through the dank streets, and Tam held his breath, listening. His heartbeat thudded, then steadied again as he realized he wasn't hearing the eerie sound of the Wild Hunt breaking between the worlds. Just mortal trouble. Just another day in the Exe.

Close to home, he skirted the abandoned building

down the block, where the yellow-eyed smoke drifters squatted. They were harmless alone, but could be dangerous in a group.

Ahead was the old auto shop—once owned by some relative, now empty except for his broken sim equip. His house perched on top, with a faded blue tarp covering the roof and rust spots on the metal walls. Still, it was home. He didn't take the rickety steps two-at-a-time—not this afternoon. The railing wobbled under his hand, but he made it to the landing, keys at the ready.

When he finally got the locks undone, he opened the door to find his mom and little brother sitting on the couch, reading a book. The sight made his heart clench. Way too many empty days stretched in his memory, too many times when Mom hadn't been around at all. But she was here now, and doing fine. That was what counted. He shoved his worry for the future into a box and locked it down tight.

His mom looked up, a smile lighting her thin face. The Bug jumped to his feet.

"Hey, Tam! Mom was worried but I told her you were ok, so she read me a story instead. It's about the alien guys on other planets."

"Sounds great." Tam mustered up a half-grin for his brother, though he was so tired all he wanted to do was sink onto the floor in a heap.

"Honey." His mom closed the book. "You look exhausted. Get some rest." She shook her head. "I knew it was too soon to send you to school."

He didn't have the energy to protest, just nodded and pulled off his shoes. Five minutes later he was in his sleeping bag. His bones felt like they'd been replaced by iron, heavy and dense. The Bug was still talking, but the words rolled off Tam, little bright marbles shining and spinning as he sank into sleep.

⬚⬚⬚⬚

Jennet's dad was late getting home—as usual. Sometimes she thought he'd stay at his office all the time, if it wasn't for her.

Of course, things were intense for him at work. VirtuMax was preparing to roll out the most cutting-edge, immersive gaming system ever, but first they had to replace the lead designer of their showpiece game, Feyland.

Her stomach clenched. She'd tried so many times to convince Dad to pull the plug on Feyland, but no luck. Even though he knew it was dangerous—after all Thomas, the original designer, had died in his sim chair—Dad didn't understand how, or why. The company thought it was a hardware glitch.

Only she and Tam knew the game was connected to the Realm of Faerie. Feyland was a gateway to a place where magic existed, and anyone who entered the game would come face-to-face with that wild, dangerous power. Jennet shivered.

She'd been one of the first to play Feyland, and the

Dark Queen had taken her essence, draining her to the point she'd almost died. In trying to rescue her, Tam had nearly lost his own life.

They couldn't let VirtuMax release the game. The thought of thousands of people flooding into Feyland, ripe pickings for the unscrupulous fey, made her bones turn to ice.

She and Tam had to do something. But what? How did two teenagers stop a huge corporation in its tracks? Two kids babbling about magic and faeries wouldn't get far, she knew that much. There were no answers, only a sick emptiness inside whenever she thought about it.

Tam was out of the hospital now, though, and together they'd figure something out. They had to.

"Miss Carter, your father has arrived home," HANA, the house network, announced. *"You are expected to appear for dinner in five minutes."*

"All right. On my way." She closed the book she hadn't been reading and went to wash her hands.

When she got downstairs, she found Dad waiting for her in the dining room. He gave her a tired smile and the usual hug.

"Hi, Dad," she said, biting her tongue to keep from commenting on how wrecked he looked.

"How was your day?" he asked.

It was what he always asked, and usually she replied with some vague, positive-sounding answer. This time, though, it was the perfect opening to find out more about Roy Lassiter. Roy, and his weird ability to make everyone like him.

"Good." She sat down and pulled her napkin across her lap. "We got a new student today—Roy Lassiter. Weren't you saying they just moved into The View?"

"Yes. Dr. Lassiter has the big house at the very back of the development."

Jennet nodded. The homes in the company compound were all big, but the Lassiter's was huge—more like a palace than a house.

"Is it just her and her son?"

"I believe so." Dad nodded as Tony, the chef, brought out their first course. "She has a husband, but he stayed behind to finish up his own work. And there's a daughter, off at college."

That huge house, for only two people?

Jennet glanced around their spacious dining room and swallowed a dry laugh. Like she should talk. Compared to Tam's tiny house—with three people living in two rooms—her house was on par with the Lassiter's. Sometimes her life pricked her uncomfortably, especially since she'd gotten to know Tam.

Tony slid a bowl of soup in front of her, rich red with a spicy-sweet aroma. Her favorite—tomato-basil. She took a spoonful, trying to frame her next question.

"How involved is Dr. Lassiter with the Full-D development… and Feyland?" She hoped her voice sounded casual.

Dad gave her a sharp look. "It's the company's number-one project. She keeps a close eye on our progress. In fact, now that she's here, things are moving forward quickly. She's brought a new content developer on board to finish up the programming. Mr. Chon. He's got an excellent background in game design."

"Oh." Jennet set down her spoon.

The original designer of Feyland had been her dad's good friend, Thomas Rimer, who had been like an uncle to her. But he had died, with Feyland still incomplete. A shiver scraped the back of her neck. Had Thomas known what he had been creating, or had he only understood at the very end?

Her dad pinched the bridge of his nose. "No one can ever replace Thomas—we both know that. Still, he laid enough of the groundwork that Mr. Chon expects to finish up the programming soon."

"Soon?" Fear zinged through her. "But… I thought you were re-testing the hardware." Not that they'd find anything, but she'd been counting on having more time.

"We've just finished running people through the sports-sims on the newest Full-D prototype." He shook his head. "I tried to extend the trial, but Dr. Lassiter took a look at the tests and said the data was sufficient. There were no issues whatsoever, even with excessive usage."

"Dad, playing virtual ping-pong isn't even close to entering Feyland! Look at what happened to Thomas, to Tam."

"I'm concerned, too—in fact, I brought this up with Dr. Lassiter as soon as she arrived, asking for more time to troubleshoot the system."

"How could she say no? The problems are obvious!"

He let out a heavy breath. "She made it very clear that the project has been delayed too long already—and that if I kept pushing, I could find myself out of a job."

"What?" Jennet set her water glass down, hard. Liquid sloshed over the side, darkening the white tablecloth. "But… you're the heart of the program, Dad. You and Thomas—"

"Thomas is gone." He looked suddenly weary beyond words. "Dr. Lassiter doesn't see any problems. She explained to me—very patronizingly—that Thomas was dying of cancer, regardless of whether or not he played a computer game. And Tam, well, we have no idea what kinds of toxins he's been exposed to, growing up in the Exe. There's no direct evidence that their problems were caused by Feyland."

A hot beast of anger rose up inside her. "Then what about me? Your own daughter? Where did these scars come from?"

She thrust her hands out, palms up. Despite the wonders of plas-skin, she would always bear the memory of Feyland, burned dark red against her skin.

He squeezed his eyes closed for a second, but not before she saw the pain reflected there. When he spoke, his voice was low and defeated.

"VirtuMax has put too much into this project, Jen. They won't stop now, not without compelling evidence that the game is harmful. Harmful to many players, not just one."

"So what, I'm statistically insignificant?" Bitterness rose up in her throat. "Why can't you *do* something?"

He was her dad. He was supposed to be all-powerful, supposed to protect her. Though that hadn't stopped her mother from taking off, never to be seen again, when Jennet was a kid. She should know better than to feel this bewildered hurt. Heat pricking behind her eyes, she turned her hands back over, resting her marked palms on the white tablecloth.

"Short of corporate espionage, I'm doing what I can," Dad said. "Putting the brakes on as much as possible—but this is what the company's been working toward for *years*. I can't stop it, any more than an ant could stop a bulldozer."

Espionage. She swallowed. Was there any way she and Tam could somehow smuggle explosives into VirtuMax headquarters? The idea flickered through her, then died. The last thing they needed was to be arrested for terrorism. Even if they managed to do some damage, that would only delay things, not halt the project altogether.

"So. What's next?" The words were dry in her mouth.

"As soon as Chon finishes up the programming, they'll begin play testing. It'll be closed beta, with handpicked players."

"And after that?" She clenched her hands into nervous fists.

"They start shipping. The pre-orders for the Full-D

have been incredible." He shook his head.

"How long…" She cleared her throat. "How long before you think the game will be released?"

"Two months, barring any more technical glitches."

Two months. Her lungs clenched and she had to force herself to breathe normally. She couldn't believe that maiming and comas counted as 'technical glitches.'

Tony came in and silently took their used dishes away, then returned with plates of Fettuccine Alfredo. Jennet poked at the pasta with her fork. It was usually one of her favorites, but tonight her stomach was full of leaden worry, not hunger.

Two months. The only thing she had to go on was a hunch about Roy Lassiter. A hunch that, somehow, had to turn into a plan.

"Um, Dad. Does anyone else besides us have a Full-D system? I mean, outside of the company headquarters."

Dad rubbed his cheek. "Well. I suppose Mr. Chon was given one, now that he's lead designer. And Dr. Lassiter, or course. She's very particular about that, collects every VirtuMax system designed to-date. And I hear she likes to provide the members of her family with top-end gear—even before release."

Heart sinking, Jennet counted. With the prototype systems, there must be at least three Full-D setups at the Lassiter's.

She and Dad had two systems—but it had only taken one to suck her into Feyland. She shivered, cold with memory.

A fantastical clearing, silvered by moonlight, where fey creatures danced around a bonfire. The haunting beauty of the Dark Queen, diamonds like stars caught in her midnight hair. A sphere filled with orange flames, while Jennet's own heart wrenched in two. A red-hot bar of iron clasped between her hands. Burning. Burning.

She shuddered. The CEO had multiple Full-D sim-systems at home. Multiple entries into Feyland.

What were the chances Roy Lassiter had been in-game? And what had he found there?

CHAPTER THREE

School the next day was a repeat of the Roy Lassiter show—with one severe exception. Instead of joining them for lunch, Marny sat at the head table, with Roy. Granted, there were a lot of other kids there too, but something was wrong if even *Marny* had fallen under Roy Lassiter's spell. Whatever kind of spell it was.

Jennet swallowed, shards of fear scraping her throat. There was only one place she knew of where magic was real—and Roy had access to it.

"I asked my Dad a bunch of questions last night," she said to Tam as he set his lunch tray on the table.

"And?" He sat across from her and rested his chin on his fist, as though his head was too heavy to hold up.

"And... Roy's mom has three models of the Full-D system at home."

"Crap." He straightened and glanced at the front of the cafeteria. "Is Lassiter a gamer?"

"I don't know."

"We need to find out."

"I don't think we can just go up and ask him about his gaming experience, do you? At least, not if we want a real answer."

She followed Tam's gaze to the table, which was packed with students listening to Roy talk. Whatever he was saying, it looked like everyone thought it was fascinating. Why were she and Tam unaffected by the new student's charm?

"Anyway," she continued, "we have more serious problems. Dad said VirtuMax is pushing for the Full-D system - with Feyland - to launch in two months."

"What? They can't do that!" Tam's face tightened with worry. "Especially after the terrible stuff that's happened."

Exasperation sharpened her words. "Apparently the company can't let little things like death and comas stand in the way of profit."

"Your dad must have something to say about this." Tam leaned forward, his voice urgent. "He's seen the damage, up close. He has to stop VirtuMax from releasing the game."

She clasped her hands together under the table. It had been nearly three weeks, but the skin of her palms was still tender. The doctors said she might not get her fingerprints back.

"Dad's doing what he can," she said. "He comes home from work every day, frustrated beyond words. But Dr. Lassiter is convinced the Full-D is safe to use. And the company techs inspected each wire and element of the prototype systems we used, Tam. They didn't find a single thing wrong."

"Because there's nothing wrong with the *hardware*,

Jennet!"

"I know that. But I can't convince Dad the game itself is at fault, and there's no proof. Of anything."

"Damn." Tam raked a hand through his hair.

She caught the haunted look in his eyes, and knew it mirrored hers. Feyland was dangerous, and they were powerless to stop it.

The bell blared, and she frowned down at her half-eaten lunch.

"Meet me after school," Tam said. "I have an idea."

Tam waited for Jennet outside, leaning against the eroded brick wall and trying not to act like it was holding him up. He was tired—but he couldn't give in to his exhaustion. As soon as Jennet walked out of the building, he straightened. The narrowing of her eyes showed she wasn't fooled.

"Maybe we should talk another time," she said.

"Meaning?" He slanted her a glance from under his hair.

"Meaning you look like you're about to fall over."

"I'm fine."

She set one hand to her hip. "Tam, it's me, remember? I know how you feel—I've been there myself. Quit being so drastically stoic."

"Alright—I'm not feeling great." He gave up on trying to seem lively. "But I'm ok for now. And I have a plan."

"Sit down, then, and I'll listen."

He looked around, at the tail end of students leaving school, then picked up his backpack. "Not here. Let's walk."

Jennet pointed with her chin as a flash of red sped past. "There goes Roy Lassiter in his new grav-car."

"Who's that with him, in the passenger seat? Long black hair."

Jennet squinted at the receding vehicle. "Keeli, I think."

Another Viewer. Of course.

Lassiter had everything—fancy grav-car, privilege, all the status money could buy. And he lived in the compound, practically next door to Jennet. Jealousy curdled through Tam. There was no way he could compete with Lassiter—and he was planning to put Jennet right in the guy's path. Yeah, a flawless idea.

He hunched his shoulders against the late-November wind, and headed down the street. Beside him, Jennet kept pace. Her pale hair blew around her face, until she pulled it back and tucked it into the hood of her coat.

"So, what's your plan?" she asked.

"We need to find out if Lassiter's a gamer. The way that people are acting around him—it's not normal. Why are we the only people who aren't affected by his charm, or whatever-it-is? What if it's connected with the game, and that's why we're immune?"

"I hate to say it—but the thought crossed my mind, too." She drew her brows together. "Still, it doesn't make sense. The Dark Queen tried to *kill* us, not make us the most popular kids in school."

Tam jammed his hands into his pockets. "Yeah, but we lost. What if Lassiter won? What if he got a real-world prize for beating the queen?"

"Could he be such a flawless player—so much better than us?" She shook her head. "I don't buy it."

"We're going to find out. Grab that fancy tablet of yours and message him. Tell him to meet us at Zeg's sim-café."

Her eyes widened. "Seriously? You're taking me to Zeg's?"

He knew she'd wanted to see the cafe, although it wasn't the kind of place Viewers went. Ratty around the edges, with older gear—at first he'd been afraid she'd scorn it. Zeg's was way too important to him. Now, though, he trusted her.

"I'd like to see what Lassiter's got," he said, "but in neutral territory. We can test him—see if he's a top-notch player. If he has what it takes to beat the Dark Queen."

"But… why would he even come?"

Tam stopped and just looked at her a moment—her intelligent blue eyes, her pale skin and high cheekbones, the silken beauty of her hair.

"You're cute," he said at last. "No way Lassiter hasn't noticed you."

Pink flushed into her cheeks. "Really? You think so?"

Her good looks were so obvious. He didn't know how she could pass a mirror and not know. Of course, he liked her for way more than that. She was brave, and smart, and a prime gamer, all rolled into one flawless package.

"Completely." He set one hand on her shoulder. "Lassiter would be an idiot not to see it. So, message him. Tell him one of the locals says he's nothing but talk, and is challenging him to a sim duel. Give him the co-ords to Zeg's. He'll come."

Tam swallowed, trying to ease his sense of dark foreboding. He hoped to hell this wasn't going to backfire all over him.

CHAPTER FOUR

Jennet's cheeks were still warm as Tam dropped his hand from her shoulder. He thought she was cute—had actually shed some of his skittishness and touched her! Hope kindled a bright flame in her chest.

"Anyway," he said, "we're almost at Zeg's. You can message Lassiter from there."

He turned and started walking, and she hurried to catch up. It meant a lot—not only that touch, but that he was letting her see Zeg's. She knew how important the sim-café was to him.

From what she could piece together, Tam had learned to sim on Zeg's equipment. Once he'd gotten good, Zeg had let him play for free, since people would come in just to watch him.

Tam was one of the best simmers she knew. Okay, *the* best. He'd won the regional tournament last year, and had a good chance at taking Nationals. If he'd gone. He didn't talk about it, but she was certain his wreck of a mom had something to do with him missing the tournament.

"Here we are," Tam said, holding open the door.

Zeg's Game Parlor was written across the large

window, and a gust of warm, coffee-scented air met her as she stepped over the threshold. The place was filled with the hum and ping of games—one side devoted to netscreens, the corner crammed with moto-sense setups. The wall by the door was covered with posters of celebrity simmer Spark Jaxley, her signature magenta hair blowing in a cyber-breeze.

A man looked up at them from behind the counter. He had long brown hair and a beard that melded together into a frizzy halo around his face.

"Hey, Tam! Good to see you," he said. "Heard you were in rough shape for a bit."

"Yeah." Tam didn't elaborate. "Zeg, this is Jennet. She's a simmer, too."

"Cool." Zeg pursed his lips and nodded at her. "Sim-systems are in the back. Tam'll show you. Don't bet against him—you'll lose."

"I'm not planning on it," she said.

"A girl with sense." Zeg winked at her. "You kids want some coffee? Tea?"

"Um…" She glanced at Tam.

"Sure," Tam said. "Your mint blend, ok?"

"I'm happy to pay, if you want to scan my chip…" Jennet lifted her wrist, her implant catching the blue light from a nearby netscreen.

Zeg looked at her arm. His eyebrows twitched into a frown, and he shook his head. "Nah, Tam's cred is good."

"Next time, then." She didn't want to coast

indefinitely on Tam's reputation.

"Come on," Tam said. "You can message Lassiter from the back."

He led the way to a second room that held a half-dozen sim-systems with color-coded chairs, helmets, and gloves. The equipment was scuffed and stained, eons behind the Full-D, but she didn't say anything. Then again, if they played here they wouldn't run the risk of getting their souls sucked out, or being chased and mangled by demon hounds.

She leaned back against the blue sim chair and pulled out her tablet. It didn't take long to craft a message to Roy and send it—but she wasn't nearly as confident as Tam that he would show.

"Shall we play something, while we wait?" she asked. "Blade-X?" The fast-paced racing sim would be a nice distraction—take her mind off the tangle of problems they faced.

"I don't want to be in-game when Lassiter comes." Tam set his hand on the back of the blue sim chair. "By the way, I don't recommend ever playing the blue system. It has severely slow response on the gloves."

"You wouldn't give me a handicap to even things up? How generous." She grinned at him, though they both knew he was the better gamer.

Not that she was wretched—far from it. Before she'd met Tam, she'd known maybe two other kids who could top her simming skills. But Tam was flawless.

He just shook his head, a half-smile on his lips.

"Come on—I bet our tea's ready."

Back at the counter, Zeg slid a couple mugs of sweet-smelling liquid at them, followed by a plate that held four crumbly cookies.

She perched next to Tam on one of the stools, and took a sip of tea. It was warm and minty—a cozy contrast to the screens and consoles surrounding them.

"Have a cookie," Tam pushed the plate toward her.

She took one. It tasted like butter and cinnamon.

"This is good. Does Zeg make them?"

"His wife does – she's more the domestic side of the business, no˜matter how Zeg acts. He's the tech guy, though he just likes to pretend to be a teddy bear."

Jennet glanced toward the man, who had moved to one of the netscreens and was helping a boy get unstuck in some game.

"He does it well," she said. "Any kids?"

"Nope. The sim-café is his baby."

Tam looked like he was about to say more, but a cold blast of wind pulled their attention to the open door of the café.

Standing there like he owned the place was Roy Lassiter.

CHAPTER FIVE

Tam scowled, a possessive jolt going through him—even though getting Lassiter here had been his idea. An idea that seemed worse by the second, especially when the other boy's eyes skimmed over him and fixed on Jennet.

There was a cluster of girls behind Lassiter. Tam blinked when he saw that Marny was one of them.

"This is my uncle's sim-café," she said, sounding breathless. "Some of the best players in town hang here."

"So I hear." Lassiter set his hands on his hips. "Not that Crestview's best is anything to brag about."

He smiled, looking totally fake, and started toward the counter. Dislike curled through Tam, and he shifted closer to Jennet. For a second he wished he had his in-game sword strapped to his side. He'd gladly use it on Lassiter.

"Jennet Carter," the other boy said, his voice dropping into a huskier register. "Nice of you to message me. I've been wanting to meet you, too."

He stared at her a little too long. Tam took a gulp of tea, trying to wash the bitterness from his mouth.

"I wasn't sure you'd come," she said. "Do you sim?"

"Of course I sim. Although I'm used to far better than this." He waved his hand, encompassing the warm shabbiness of Zeg's.

Jennet nodded, clearly playing along. "I bet you have some pretty flawless gear at home."

How could he not? Lassiter's mother was the freakin' CEO of the top gaming-tech company in the world. The question was—had he gone into Feyland? Had he actually beaten the Dark Queen in battle?

"Nothing can beat my sim equip. Or me." He turned, fixing Tam with a look as cold as a snake's. "Is this the local who thinks he can outplay me?"

Marny stepped up. "This is Tam Linn, Roy. He's one of the best."

"Yeah?" The other boy eyed him up and down. "Don't look so special. Are you sure you can play with the pros?"

Tam slid his stool back and got to his feet. He was an inch taller than Lassiter, and glad of it.

"Yeah," he said. "I can take you."

Lassiter let out a snort. "You won't know what hit you. At least it will be over fast, Exie."

Jennet stood abruptly, shoulder-to-shoulder with Tam. "I've simmed with Tam, and I've no doubt he's as good as you, if not better."

Her defense took some of the sting out of Lassiter's words. While it was true the taint of the Exe clung to Tam—in the clothing he could never quite get clean, in the shadow of poverty that haunted everyone in that part of town—he was the best player in the region.

But how good was Lassiter, the boy who grew up in VirtuMax's pocket?

"Heh." Lassiter narrowed his eyes and stared at Tam. "We'll see about that. The equip here isn't what I'm used to—but it'll be enough to put you down. Ready for a sim-duel?"

"You're on."

They had Lassiter right where they wanted him. Too bad it didn't feel very satisfying. Tam hoped he could wipe that arrogant smirk off Lassiter's face, instead of being the one to eat dirt. The adrenaline of upcoming battle fired his blood, and he curled his fingers into his palms.

Marny looked at him, wide-eyed. "But, Tam. This is Roy Lassiter." She said Lassiter's name like he was president of the galaxy. "Do you really think you can beat him?"

They'd know soon enough. The key was to show no weakness. He nodded, projecting confidence.

"The sim-systems are in back," he said to Lassiter. "Come on."

The group moved forward, the girls whispering excitedly. Lassiter was probably strutting like a rooster, but Tam didn't care to watch. He glanced at Jennet. She had her lips pressed together in that anxious way of hers.

Lassiter stopped beside the blue sim chair. "Leet gear," he said, the contempt in his voice clear.

"If you're not up for it…" Tam shrugged.

"Oh, I am." Lassiter reached for the blue helmet.

Jennet shot Tam a wide-eyed glance. For a half-second, he was tempted to let the other boy choose the slow system. But that wouldn't be a fair test, would it?

"I'll use that one," he said.

"Tam…" Jennet widened her eyes and shook her head at him.

"Uh huh," Lassiter said, with a mocking smile. "I see what you're up to. Trying to take the best gear for yourself, aren't you? I think blue's my color."

"Stop it," Jennet said. She pulled the helmet from Lassiter's grasp. "I'll use this system, to watch the fight. All the others are equal, ok?"

He looked at her. "If you say so, blondie."

Tam could hardly wait to pound him.

Zeg ambled into the room. "Everything all right back here?" he asked in a deceptively quiet voice.

"We're good," Tam said.

Though Zeg seemed mild-mannered, Tam had seen him throw trouble out on its ear. If things got nasty, the owner would step in.

"Hm." Zeg glanced at Lassiter, then back to Tam. "I've just installed the new sim-version of Rumble. That might be what you boys are looking for."

"Perfect," Lassiter said, giving the owner a toothy smile. "I'm in the mood for some player-versus-player action."

"If you want, I'll put the feed up on the flatscreen, so everyone can watch," Zeg said.

"Good." Both Tam and Lassiter spoke at the same time.

Jennet wrapped her arms around the blue helmet. "I'm still going in as a spectator."

"No problem," Lassiter said. "I appreciate the support. It'll be nice to have you with me, blondie." He put his hand on her arm.

"Stop calling me that." Jennet twitched away from his touch and slid into the sim chair. She looked up at Tam. "See you in there."

"Listen, Exie." The other boy faced him. "I know you might be a decent player, but you don't want to beat me. Really, you don't."

There was an odd light in Lassiter's eyes. Tam's ears itched, like something was buzzing inside his skull. He blinked, then shook his head, trying to clear it.

"Right." He meant the word to be sarcastic, but somehow it came out as agreement.

"I knew you'd see it my way," Lassiter said. He winked at Tam, then settled in the red sim chair and pulled on the gloves.

Whatever. Tam let out a deep breath, then took the yellow system on Jennet's other side. No matter what Lassiter said, there was no chance Tam was going easy on him.

In-game, Tam flicked through Rumble's fighter avatars and chose his favorite: Sascha the marksman, who was equipped with jet boots and two gigantic swords for close fighting. Just for fun, and because he thought it would throw Lassiter off, he switched up the gender.

Now, instead of a tall, muscled man, Sascha appeared as a buxom woman in scanty armor. Not that it changed her fighting abilities one bit, but her appearance could be a distraction. Anything that might unbalance Lassiter was good with him.

The challenge summons rolled across his helmet screen, and he accepted. The game would place him and Lassiter in a random battle arena. Depending on which one, there would be various traps and pitfalls, as well as items the fighters could use to their advantage.

A red flash of the visuals signaled that the fight was about to begin. Tam took a deep breath and entered the game.

Sascha materialized on one side of a paved courtyard ringed with columns. The place looked vaguely Roman, and was one of the barest arenas Tam had ever seen. There was no time to check out his surroundings, though. Lassiter's character appeared across from Sascha, and Tam almost laughed out loud. From dozens of possible fighters, his opponent had *also* chosen Sascha— though he'd stayed with the male version.

A flutter of black cloth caught his eye, and he glanced up to see the character Jennet had chosen. Nika, the ninja assassin. Her avatar was in spectator mode, suspended above the arena and able to see everything, but prevented from interacting with the environment in any way.

"You have good taste, Exie." Lassiter's voice sounded smug through the helmet's speakers. "Although, it's not going to save you."

Tam didn't waste time answering. He drew Sascha's gun and sighted for his opponent. Just as he squeezed the trigger, Lassiter activated his boots and flew up into the air. At least the guy wasn't a complete noob.

He saw Jennet move out of the way, taking her character to hover by the edge of the combat zone.

Now Tam was the target. Did those columns offer any protection? He sprinted for the side of the arena and tucked himself beside a column. Shrapnel exploded, stone chips flying past his shoulder, but Lassiter's shot didn't touch him. Tam crouched and fired off a quick volley, back along the trajectory of his opponent's bullet. He heard Lassiter curse under his breath, but his character seemed unharmed.

There wasn't enough cover in this arena for a sniper shootout. Time for a change of tactics. Tam flexed his fingers inside the gloves, and Sascha leaped into the air, drawing her double swords. Keeping her jet boots at max speed, Tam steered her through the air, straight toward Lassiter.

The other Sascha fired, and Tam somersaulted out of the way. Then he was on Lassiter, swords flashing.

"Hey," the other boy said, voice strained.

Lassiter drew his blades, too, but he was surprisingly slow, as if Tam had taken him unaware. As if he'd expected less of a fight.

Still, he managed to deflect Tam's first assault. The two Saschas danced around one another, feinting and lunging and parrying. There was something about Lassiter's play-style …

Tam watched closely. Ah, right—the other boy moved his character in a linear way, playing as though he were standing on a floor, not floating in three dimensions. Time for the kill. Tam cut the power to his boots, dropping suddenly toward the pavement. He heard Jennet gasp.

Before Lassiter could react, or re-target him, he turned the boots back on and surged forward, angling to come up behind his opponent. A stab to the back, another quick slice across the neck, and the male Sascha gave a gurgling cry and slumped over, dead.

:GAME OVER: The words blinked red across Tam's field of vision.

"Rematch?" he asked.

"Nah." Lassiter sounded like he'd eaten something nasty. "Another time, maybe."

The dead Sascha disappeared as Lassiter left game.

"Nice job," Jennet said. "I don't think he was expecting you to beat him."

"Me either. I mean, he was a competent player, but he didn't really push."

"I got that feeling, too." She sounded thoughtful. "Well, see you out there."

Tam pulled off his helmet and gloves, then stood. Roy Lassiter was already at the door, the cluster of girls around him making sympathetic, cooing noises. Even Marny. When she noticed Tam was off the system, she narrowed her eyes at him, then pointedly turned away.

Nice.

"Don't let it bother you," Jennet said from behind him. "Marny's not herself."

"Well then, who is she?" He hadn't realized how much he'd counted on the big girl's friendship, until it was gone.

"We'll find out." There was steel in Jennet's voice.

She headed over to where Lassiter was holding court, and Tam trailed behind. The other boy turned his attention to Jennet, again completely ignoring Tam. Jerk.

"So, blondie, want to come see me play on a *real* system?" Lassiter asked. "I only live a few blocks from you. Tomorrow afternoon's good. What say?"

The other girls pouted, and Tam could tell Jennet was considering saying no. He poked her in the back.

"All right," she said after a pause. "I could come over after school." Her words were reluctant, but Lassiter didn't seem to notice—or if he did, he didn't care.

"Great." He grinned at her. "I'll be counting the hours."

"Right," Tam muttered.

"You know it, Exie. Why would she hang with you, when she could be with me? The choice is so obvious." Lassiter turned to his admirers. "Come along, ladies. We have fun waiting for us—elsewhere."

The door slammed closed behind the Viewer and his entourage, and Jennet let out a low breath.

"I don't want to spend any more time with that walking ego," she said. "Especially if he keeps calling me blondie."

"You have to go." Tam shoved his hair out of his face and gave her a serious look. "We didn't find out nearly enough about Lassiter's playing abilities. And if there's a way to stop Feyland from being released, becoming friends with the CEO's son could help us find it."

"You're right. How about *you* become his buddy, then."

"Other than the fact he hates me for beating him? He's a Viewer and I'm from the Exe." Lassiter had made sure to pound that point every chance he got.

She folded her arms. "So? I'm your friend."

Against all the odds, really. He tried not to think about the distance between their lives, but it was hard, with Lassiter in the way.

"Then you can go be Roy Lassiter's friend, too. Admit it—it will be a lot easier for you. You belong in his world."

She made a face. "Fine. I'm not thrilled with the idea."

Neither was he. Pushing Jennet at Lassiter was the last thing he wanted to do—but he had no choice.

CHAPTER SIX

Jennet rode her g-board slowly up the flagstone drive that led to the Lassiter's front door. The place was the biggest mansion in The View, no question. Impeccable landscaping framed a building that could easily, in a different setting, be a 5-star hotel—all gleaming glass and sharp angles.

Her dad might be the lead project manager for Feyland, but Dr. Lassiter was VirtuMax's CEO—and clearly wanted everyone to know it.

The entryway was designed to make people feel small. At least, that's how Jennet felt, standing in front of the huge double-doors. There was no need to knock. Security cameras had swiveled onto her the moment she'd entered the wrought-iron gates out front. The system had probably scanned her wrist-chip within seconds.

"*Miss Carter,*" a metallic voice said from a hidden speaker by the door. "*You are expected. Please enter.*"

Definitely a House-Activated-Network-Assistant, though her own HANA had a better voice program than the Lassiter's interface. But maybe they liked it that way—cold and impersonal.

The doors swung open to reveal Roy Lassiter, aiming his even-toothed grin at her.

"Welcome to the palace," he said. "Come on in."

He reached for her arm, but Jennet strode past him into the foyer. Inside, it was cool and hushed and dim. How many empty rooms did this place have? The tomblike silence was broken only by the distant hum of a robo-vac.

"Thanks for the invite," she said, propping her board in the corner.

"Anytime, blondie." He glanced at her g-board. "Nice ride—though not quite as prime as my Quell. I'll take you out and show you some real tricks sometime. You'd like that."

"Um, yeah."

She didn't like *him*, or the assumptions he made. Still, she had to at least act friendly.

"Maybe next time." He winked at her. "Today you get to see an expert simmer at work."

If his head got any bigger, he'd fall over from the weight. Jennet folded her arms.

"I sim, too, you know," she said.

He laughed. "G-board, simming… I didn't figure you for such a techie girl. Not with your looks."

That statement was so full of wrong, she barely knew where to begin. "Just because I have blond hair doesn't mean I'm stupid—about tech *or* about gaming."

"Hey." He held his hands up in mock surrender. "It was a compliment, get it? But whatever. The theater is this way."

Without looking to see if she was following, Roy headed down the tall corridor to his left. Sconces along the walls shed a faint illumination, and she felt like she was walking into a deep canyon.

"The theater?" she asked. Her voice echoed hollowly off the glass and polished stone. They had a media room at her house, but it couldn't be called a *theater* by any stretch.

"My mother's a fan of gear," Roy said. "After all, it's made us rich. She designed a space for all the media interfaces and systems we have. Which is a lot."

Sounded like her dad was right about Dr. Lassiter collecting every system VirtuMax ever made.

At the end of the hall was another massive set of double-doors. They swung silently open as Jennet and Roy approached. It was creepy. Sure, the house-network could be programmed to open doors whenever people got close, but Jennet and her dad both preferred to be in charge of whether or not a door was going to swing wide.

Roy paused on the threshold and gave her an ironic half-bow. "Behold. Lassiter central."

She felt her eyes widen as she stepped inside. It really *was* a theater, with forty-foot ceilings and rows of seats in the middle, facing a floor-to-ceiling screen that dominated the space.

The seating area was only a portion of the huge room, though. Along the sides, dozens of gaming systems were lined up: netscreens, and moto-sense setups, and sim-systems. She was used to cutting-edge tech, but this—this was drastically over the top. Roy had his own private arcade, with equip she hadn't seen in years, or *ever*.

"This is…." She turned in a circle, trying not to let Roy see her amazement.

"Pretty prime. I know." He sounded smug. "But the best part is over here."

He led the way to an area partitioned behind frosted glass panels. With a wave of his wrist, the glass slid aside to reveal VirtuMax's crowning achievement.

The Full-D sim-system.

Actually, three models of the Full-D, perfectly lined up. Spot lighting from above illuminated them, making the helmets gleam and the synth-leather of the chairs glow. The LEDs on the gloves shone like gemstones.

"It looks like a museum," Jennet said. Or a shrine to a digital god.

"All these systems are playable—though I do like the most recent equip the best." Roy patted the back of the middle system's chair, the way someone would touch a favorite pet.

Her breath tightened and fear shivered across her nerves. So, he *had* been simming on the Full-D. Somehow, she wasn't surprised.

There was a part of her—spirit, soul, whatever—that had been held captive in Feyland by the Dark Queen. That part had prickled with wariness the moment he'd stood up in Ms. Lewis's class. Roy Lassiter had been touched by the Realm of Faerie. Did he even know it?

Too many questions, not enough answers.

She cleared her throat. "You play a lot?"

"Of course. It's a gamer's paradise here." He leaned toward her. "I knew you'd like it. But then, you've used a Full-D system before, haven't you?"

"I…" She swallowed. Maybe Roy was more clever than he seemed. "Yeah, my dad brought one home." Two, actually, but why reveal more than she had to? "I've messed around on it. A little."

He bounced up and down on the balls of his feet. "Well, Jennet Carter, it's your lucky day. I'm going to show you something so astounding, you won't believe it."

"Are you talking about Fey… about the new game the company's working on?"

"Feyland, yeah." He shot her a speculative look. "Your dad's the project manager. I'd expect you to know all about it."

"Not really." She forced a laugh and took a step away from him. "Dad spends a lot of time at work, and when he's home he doesn't talk much."

Although recently they'd had some real conversations. She was still trying to explain what had happened to her and Tam in-game, and sometimes it seemed like she was getting through. She had to admit, though, the whole thing was pretty hard to believe.

Roy nodded, the doubt clearing from his expression.

"Ok then, have a seat. I'm taking you in-game with me."

Fear clenched her ribs. "I, um... I don't think it's a good idea."

Way too much trouble could happen in Feyland. *Had* happened in Feyland. Some of the creatures there were her mortal enemies, and she didn't dare encounter them—especially not without Tam at her side. She pressed her lips together, trying to keep the panic at bay.

"Oh, right." He rolled his eyes. "Your dad's convinced there's dangerous hardware issues. Listen. I've been simming on this equip for a long time, on all three prototype systems. Nothing bad has happened to me, not once. That's weeks—ok, months—of playtime, and no evil effects. Nothing to be scared of."

It sure didn't sound like Roy had gone all the way to the Dark Court. Either that, or he was an excellent liar.

She shook her head. "I still don't think—"

"Look, Jennet. As long as you're not a total noob, you'll do fine. You know how to sim—you said so yourself. Right?"

"Yes."

"Then what's the problem?"

The problem was that the Dark Queen had tried to kill her. Twice. The fey-folk knew her name, knew *her*. They would recognize her no matter what kind of character she played in-game. Going into Feyland was beyond dangerous.

She made herself breathe past the tightness in her lungs.

"Tell me about the game," she said. "You know, monsters we might encounter, stuff like that."

Wicked water-hags and redcap goblins. The dread Wild Hunt. The sharp-edged, terrible beauty of the Dark Queen in her Court.

"No worries," he said. "In the early levels of the game, there's nothing fierce. And you'll have me to protect you."

"So… we won't reach the final boss or anything?" She didn't care if Roy heard the tremble in her voice and thought she was a timid player.

He frowned. "The final boss? Nah. It takes days of playing to get that far in-game. He's way deeper in than we're going to go."

He?

Her heart gave a thud, and shock rippled through her like lightning. She blinked at Roy. Had she heard him right? *He?* Had Roy actually encountered a different enemy at the end of Feyland, not the Dark Queen?

"If we *do* end up meeting the boss," she said, lacing her fingers tightly together, "I should know more. Tell me about the fight, the strategy."

"Nah." He shook his head. "There's no way we can play that far in one session. Unless you want to stay here all night." He gave her a look that was probably meant to be smoldering.

"I've got homework tonight. Sorry." No way was she spending any more time with him than necessary. "But this boss—"

"Don't stress it," he said. "Feyland is easy, especially at the beginning. Though if you really don't feel like playing, we could go up to my room, instead." He winked at her.

Ignoring his suggestion, she bit her lip and tried to think past the fear swirling through her. What if Roy hadn't come to any harm, hadn't met the Dark Queen... because his Feyland wasn't the same game? Was that even possible?

What if—her pulse sped at the thought—what if Feyland was actually *safe* to play? Maybe her version was the tweaked one, the buggy one. What if all her and Tam's fears were groundless? The idea trembled through her, promising a relief so great she could barely breathe.

The only way to find out was by going in-game with Roy, right here, right now. She didn't have to go very far. Just beyond the fairy ring, just enough to see if the world was different. If things got severe, she could always run back out.

She had to know.

"All right," she said. Her stomach in knots, she walked over to the Full-D systems. "I'll play Feyland with you."

CHAPTER SEVEN

"**T**here you go." Roy's grin was firmly back in place. "Don't worry, I'll take care of you. All you have to do is follow me around. Here—take the newest system. The interface is easier to use."

Didn't she know it.

Throat dry as sand, she slid into the chair. When Roy stepped forward, like he was going to help her with the helmet, she hurriedly pulled it on, then donned the gloves. Her hands throbbed with the memory of searing fire.

"Ready," she said.

Though she wasn't, not at all. She wished, with a yearning that made her bones ache, that Tam was with her. But there was no scenario she could imagine where Roy invited "the Exie" over for a gaming session. It was up to her.

Through the dark glass of the visor-screen, she saw Roy settle into the system to her right—the second prototype. He geared up, then looked over at her.

"At the main screen, choose the *F* icon from the menu." His voice came, crystal-clear, through her helmet's speakers. "And prepare to be amazed."

The *F* icon glowed, softly golden, like it was made of flame. It took only the slightest flex of her finger to select it. The menu faded out, replaced with the blinking words she'd seen a hundred times:

Feyland: A VirtuMax Production
Alpha 1.5.0486

The visor-screen went dark. Faint, mysterious music began playing. Light slowly etched across her vision, a delicate tracery like webs or tree branches.

WELCOME TO FEYLAND

The words unfurled across the screen. The letters glowed a rich gold that deepened to crimson. Flames flickered along the sides, then the words faded to grey, as though they had burned down to ash. The music twisted, and the dim letters suddenly whirled up into a flurry of dark-edged leaves. Behind them... she squinted. Was that a pair of eyes, gleaming from the shadows? She'd never seen that before.

Then the screen cleared, showing the familiar character-creator interface.

"Now make your avatar," Roy said. "Spellweaver would be a good choice for you."

Well, yeah. It was what she played all the time in-game, but she wanted to do what she could to disguise herself. Maybe, by using Roy's system, she'd get a layer of protection from the creatures of Feyland, if his game in fact led to the Dark Realm.

And if it didn't? She still didn't want Roy to know how familiar she was with Feyland—at least not until she knew more. Choosing an untried class would help with that.

"What type of character are you?" she asked.

No way did she want to inadvertently pick the same kind as Roy. For one thing, having him tell her exactly how to play would be insufferable.

"Mercenary. Best warrior in the game. Whatever class you choose, I'll protect you."

He wasn't a Knight, then. She should have guessed. Knight was what Tam played—and it fit him well, no matter what he thought of himself.

The same way Mercenary fit Roy. Someone interested only in their own gain. She'd never met a more self-centered person than Roy Lassiter.

All right—time for a decision. She scanned the character classes, paying more attention to the hybrids listed at the bottom. *KITSUNE.* That looked promising. And potentially a way to hide her identity in-game. Lifting her index finger, she highlighted the choice.

KITSUNE: Attuned to the wild magic of the elements, the Kitsune can wield fire, cast illusions, and shape-shift into the form of a fox. Clever and cunning, Kitsune prefer to win their battles without the use of brute force.

"Are you done?" Roy asked. "Is the interface confusing you?"

"No, no. Give me a minute."

Quickly, she created her avatar. A petite blond-haired girl with a pointed chin and high cheekbones appeared on the screen. She was wearing a green leather vest trimmed with leafy patterns, dark leggings, and tall boots. Not bad—but what were the character's weapons? Jennet rotated her avatar. A thin dagger was strapped to her belt, and she carried a slender curved bow and quiver of arrows on her back.

Not a class made for close fighting. She'd have to experiment with the fire and illusion bit, but that was good—keep her looking like a novice.

Choose character name, the game prompted.

What should she pick? Not her own name, for sure. That would be the first test. If the creatures in Feyland called her Fair Jennet, she'd know that Roy's version was more than just a game.

She needed something fox-like. Vixa—yes, that was good. Jennet double-clicked her thumb and index finger, the universal glove command to bring up the keyboard, then typed the name into the interface.

VIXA—character complete. Enter game?

Ready or not, here she went. She took a steadying breath, then tipped her thumb up. *Yes.*

A fanfare of trumpets blared as the visor-screen went golden. Even though she was prepared for it, her stomach gave a queasy lurch. The first few times she'd simmed on the Full-D system, she hadn't realized the weird sensation had anything to do with the game. Later, she'd thought it was an interface glitch. But now she knew better. Going in-game was no simple thing. And in this case, it wasn't a hopeful sign.

The golden light dissolved, and she found herself at

the regular starting point—a clearing surrounded by white-barked birch trees. The sky was bright blue overhead, the grass a vivid green. Wind moved across the leaves of the trees, shimmering silver as they rustled in its wake, and she could feel the warm breeze against her face.

Her avatar stood within a faerie ring of mushrooms, as usual. *Hold on a sec...*

She looked again at the ring. Instead of the expected moon-pale mushrooms, this was a circle of white-spotted red ones. The poisonous kind.

But that was a good thing. It meant that Roy's version of Feyland wasn't exactly the same as hers. Still, how different was it?

She shivered. Gripping her bow, she turned in a slow circle. The weapon felt unfamiliar and awkward. Maybe selecting an untried class wasn't such a great idea, after all.

"I'm in," she told Roy.

"Sweet. Be right there—I was checking out some character specs."

A moment later the air beside her shimmered, and his avatar appeared. Surprise wrapped around her lungs and it took her a second to catch her breath. The character was Roy, but he looked—well, he looked amazing. Not just an enhanced version of himself, the way she and Tam did in her game.

No, this Royal Lassiter resembled a prince of old. His hair was coppery and perfectly tousled, like a vid-star's. His eyes were deep indigo, his features flawlessly hewn. Was *this* how the other students at school saw him? If so, she could totally understand the appeal.

He wore gladiator-style armor—a chest plate and vambraces that revealed his muscular upper arms. A golden armband with an intricate Celtic design encircled his left bicep, and he had an ornate torc around his neck.

"Like what you see?" He flexed, then drew his two-handed sword and went through a fighting sequence, attacking and parrying an imaginary opponent. Much as she hated to admit it, he looked good, all smooth moves and rippling muscles. Like he *would* be able to protect her, if things got dangerous.

"Impressive," she said.

"Let's check you out." He sheathed his weapon, then looked her up and down. "Didn't roll a caster, huh? Well, this isn't bad. I'm interested in seeing how the Kitsune work. And you make a cute fox-girl, with those pointy ears."

Her ears were pointy? Jennet felt one. Sure enough, they were sticking up through her hair. The character graphic hadn't shown that feature, but she was a fool to trust any part of this game. Things could change from minute to minute—and did, with unsettling frequency.

"Follow me, and don't step on the mushrooms," he said. "First quest is down the trail."

He jumped over the faerie ring and strode to the edge of the clearing. Even though the mushrooms were changed, a mossy path led between the trees—just like in *her* Feyland. Ferns grew along the edge, and the sunlight sifted long beams of light into the forest. So far, it was impossible to tell if this were truly a different game.

She took a deep breath and leaped over the mushrooms. The avatar felt lighter, more agile than her Spellweaver.

Roy turned to watch her. "Good job with the interface," he said. "At first I was annoyingly clumsy in here, but you have a feel for it."

Drat. She'd have to remember to stumble sometimes. "Maybe it's this character—it seems pretty easy to move around."

"Well, stay close." He shifted, and for the first time, a hint of unease crossed his handsome features. "Feyland can be a little... unpredictable."

She widened her eyes and tried to look innocent. "I thought you said it was amazing."

"Oh, it is. Come on, I'll show you things you're not going to believe."

Except she could believe them. She'd seen more than her fair share of freakiness in-game. She skirted the edge of the circle, following Roy as he started down the path.

The quiet of the forest was punctuated by the liquid trills of some hidden bird. The pale trunks began thinning out, showing glimpses of rolling green hills beyond. When she and Roy stepped out of the trees, there was a cottage right in front of them, complete with thatched roof and diamond-paned windows.

It looked a lot like the cottage she and Tam had encountered when they'd played together. And yet, there were differences. The brownie called Fynnod wasn't sitting out front, for one thing. Instead a small, goblin-like creature squatted on the doorstep. It had skin like old leather, long ears, and a nose that curved sharply downward, almost meeting an equally pointed chin. It watched them approach with dark, unblinking eyes.

She had never seen this particular denizen of Feyland before, but that was no guarantee it didn't know who she was. Jennet edged behind Roy, trying to keep him between her and the creature.

"First quest-giver," Roy said over his shoulder to her. "Don't be scared—these starting quests are dead easy."

She flinched at his choice of words. "As long as *we're* not dead."

"Not to worry." Roy patted his sword. "Like I said, I'll protect you. Besides, I know this game inside and out."

He strode to the front steps, and she trailed behind him, keeping her head ducked low. Fear drilled through her, fast and insistent. If this creature recognized her, what was she going to do?

"Greetings, Hob," Roy said.

Jennet glanced up, to see the goblin rise and make a flourishing bow. So far, it hadn't seemed to notice her.

"Greetings, Royal one. You return to the realm." The goblin spoke in a high, creaky voice, then looked over at Jennet. "And you have brought a new companion."

There was no sign of recognition on Hob's ugly face, no sign that he was going to point his clawed finger at her and denounce her as an imposter. Her heartbeat notched down from panic mode.

"Indeed," Roy said. "Lady Jennet will accompany me on my adventures. Grant her the courtesy that is her due."

Annoyance stabbed through her. Great. He'd blown her cover first thing. So much for her first test of the game—seeing if her character name stuck.

"Roy," she whispered, leaning close, "my avatar is called Vixa."

"Sorry," he said. "I forgot to check—but it's all good. You can be a lady, it suits you. Anyway, it's too late to change—from now on the interface will recognize you as Lady Jennet."

The goblin turned and bowed to her. "Well met, Lady Jennet."

The creature gave no sign that her real name carried any importance. And it hadn't greeted her as Fair Jennet, the name she was called in *her* version of Feyland. Maybe this was going to work, after all.

"We seek a quest," Roy said, sounding like a bad English actor. The first encounters in Feyland were highly scripted, and he clearly had the role-playing aspect down.

"A quest?" the goblin said.

"Aye. Lay upon us some service, that we may prove our worth." Roy glanced at her, and added in a quieter voice, "This is how the game goes. Do a quest, have an adventure, and it opens up to the next level."

She swallowed and tried to keep her tone light and curious. "Until you get to the end, right?"

For a second, the icy laughter of the Dark Queen echoed around her. Jennet shivered and forced her attention back to Roy.

"Yeah," he said. "You go through all these areas, and battle fantastical things, and at the end you make it to the Court."

"The Court?" She squeaked the words, but he didn't seem to notice. "What's that like?"

Her hope that Roy's game was different started to dissolve. Maybe the gender of the final boss changed, depending on the player—which would mean Roy had met the Dark King, instead of the Dark Queen. Either way, the Dark Court was trouble.

"I have a quest for two such bold adventurers," Hob broke in. "Heed what I now say."

"I'll tell you later," Roy whispered.

The goblin snapped his fingers, once, twice, and two lengths of silken cloth appeared on the steps beside him. One was white as snow, the other a deep crimson.

"Take these," Hob said, gesturing to the cloth, "and wash them in yon stream 'til the red becomes white, and the white turns to red. Then I shall deem you worthy of my reward."

Another tricky faerie quest. Where did they come up with this stuff?

"We shall return shortly." Roy picked up the lengths of silk, then held them out to her. "You better carry them, so I can get to my sword when we're attacked."

Her stomach clenched. The last time she'd done a quest involving water, she'd been pulled under by a water-hag and nearly drowned. Tam had been there, though, and had saved her. Longing ached through her. How she wished Tam were here beside her.

"We'll be attacked?" she asked.

"Of course," Roy said. "Nothing I can't handle. We're in the starting zone, remember?"

Yeah, well. That didn't necessarily mean anything, not in Feyland. She took the cloths and wound them together into a compact bundle. Roy wasn't the only one who could fight, if needed. She didn't know how the Kitsune magic worked, but she would figure it out. Plus, she had her bow and dagger.

They headed away from the cottage. Jennet glanced over her shoulder, to find that Hob was still sitting on the front step, knobby knees crossed. Watching them. She was glad when the path curved between two hillocks, taking them out of sight of the cottage.

"So, Roy, about the Court—"

"Sec." He lifted his hand. "This is usually where the ambush happens. Go slow."

He drew his sword and, gripping the hilt in two hands, held the naked blade before him.

"Um…" She glanced around, but saw only flower-spangled grasses and the curve of blue sky overhead.

"Don't be nervous, blondie." Roy flashed her a perfect smile. "I'm really good."

She had her mouth open to reply, when the ground before them erupted. Dirt sprayed everywhere, and three hideous creatures clambered out of the hole. They were squat and ferocious-looking, wearing rough leather armor and carrying long pikes. The one in front grinned, sharp-toothed and evil-eyed, and lifted his weapon.

CHAPTER EIGHT

"**B**ogles!" Roy said. "Stay back. I got this."

Jennet retreated a few paces, but no way was she just going to stand there like a noob and watch while Roy fought. She dropped the bundle of cloth, pulled her bow off her back, and nocked an arrow to the string.

With a guttural cry, the bogles surged forward, concentrating their attack on Roy. He blocked their strikes with his blade, the clang of metal-on-metal ringing through the air. The bad odds didn't seem to bother him as he ducked, parried, and stabbed.

One of the bogles hung back, poking at Roy from the edges of the fight. Ok then—that one was her target. She pulled back on the bowstring and sighted down the arrow. Aim for the middle of the creature—surely she could at least hit it? She let the arrow fly. It struck the bogle in the shoulder, and it gave a yelp.

Not exactly what she'd intended, but better than nothing. Quickly, she snatched another arrow from her quiver, aimed a bit lower, and this time hit the bogle in the leg. It snarled and headed toward her.

In her peripheral vision, she saw one of Roy's opponents go down. Her third arrow was nocked and ready, centered on the bogle's chest, when the ground shook. A cloud of dust billowed out from where Roy was standing.

"Roy!" She couldn't see a thing. Coughing, she started forward.

"Relax." His voice came from just ahead. "Wait a second. It'll clear."

Sure enough, the dust dissipated fast. In a moment, it was gone—and so were their enemies. Jennet glanced around, but there was no sign of the creatures. Even the path was undisturbed, as if the earth had never belched out bogles to attack them. Slowly, she lowered her bow, then tucked the arrow back into her quiver.

"That's it?" she asked. "Where'd they go?"

"I told you, it's easy fights. You don't have to kill things at this level, only injure them. Do enough damage, and they just disappear." He eyed her bow. "Not bad with the shooting—but you didn't need to fight."

"Hey. It's how I play."

She wasn't a fan of playing the helpless maiden, even if Roy kept trying to shove her into that role. She'd been getting the hang of the bow, too. Next fight, she'd be able to hit things much better.

"Whatever." He shrugged. "Grab the cloth—the stream's up ahead." He started forward again, not waiting for her.

She slung her bow across her back, picked up the silk, and followed. It stung a little, that Roy was annoyed with her for fighting. His self-importance was so big, it squeezed out everyone else around him.

The path dipped down into a small vale. Saplings grew here, and she could hear the bright chuckle of running water. Lengthening her stride, she hurried to catch up with Roy. He stood by the waterside, illuminated by a beam of sunshine that made the copper in his hair glow. Probably he'd picked that place to stand on purpose.

"Alright," he said. "Give me the stuff."

Jennet handed over the bundle of silk. Thankfully, the stream was small, maybe two feet across at its widest. The bright water was clear enough that she could see the sandy bottom—no deeps and shadows where wicked water-hags could lurk. On the bank grew delicate ferns and long-stemmed purple flowers shaped like hoods. It seemed peaceful. She took a deep breath.

"So," she said, "what do we do?"

She half-expected him to suggest they just switch the cloths and tell Hob they'd washed them. But the little goblin would know.

"I'll wash the red one, you do the white." Roy handed her the pale silk. "It's simple. Dip it in the water and imagine it changing color."

Roy knelt and submerged his cloth. She was a little surprised he hadn't remained standing there like some fancy statue and delegated the menial parts to her. Then again, they were both supposed to complete the quest. It probably wouldn't succeed if only one of them did it.

His silk turned a deeper hue of crimson beneath the

water—but as he pulled it out, the color seeped away. She expected to see swirls of red in the stream, but the water ran as clear as ever. When Roy finished pulling the silk out, it was pure white.

"See?" He winked at her. "Your turn."

The stream was so cold it made her gasp. Right—she'd forgotten how much sensation was programmed into Feyland. It felt real—it *was* real, in a crazy way.

"You can feel the water, right?" Roy smiled at her. "I told you this game was flawless. Ok, now think *red*."

Jennet swirled the white silk under the water and pictured it turning deep crimson. Red as rubies. Red as fresh-spilled blood. Slowly, she pulled the cloth up.

Droplets ran like crystals back into the stream. As she watched, the white turned a pale pink. Then rose-colored. She held her breath. *Red*. The silk deepened to scarlet. Kept going.

"Whoa!" Roy grabbed the cloth out of her hands. "Not black, Jennet."

He held it up by the corners. The silk was red, mostly. But the middle was marred by a swirl of darkness—burgundy, shading to midnight at the very center. She shivered.

"Is the quest ruined?" she asked.

There was a shadow of uncertainty in Roy's expression. He stared at the silk a moment more, then gave himself a shake.

"We're good. Don't worry." It sounded like he was trying to convince himself.

She stood. "Let's go back."

Roy nodded, his face tense, then turned and tromped up the path. This time, he didn't hand the cloth off to her. Was he worried she'd wreck the quest even more if she touched it? Maybe he was right.

"Hey," she said, hurrying after him, "why don't you tell me more about the game?" A little flattery wouldn't hurt, either. "This place is amazing, just like you said. You were really good in the fight, too."

He slowed down and gave her a warm smile. Too bad he wasn't this handsome in the real world—though he sure acted like he was.

"I've spent a lot of time playing Feyland," he said. "But if you think this is sparked, wait til the next time we play, when we get deeper in-game."

She wasn't so sure she wanted there to be a *next time*, or if she wanted to keep playing with Roy. Then again, none of her questions had been answered. Was this really a different version of Feyland?

Just when she thought it might be, weird things happened, like the silk turning dark in the middle.

"You were going to tell me about the Court—ow!" A sharp tug on her hair made her whirl around, hand going to her dagger.

Nothing was there. Except… she squinted. There were brighter places in the air, shimmery bits that hovered and fluttered. Out of the corner of her eye, she saw one move close to her arm. Ouch!

She swatted at the air, and was rewarded with a high-pitched giggle.

"It pinched me! Roy, what's going on?"

"It's just the pixies. They're harmless." He looked amused now, instead of worried.

"They don't seem harmless." She ducked as one of the shimmers flew at her face, then winced as her hair was yanked again. "Why aren't they bothering you?"

She had seen pixies in Feyland before, glowing winged creatures that were as innocuous as fireflies. They had always seemed more like stage props than actual fey-folk.

"I guess they like you better," Roy said.

"I don't think *like* is the right word here." She batted another glow away. "Ok guys, you've had your fun. Now stop."

Her answer was a spate of giggling, and a pinch on her thigh. This was getting seriously annoying. She had to drive them off, but her bow and dagger weren't much help against glowy bits of light. Roy wasn't much help, either, standing there with his arms crossed and laughing.

Obviously she was on her own. What could she use against the pixies?

Her Kitsune magic. She thought back to the character creation interface. Shapeshift, wield fire, and cast illusion. Turning herself into a fox didn't seem like the right solution, and fire was too drastic. She wanted to drive the pixies away, not torch them.

Doing her best to ignore the pokes and pinches, she closed her eyes and focused her imagination. She needed something the pixies would fear—an enemy, coming at them out of the sky. She took deep, even breaths, and pictured a hawk circling the thermals above. Sharp beak and talons, the deadly shadow of wings rippling over the meadow.

She opened her eyes and squinted up. The shape of a raptor was outlined in the sky above them. She'd done it! Grinning, she brought her illusion diving down, talons extended.

The pixies' giggles turned to shrieks, their shimmering lights swirling in consternation as the bird attacked. The hawk scattered them, then banked sharply above the tall grasses and began to climb. Two of the pixies hovered uncertainly, but the rest were fleeing. When Jennet made the bird dive again, the remaining shimmers gave a squeak and streaked away.

She watched until all the glowing specks had disappeared over the hills, then let her illusion fade. Sudden weariness washed over her, and she lowered herself to sit, cross-legged, on the ground.

"You ok?" Roy asked.

"Yeah," she said. "Just tired. I guess illusion-making takes it out of you."

"Wait… the hawk. You did that?"

"You don't have to sound so surprised. I had to get rid of those pixies somehow. They were severely bothersome."

"I'm impressed," he said.

There was a look in his eyes that made her

uncomfortable—as though she were suddenly coated with sugar and he had a raging sweet-tooth. Jennet hurriedly got to her feet.

"Anyway," she said, "let's turn in this quest."

"Ok." He tucked the bundle of silk under his elbow. "Hob's cottage is around the corner."

He was right, of course. The cottage came into view as soon as they rounded the next bend. The goblin sat on the doorstep, exactly where they had left him. As they approached, he rose and held out his spindly arms.

"Have you completed the quest I set you?" he asked in his creaky voice.

"We have." Roy handed the cloth over, then glanced at her.

She knew they were both thinking the same thing. Would the quest fail because of her dark-marked silk? Her heart sped, like she'd been running.

Hob unfurled the lengths of cloth. He held the white one up and nodded, the motion bobbing his long, curved nose. When he picked up the red one, he gave a small grunt.

"What do I see? How comes this stain upon the silk?" He looked up at Jennet, pinning her with his dark gaze.

"I…" Jennet swallowed. "I don't know." The words came out more like a question.

Roy stepped forward. "Look. It's red, right? That's what counts. Just call it done and send us to the next level."

He was arguing with a Non-Player-Character? That was a little extreme—but then, when had Roy ever acted like anything but the center of his own private universe.

The goblin stared at Roy for a long moment before lowering the cloth. "Very well, Royal one. But take heed—the King awaits his tithe. His patience wears thin."

"I'm getting it." There was a defiant edge to Roy's words. "Tell him I'll be there soon."

"Soon," Hob echoed, his voice scraping the word. "But will it be soon enough?"

Roy folded his arms. "Tell the king—"

"Enough." The goblin held up a clawed hand. "I delivered my message—I do no more." He scowled. "Your quest is accepted, adventurers. You have won access to the second circle. Prepare yourselves."

Roy glanced at her. "Hold on," he said. "This gets a little wild."

Didn't she know it. There was just time to nod before a golden glow surrounded them. Then the world spun, a sudden vortex of glittering light. It wasn't dangerous, traveling the rings, but it could be disorienting. To her surprise, she felt Roy reach out and catch her hand. It was an annoyingly kind gesture.

The whirling stopped, the light fading away to reveal a deep forest. They stood in the center of a ring of mushrooms—still the white-speckled red ones instead of the pale mushrooms she was used to.

"You alright?" Roy asked, still holding her hand.

"Yeah." She pulled away, conscious of his stare on her. Think. What would someone unfamiliar with the game say? "Um, that was weird. So, where are we now?"

"We're at the next fairy ring—the second level of Feyland. Want to keep going?"

She eyed the dark pines towering above them. "No. Let's log off. I need to get home."

A minute later, she pulled off her sim helmet, questions burning through her. As soon as Roy was off the system, she turned to him.

"The king that Hob mentioned—is he the final boss?"

"Yeah." Roy slid out of the chair, not meeting her eyes. "I thought you had to go."

"So, we can't talk about Feyland?" She followed him out of the Full-D enclosure. "What's the tithe thing you're supposed to pay? It sounds serious."

"Look, it's just a game." His voice was cold. "I'll walk you to the door."

Wow, where had Mister Super-charm gone? Whatever the tithe was, he obviously didn't want to discuss it. Did that mean it had something to do with the real world?

She had to talk to Tam, right away.

CHAPTER NINE

Tam lay on the couch, his sleeping bag draped over him, but he couldn't rest. Even though his body felt heavy with exhaustion, his brain buzzed, thoughts circling like bees.

Jennet was at Lassiter's house.

What were they doing? Probably eating something delicious that both of them completely took for granted. Playing on his no-doubt amazing systems, laughing. Lassiter showing off for Jennet, dazzling her. Gaming skills counted for a lot in her world. Just because Tam had beat the Viewer yesterday, it didn't mean Lassiter wasn't a prime player.

She said she didn't see anything special about him—but what if that changed? If Jennet came back to school tomorrow all starry-eyed over Lassiter, Tam didn't know what he would do. Other than hate himself for pushing her at the guy.

He was worrying too much, he knew it. Jennet could take care of herself—and it wasn't like he had any claim on her, beyond being her friend. *But you want to*, part of him whispered. He moved restlessly, the sleeping bag making shushing noises, but there was no getting away from the thought. Even though he knew it was hopeless, he wished… he wished…

"Dammit," he said, throwing the sleeping bag off and sitting up.

No more lying around, thinking about her smile or how soft her lips would be, if he ever kissed them. Next thing, he'd be wearing black and writing emo poetry about love and blood. He scrubbed his hands through his hair, then let it fall back over his eyes.

The afternoon was shading to dusk, the house quiet and empty. Mom and the Bug had gone out so that he could get some rest—much good that had done. Tam got to his feet and went into the kitchen, flipping the kettle on to make instant coffee. Strong and black, so he could cover the bitter taste in his mouth with something real.

Outside, the stairs creaked, signaling that someone was coming up. He went to the door, bracing himself for Mom's clinging hug and the Bug's excited chatter about wherever they had been.

Instead, there was a knock.

"Tam?" It was Jennet's voice. "Hey, are you there?"

He slid the peephole aside, just to be sure. Yep, Jennet Carter stood outside his door, her hair shining in the last bit of sun.

"Jennet." He undid the deadbolts and wrenched the door open. "What are you doing here? The Exe isn't safe for you. You didn't walk, I hope."

She made a face. "Thanks, I'd love to come in. Good to see you, too."

"I'm serious." He stepped back so she could come inside, then closed and locked the door behind her. "It's getting dark. You shouldn't be here."

He sounded like a grumpy old man, but he couldn't help himself, even though he was beyond glad to see her.

"I had George drive me. Don't worry so much."

Like being chauffeured around in a grav-car wasn't incredibly conspicuous, especially in the Exe. He bit his tongue to keep from scolding her even more. She didn't deserve to be a victim of his bad mood.

"Want something hot to drink?" he asked.

He went back to the kitchen, trying not to notice the mess in their two-room house. While he'd been in the hospital, Mom had let the Bug trash the place. Maybe if he ignored the mess, Jennet wouldn't see it, either. Yeah, right. One of these days, when he got his energy back, he'd start picking up.

"Tea would be good," she said, following him into the kitchen alcove. "Um, is your family here?"

She glanced at the narrow door to Mom's bedroom—the only other place they could be, since they clearly weren't in the living room.

"No," he said, getting down two mugs. "Black tea?"

She nodded, looking at him with her serious blue eyes. "I have to tell you what happened at Roy's."

Did he even want to know? Roy Lassiter wouldn't be shy about kissing Jennet. Then again, she'd probably slap him. He concentrated on pouring the hot water with a steady hand. Steam curled up, warming his skin.

"Alright," he said.

"Let's go sit down," she said, accepting her mug of tea.

Tam finished stirring his coffee. For a second he stared at the little whirlpool in the center of the liquid. Damn, he was tired. He set the spoon down and followed her into the living room.

"Just push the sleeping bag off the couch," he said. At least none of his dirty clothes were obviously visible.

She sat and patted the space beside her. "Sit down, Tam. You look terrible. Are you sure the doctors said it was ok for you to be back in school?"

Great. He looked as bad as he felt. He lowered himself onto the thin cushions, and took a scalding sip of coffee.

"Go ahead," he said. "Tell me about your afternoon with Roy Lassiter."

"Oh, Tam. You would not *believe* his gaming setups." She shook her head. "But the most important thing is he has the Full-D systems. All three prototypes."

He swallowed, tasting fear along with his coffee. "That's not good. Are they just for show, or do you think he plays?"

"I *know* he plays. He took me into Feyland."

"What?" Hot liquid splashed onto his wrist. He winced and carefully set the mug down. "How could you go back in-game, Jennet?"

Especially without him.

"I had to." She looked down at the threadbare

carpet. "More than anything, I wished you were there."

He wanted to shake her for being so dumb. He wanted to hug her, for coming out safely. Instead, he gently took her hands. Those hands were damaged now, because she had saved him. She had held him, in-game, had wrested him from the power of the Dark Queen. He owed Jennet his life.

"Are you ok?" he asked, keeping his voice calm. "Any injuries carrying over into the real world?"

"No carryover," she said. "The fights were easy. I emerged without a scratch."

She met his eyes and curled her fingers around his. Warmth pooled between them and his breath hitched. It felt good, their skin touching—almost too good.

"Why the hell did you go in?" If anything happened to her, he would never be able to forgive himself.

"When Roy was talking about the game, he called the final boss 'he.' It made me think that *his* Feyland might be different. What if my version is the only bugged one? Maybe faeries aren't trying to take over the world, after all."

"And? Is his game different?" Tam squashed down the hope her words kindled. It couldn't be that easy. Life never was.

She shook her head. "It was hard to tell. Some things, like the starting area, were changed—but the game was still pretty unpredictable. At the end, I got Roy to tell me that the final boss was a king of some kind. A king that's apparently waiting for Roy to bring him a tithe."

"And you came straight here." The knowledge eased the knot inside his chest.

"Of course I did. We're in this together, Tam." She gently squeezed his hands, then let go and took a sip of her tea.

He cleared his throat. "What's a tithe, anyway?"

"A payment, a tax." She frowned. "The way Roy acted when I asked him—the subject was completely off limits."

"Alright." Tam leaned back. "So, Lassiter found a king, instead of a queen. And he owes this king something."

"I still can't believe he didn't encounter the Dark Queen. She's the end boss."

"In the Feyland we played, yes. But you already said his game was different. Maybe…" He picked up his coffee and turned the mug back and forth between his palms, thinking. "Maybe he went to a different court."

Her brows drew together, then snapped up, her eyes going wide. "That's it! Remember the old book Thomas gave me, *Tales of Folk and Faerie*?" He nodded, and she continued, her voice fast with excitement. "The fey-folk have two courts—we talked about it in-game once. There are the Unseelie, or dark faeries, and the Seelie."

"I remember." Understanding sparked through him. "So, if the Dark Queen is Unseelie…"

"Then this king might be the leader of the Seelie Court," she finished. "It explains a lot. Why Roy isn't as damaged as I was after fighting the final boss, but why he still seems to have the magic of Feyland around him."

"Because the Seelie faeries aren't nearly as bad as the Unseelie." Tam nodded. "It makes a tweaked kind of sense. So, how did Roy get there, instead of the Dark Court?"

She pressed her lips together. "I don't know—but maybe the different landscape influences where the player ends up."

"I bet your connection to Thomas is part of it, too," Tam said. "You went to the Dark Court."

"And he's the Dark Queen's Bard." Jennet's voice was solemn. "Do you think the Seelie faeries have the same problem as the Dark Court—that without enough human contact, they're fading away?"

"It makes sense." He took another swallow of coffee. "Both courts are part of the Realm of Faerie, which Thomas said is starting to die."

"I don't like the sound of this tithe that Roy owes the king." Her voice trembled, ever so slightly. "The last faerie payment was you, Tam."

Coldness crept up his spine. "Then we better hope the Seelie Court isn't into human sacrifice. Or Lassiter's in severe trouble."

CHAPTER TEN

Jennet got home a few minutes before her dad, which was a relief. He didn't mind her spending time with Tam, but her going into the Exe would have made him furious. Luckily George, the chauffeur, was on her side—sort of. He wouldn't tell Dad where she'd been unless directly asked.

When Dad walked in the door, it was clear that asking about her afternoon was the last thing on his mind.

"Welcome home, sir," HANA said. *"Dinner will be served in fifteen minutes."*

Instead of responding like he always did, he just stood there in the entryway holding his briefcase. His face was set in a grim expression.

"Dad?" She went over to him. "Are you all right?"

"Jen." He gave himself a little shake. "Sorry, I didn't see you."

Moving like his bones hurt, he put his briefcase down and slowly removed his coat. One of the maids bustled up—no doubt alerted by HANA that Mr. Carter was home—and whisked the coat away.

"Sit down." Jennet took his arm, worry pulsing

through her. "What happened? HANA, send my dad something to drink, please."

"Whiskey," her dad added.

"Right away," the house replied.

When he got to the couch, Dad sank down and stared at his hands. "I can't believe it. After all that work, all those years…" He shook his head.

"What?" She sat beside him, suddenly chilled. "Did VirtuMax *fire* you?"

"No—it's worse than that."

"How could it be worse?"

"They pulled me off the project."

"You're…" she swallowed, her throat dry with worry. "You're not in charge of Feyland any more?"

This was bad. Even though Dad hadn't been able to stop Feyland, he had done what he could. Now there was nothing standing in the way of the company releasing the game.

He gave a thin laugh. "It would be better in some ways if they had, in fact, fired me. But no—they've shunted me off to work on the Virtual Conferencing beta."

"What happened?"

"They're moving the Full-D release forward, again. When I heard that… well, I lost it. I'm the project manager and they're making all these decisions without me. I stormed into Dr. Lassiter's office and demanded she listen."

Obviously, she hadn't.

One of the maids came in and set a glass of amber liquid on the low table. Dad grabbed the glass and took a long swallow.

"I told Dr. Lassiter the equipment is dangerous," he continued, "told her she's opening up the company to enormous lawsuits in the future. She shook her head and said the Full-D is perfectly safe—that her own son has played it for almost a year now, with no problems."

"Right," Jennet breathed.

It explained a lot about why VirtuMax was so determined to go ahead with the launch. The CEO's own son had been playing, and hadn't had any issues with the system. No wonder the company wouldn't listen, not with that example in front of them.

"I…" He took another drink, then set the glass down. "I started yelling at her then. How the hell could she tell me it was safe? She wasn't there in the hospital, she didn't see the burned hands, the boy in a coma." His voice broke. "Her best friend dead in his sim chair."

"Oh, Dad." Jennet put her arms around him and squeezed, tight.

He leaned against her for a moment and took a deep, shuddering breath. "She made me sit there while she called in the company counselor. They asked me a bunch of questions, and decided that Thomas's death had obviously affected me deeply, I hadn't dealt with it properly, and I couldn't handle the stress of the accelerated timeline. I'm required to go in for regular psych-evals. They took me off the project, and reassigned me to one without the 'taxing personal issues' of Feyland."

"But," her voice was shaky, "who's in charge of Feyland now?"

"Dr. Lassiter herself. And she's set a firm launch date for the game."

"When?" She could barely say the word.

"January second—just in time for the new year."

Fear stabbed into her lungs, stealing her breath. January second? She made a quick calculation. Five weeks. She and Tam only had five weeks to figure out if Feyland truly posed a danger to the mortal world. And if it did?

When the game went live, the Wild Hunt would rampage, the Dark Queen would rule, and humans would be at the mercy of her fey magic.

Time was running out.

The cafeteria was noisy, but not as loud as the clamor of worry in her head. She'd explained to Tam what had happened to her dad, and that the company had accelerated the schedule for Feyland's launch.

"What now?" she asked, leaning over her tray of mushy vegetables.

Maybe Tam had some ideas, though she had the sinking feeling there was only one thing they could do. She'd spent half the night awake, trying to think of a solution, and had finally come up with the answer.

Tam was going to hate it.

He stopped prodding his lunch and met her eyes. "We need to get back into Feyland."

She nodded. "I agree, but if we go on my systems, we won't learn anything. I think… I have to go back in-game with Roy. Get him to take me to the Court."

"No." He shoved his tray away. "No way—you're not going without me. What if our theory about the Seelie Court is wrong? What if you meet the Dark Queen? I can't let you do that alone."

She shivered. "I know—but we still don't understand enough about Roy's version of Feyland. He could be in serious danger. The whole world could… or not. The only way to find out is by going back in-game. *His* game."

"Fine. Then I'm coming, too." He stood. "In fact, I'll go ask Lassiter right now if he'd like to game again. I bet he'd love to even the score between us."

"Wait…" It was a decent idea, but she knew enough about Roy to know it would never work. In fact, it would kill any chance of slipping Tam in under the radar.

Before she could stop him, Tam strode to the front of the cafeteria, halting at the long table Roy had claimed as his own. He spoke, and Roy responded, shaking his head. Tam lifted his hand, as if asking a question. Whatever the answer was, it disappointed him. His shoulders fell. He said something else to Roy, then turned and walked back to where Jennet sat.

"No luck?" She could tell from his expression.

Tam sat down and folded his arms. "Prince Lassiter made it clear that no Exies were allowed at his pristine mansion. But if we wanted to meet at Zeg's again, he'd be glad to teach me a lesson in defeat."

"You refused."

"Yeah." He let out a heavy breath. "I don't care what he says. I'm coming along with you anyway."

"Then he'd just turn us both away. Tam—"

"Hi, guys." Marny set her tray down next to Jennet's, effectively ending their conversation.

"Hey, Marny," Jennet said. "Glad you could join us."

It had been a few days since the other girl had eaten lunch with them. Maybe whatever weird hold Roy had over her was fading.

"Did you get kicked out of the harem?" Tam asked.

Marny made a face, looking almost like her old self. "I got tired of watching Keeli make a fool of herself. I can't believe she got his attention! Roy could do so much better."

Jennet glanced to the front of the cafeteria. She hadn't noticed before, but Keeli, the black-haired girl from The View was sitting right next to Roy—and he had his arm around her. Did that mean the rest of the girls would become immune to his dubious charm? Judging from the adoring looks around him, it didn't seem so.

"Better than a good-looking Viewer?" Tam shook his head. "You don't need him anyway. Come on, Marny, it's not so tragic. He just went with his own kind."

A doleful expression crossed her round face. "But Roy is great, and she's nothing but an over-privileged, empty-headed, rich—ow! Tam, don't kick me. You know I don't think Jennet's like that."

Jennet shifted. There was enough truth in Marny's words to hit close to the bone. And Tam approved of Roy's choice. *His own kind.* Like that was the only option for someone who lived in The View. Tears made a sudden lump in her throat.

She grabbed her tray and stood up. "I have to run... catch up on some homework. See you later."

"Wait," Tam said as she turned away. "Jennet..."

"Talk to you after school," she said, not looking at him. "Bye."

She walked past the table where Roy was laughing at something Keeli had said. The black-haired girl looked blissfully happy, and the hurt inside Jennet scratched even harder.

She was a fool for hoping, but somewhere along the way the warmth of their friendship had changed. At least for her. It was getting more and more difficult to pretend things were still the same.

CHAPTER ELEVEN

Tam slung his battered pack to the ground, leaned one shoulder against the wall, and tried not to look like he was waiting for Jennet. Still, he knew it the moment she walked out of the school.

She glanced up and saw him. For a second, she hesitated. His breath tightened, then eased when she came over to join him.

"Hey," he said.

"Hi." She didn't meet his gaze.

She looked like she'd been crying. Not obviously, but there was a puffiness around her eyes, and her lashes were stuck together with the memory of tears.

He jammed his hands into his pockets, feeling toxic. Here was Jennet, who had so much going for her, and all he could do was drag her down.

She stared at the ground, and there didn't seem to be anything to say. He looked at her, tongue glued to the top of his mouth. A couple more students came through the doors.

"Look," he said, grateful for the distraction, "there goes Lassiter with his new girlfriend." They had their arms around each other, and Keeli was staring up into

Lassiter's face.

"Guess that means he won't be inviting me over," Jennet said.

"Good." The word was out before he could think. "Listen, about what I said at lunch... I just wanted to make Marny feel better."

She folded her arms across her chest. "That doesn't mean you didn't believe what you were saying. That Viewers belong with *their own kind*."

"I wasn't thinking. I'm sorry, Jennet." He swiped the hair out of his eyes. "But we're still friends, right?"

"Friends." She said the word like it was dirt in her mouth. "Is that what you want? A pet rich-girl for a friend?"

"Of course not! You're so much more than that. You deserve the best."

She met his eyes, anger sparking her gaze. "Do I? Is Roy Lassiter the best, in your book? Is that really what I deserve—an egotistical, shallow guy who treats me like an idiot? You think that highly of me, huh?"

She had a point. "Well—"

"What about a guy who stands by his word? A guy who always tries to do the right thing? Who risked his life to save me? Maybe I deserve someone like that, Tam Linn. Maybe I deserve *you*. Ever think of that?"

"I..." He swallowed and glanced at the ground. "I hadn't thought about it that way."

"So, start thinking." She let out a low breath. "That's all I ask."

Part of him wanted to turn on his heel and head for the Exe. This was too hard. He was going to let her down anyway—it might as well be now. But the part of him that had battled monsters and braved dark magic was too stubborn to let go. Jennet was worth it.

Her words knocked around inside him, chipping the edges off of things he'd always believed were true. He didn't believe her, not quite, but he couldn't just walk away.

"Alright." He met her gaze, held it. "Forgive me?"

The frustration in her expression faded, the heat of anger in her eyes softening to warmth.

"Okay," she said, after a moment. "Now grab your stuff and come on—George is waiting with the grav-car."

"What? Where are we going?"

"My house. I want to try something. That is... if you're free."

His head was whirling. One minute, he and Jennet were barely speaking, the next, she'd given him a royal talking-to and was taking him home with her. That was progress, right? He bent and scooped up his backpack. At least nothing was permanently broken between them.

"Mom's around," he said. "For now, anyway. I don't have to take care of the Bug after school. So, yeah. I'll come over."

She smiled at him, just a wisp of a smile, but it was enough to lift his mood out of the shadows. He slung his pack over his shoulder.

"Do you still have that temporary badge for me to get into The View?" he asked.

Peons from the Exe couldn't just go waltzing into the VirtuMax compound without some kind of security access. The pass certainly had a tracker in it, in case he got unruly and went someplace he wasn't supposed to, but at least it would let him through the gates.

She dug around in her bag, then handed him the guest badge. Tam waited until he got in the grav-car to clip it on. No matter how many times he'd ridden in the vehicle—and it had to have been nearly a dozen by now—he still couldn't get used to how plush it was.

"Hello, Mr. Linn," the chauffeur said. "It's good to see you back on your feet."

"It's good to be here," Tam said, giving George a half smile.

The chauffeur didn't say much, but he didn't miss much, either. Unlike Jennet's house manager, Tam got the feeling George sort of liked him. Well, didn't despise him at least, which went a long way in The View.

The quiet smoothness of the ride still took Tam by surprise. That, and the drastic way the neighborhoods cleaned up on the way to Jennet's. By the time they whooshed under the plas-metal archway of The View, things were pristine. Clean and newly-painted, with eerily similar mansions lining the street and not a single person in sight.

Jennet had been staring out the window the whole time, which was fine with him. They couldn't talk freely with George listening, anyway. The grav-car pulled into the circular driveway and the back doors slid open.

"Thanks," Tam said.

The chauffeur nodded. "Glad you could come for a visit."

"Could you take Tam home, when we're done?" Jennet asked.

"Certainly, Miss Carter. Just inform me when you're ready."

Tam got out of the car. He didn't like George taking that gleaming machine into the Exe, even the outskirts where he lived. It was too conspicuous—a nice juicy target—but every time he argued with the driver to just drop him off in regular Crestview, George refused.

"We will," Jennet said. "Thanks."

She grabbed her bag and led the way up the wide stone path leading to her house. The place was four stories high, with balconies that jutted out on the upper levels and dozens of windows. The fountain in the front was lit up, a sparkle and cascade of water that seemed like it belonged somewhere public, not as a lawn decoration that maybe five people ever saw.

Jennet held her wrist up to the front door and it opened with a soft chime.

"Welcome home, Jennet," a perfectly modulated female voice said as they stepped over the threshold. *"You have brought Mr. Linn. Staff has been notified."*

"Right," Jennet said. "We'll be up in the game-room."

"Confirmed."

Tam shook his head. He couldn't get used to the house network, either. No matter how complicated things got at home, at least his place didn't talk to him. He liked it that way—no machines peering over his shoulder all the time.

"One moment, please. The house manager wishes to speak with you," the computer said.

"Great." Jennet pressed her lips together. "I wonder what Marie wants."

Tam had a pretty good idea.

The click of heels announced the house manager's arrival. She was dressed in a suit, and was as short as Tam remembered—though there was nothing small about the scowl she sent him.

"Miss Carter," she said in her clipped accent. "As you recall, the last time you brought this person as a guest, we discussed the need for a more in-depth security clearance."

"Ah, yes," Jennet said.

At least this time she didn't look nervous at the thought. Guess she trusted him enough now to believe he didn't have a criminal past.

Marie, though, was clearly convinced that he was going to go home with his pockets full of small valuables if she didn't fingerprint him right away. She whipped out her sleek tablet and held it out toward him.

"Place your right hand on the screen," she said. "Hold still until the scan is complete."

He did, trying not to notice how Marie's gaze catalogued every fray and rip in his clothing. She wrinkled her nose, as if she could smell the Exe on him.

The tablet beeped softly, and the house manager snatched it back and took a few quick steps away. She studied the screen, the soft light illuminating the disappointment on her face.

"Well, Mr. Linn, it looks like the system has no record of your illegal activities."

"Marie!" Jennet set her hands on her hips. "Tam's my guest. Don't speak to him like that."

The house manager looked up, her ink-thin eyebrows lifting. She stared at Tam until he felt reduced to a little black beetle, an unwanted insect on the polished floor of the Carter's entryway. One that Marie would squish with the pointed toe of her shoe, if she could.

"Miss Carter. I cannot say I approve of you spending time in this person's company."

Jennet lifted her chin. "It's not your choice. Tam's going to be a regular guest here. I require that you treat him civilly, and see that he's issued a permanent pass."

She blew an impatient breath through her nose. "Very well. If you insist."

"I do," Jennet said. "That will be all."

Marie shot Tam one last, sour look, then turned and stalked down the hallway. Her footsteps were sharp enough to crack stone. Tam half-expected to feel the house shake from the force of her displeasure.

"Sorry," Jennet said. "Marie gets full of herself sometimes. It's all good now."

He doubted it.

Tam followed her up the stairs, the thick carpeting cushioning his footsteps as if he were walking on clouds. At the end of the hall, the wide double-doors of the game room stood open. Inside, he glimpsed the gleam of LEDs, the shine of a sim helmet—a techie's treasure trove. Jennet's game room was as big as his house, and almost as well equipped. Put in a fridge and micro, and you could live here, easy.

She hit the jamming switch beside the Full-D systems, activating the privacy frequency VirtuMax had installed to keep corporate spies and hackbots out.

"So," he said. "What's your plan?"

She tucked a strand of hair behind one ear. "I was thinking... When I played with Roy, I made a different character. If I re-create her and go in-game here, that might help change things."

"Should I switch, too?"

He slung his backpack into the corner by the door, then glanced at the sim-systems. His pulse notched up at the thought of re-entering Feyland. Even though he'd almost ended up as a sacrifice to the Dark Queen, he and Jennet had beaten her. They'd won. It was dangerous, true, but it also made him feel alive in a way nothing else did. A part of him—a big part—couldn't wait to return to Feyland.

Jennet tilted her head and considered him. "No,

don't change—I think we still need your Knight. He's the best heavy-armor fighter class in the game. And one of us should be on our strongest character. I'm still getting the hang of the Kitsune."

Tam headed for one of the sim chairs. "What kind of character did Lassiter play?"

"Mercenary, of course." She made a face. "Decent fighter, but way full of himself."

"I'm not surprised."

"Hold on," she said. "One of the maids will bring up a snack. We don't want to go in-game until after she's gone."

"Oh, right." He veered away from the sim equip, though he felt their pull like a magnet. "After we eat, then."

He'd forgotten how Jennet lived. Like a princess— driven around, cooked for, her every need anticipated. It was amazing she'd ended up such a competent person, with all that pampering.

Just one more way their lives were ridiculously different.

At least when he was in-game he could forget about that for a little while—could leave his flawed life behind and be his best self. Someone worthwhile. Heroic, even.

"Miss Carter?" A timid-looking woman in a uniform hovered in the doorway, holding a tray of food.

"Thanks, Tish—set it over there." Jennet gestured to the low table by the seating area.

The maid scurried in, put the tray down, and left.

She didn't even glance at Tam. Was it a good thing to be invisible to the staff? Or did it mean he wasn't even worthy of their notice? He shook his head. Either way, it didn't matter. Jennet wanted him here, and that was enough.

"Smells good," he said.

His stomach growled at the aroma of something fresh-baked. Now that Mom was around he ate a little more regularly, but meals were still scanty. He headed for the couch.

"Guess Marie doesn't want us to starve," Jennet said.

Tam picked up a blueberry muffin. It was still warm, and smelled delicious.

"Are you sure she didn't poison mine?" He was only half joking.

Jennet rolled her eyes. "And risk killing me, too? I don't think so."

"Maybe she's already fed you the antidote."

"Tam, you're too sensitive. Marie doesn't hate you."

She didn't see it—but then, he doubted Jennet had been the target of serious dislike very often in her life. Maybe when she'd first come in as a new student to Crestview, but soon enough she'd been accepted. Grudgingly, maybe, but nobody despised her—especially once they saw she wasn't a rich-bitch entitlement diva, even if she was a Viewer.

"Alright," he said. "I'll take my chances."

He took a bite of still-warm muffin, trying not to groan at how good it tasted. He ate three muffins, four slices of cheese, and a bunch of grapes in the time it took Jennet to finish one muffin.

"More?" She slid the tray toward him.

"No. Let's get in-game." Anticipation spiked through him.

She stood and went to wash up at the small sink in one corner of the room. Tam brushed the crumbs off his hands.

"Aren't you going to get in trouble for playing?" he asked, heading for the Full-D systems.

"Probably." She pressed her lips together, then picked up the gloves. "But this is important. And if it works, well, maybe there's no danger after all. We *have* to find out, Tam. You know that."

"Yeah."

He slid into his usual gaming chair and pulled on the gloves, taking a deep, surreptitious breath. In addition to the sheen of metal and the jewel-bright LEDs, the system even *smelled* good—a mix of machine and opulence that he couldn't quite describe. Did Jennet notice it, too, or was it just one more thing she took for granted?

He pulled on the helmet, his pulse doing a happy-dance at the thought of simming again. It had been way too long—that duel with Lassiter barely counted.

"See you in there," she said. "And keep your fingers crossed."

"Not that easy to play with crossed fingers," he said, trying to make her smile.

It worked. She shook her head at him, a smile at the

corners of her mouth, then pulled down the visor of her helmet.

At the sim interface, he selected the *F* icon from the menu. His nerves tingled with excitement as the visor-screen went dark. Back in-game.

CHAPTER TWELVE

WELCOME TO FEYLAND

The letters glowed against the blackness, turned from gold to deep crimson, then faded to gray. Tam braced himself for the transition as the music swelled. A blare of brightness across his senses, a sick churning in his stomach—the indicators that he was going *elsewhere*. A place between, as the ghost of Thomas had once described it.

That was another good thing about going back in-game—maybe they could talk to Thomas. Surely the former designer would be able to help them out, the way he had in the past.

Tam's vision cleared and he found himself in a glade surrounded by white-barked trees. Everything looked the same as usual, and his thrill faded. If Jennet couldn't change the game, no way were they going to go quest. If the Dark Queen saw them again... A chill shuddered through him.

Her parting threat had been to rip out his heart.

The air beside him shimmered, and Jennet's character appeared. He blinked. Even though he knew she was going to change characters, it was still a surprise not to see her Spellweaver.

The spell-caster had been replaced with a more feral avatar. She seemed smaller, lighter-boned—though maybe it was because she was wearing close-fitting armor instead of long, flowing robes. Delicate ears pointed through her hair, and she had a wicked-looking bow strapped to her back.

"Nice," he said. "You look fierce."

She nodded at him. "So do you. Doesn't look like your armor tarnished while you were gone."

"Knights don't rust. So…" he glanced around at the clearing, "looks like we're in the same old Feyland."

Jennet turned in a slow circle. When she came back around to face him, her eyes were alight.

"Don't be too sure," she said. "Check out the mushrooms."

He took a closer look at the fairy ring encircling them. Instead of the usual pale, glowy mushrooms, these were red with white spots.

"That's not a big change," he said, trying not to hope. "We could still be in your version of Feyland."

"Maybe—though these are exactly like the ones in Roy's game. What if this worked?" Her voice held suppressed excitement.

The breeze blew a strand of hair across her cheek. Without thinking, he reached to tuck it back in place. The edges of his fingers brushed her face, and his heart gave a painful lurch. Did she deserve him? Did he deserve her?

She stilled, her eyes wide.

Pulse racing, he pulled his hand back—although crazy thoughts prickled under his skin. What would happen, if he kissed her in-game? Would it count, in the real world? And how far did the sensory interface go, anyway?

She looked at him a moment longer, then let out her breath and stepped out of the circle. One hand on his sword, Tam followed. A mossy path spangled with white flowers led between the trees. The wind whispered in the leaves overhead, and he heard the chiming laughter of pixies.

Jennet glanced up at the sound. "The pixies attacked me, when I was in-game with Roy."

"Attacked you? How? They're tiny specks."

"I know." She shook her head. "But bees are small, too, and you wouldn't want a swarm of them on you. Anyway, I think the pixies recognized me, from playing before."

"So, maybe there is a connection between the Courts. And between the games."

He glanced up at the shimmers dancing through the trees. Time to find some answers. He just hoped Feyland would cooperate.

Senses primed, he started down the path. Behind him, Jennet's footfalls were light. The pixies floated, keeping pace with them, but didn't come any closer. Was that a good sign, or not? It felt as though the game was holding its breath.

After a minute the forest thinned, revealing glimpses of rolling green hills beyond. They came out of the trees, and he looked around. Nothing but waving grasses and scattered clumps of bushes.

"No cottage," Jennet said, coming up beside him. She glanced around, then frowned. "Either Hob or Fynnod should be here. Something, anyway. Do you think we broke the game?"

"No—it doesn't feel broken. Maybe Feyland hasn't made up its mind where to take us."

She folded her arms. "We need a quest-giver."

He shaded his eyes with one hand and scanned the horizon.

"I think I see something," he said. "There, where the hills dip down. Can't tell if it's a building or what, though. Let's go see."

"All right, but be on guard," she said. "In Roy's game, we were jumped by some creatures right after we left the cottage."

"Then stay close."

He set off, heading toward the low hills. The meadow sloped up and down, and in a few minutes the forest was a distant smudge behind them. Time and distance were weird like that, in-game.

"Tam, wait." Jennet stopped, glancing at the hillocks to either side. "This looks like the place where Roy and I were ambush—"

The ground in front of them exploded, sending clods of earth spraying around them. Three red-cap goblins scrambled out of the dirt, brandishing wickedly-barbed spears. They bared their pointed teeth and rushed forward.

"Get back!" Tam yelled, pulling his sword.

His shield appeared, strapped to his arm—just in time. Two of the spear-points met it with a clang, and he felt the shock down to his toes. He ducked, and the other spear whistled past his helm.

Behind him, he heard the twang of a bow-string. A blue-shafted arrow sped by and glanced off the leather armor of the right-hand goblin.

Tam moved to the side, weaving around the spears and trying to give Jennet a clear shot.

"Aurgch!" cried the lead goblin as an arrow struck his arm. He stopped attacking and tried to pluck it out.

Ignoring the assault on their leader, the other goblins didn't hold back. Tam parried their spear thrusts, dancing back, ducking. Frustration sizzled through him. He couldn't attack—those nasty spears held him at a distance, making his blade pretty much useless. Jennet's arrows were slowing the first goblin, but the others were a problem.

He raised his shield and charged forward. Metal screeched as one of the spears slid across his armor, but he was close enough now—inside the reach of the points, where his sword could finally be useful. He stabbed the goblin in front of him, and green blood spurted from its shoulder. It fell back with a cry, only to be replaced by the second creature.

This one seemed to realize it couldn't poke at Tam. It brought the spear haft up with both hands, using it like a quarter-staff to block Tam's attack. The two of them circled, making quick feints. Tam landed a strike, cutting the goblin's arm, and was rewarded with a blow to the side of the head that made his ears ring.

The wounded goblin, clutching his shoulder, came up on Tam's right. On his left, the leader moved forward, with four arrows sticking out of him. The creature in front of him raised his spear and grinned.

Tam swung, hard, just as the three goblins rushed him. His sword imbedded itself in the leader's chest armor—and stuck. The goblin staggered, then gained his balance and gave Tam an evil grin.

"Jennet," Tam called, "keep shooting!"

Where were the arrows? Why had she stopped?

He wrenched his blade free, but it cost him a blow to his ribs that nearly took his breath. Before he could recover, the leader swept his spear low, tangling Tam's legs.

"Jennet!" he cried again, trying to keep his balance. "Shoot him, now!"

The goblins hefted their spears, a killing light in their eyes. Tam was at their mercy—and they knew it.

"Hold on," Jennet called. "One more second."

He didn't have a second. Praying he wouldn't stab himself, he threw himself into a roll. A wicked spear point swished past his ear, and everything seemed to slow down. The goblins leered and advanced, while he scrambled to his feet. Too slowly. There was no way he could deflect all three spears, poised to jab and rend. Regret seared through him. He'd failed Jennet.

A horn sounded, clear and silvery. From behind him came the thunder of hoof beats. The goblins looked up, and their faces went slack. A moment later, they turned and fled, clutching their spears and making high, whimpering sounds.

Tam froze in place as a tide of mounted knights swept by on either side of him. The ground shook under his feet, the white horses passing a hair's breadth away. As they flew past, he saw that the knights were wearing white tabards with red crosses emblazoned on the front. They held their glowing swords aloft, pursuing the fleeing goblins over the rise.

Two heartbeats later, the crusading knights were gone. The grass ahead was flattened, the only sign that anything had just happened.

"Did you see that?" Tam turned. "Jennet!"

She lay crumpled in a heap on the ground. Panic spiked his heartbeat as he sprinted to her. Had the mounted knights trampled her? He tossed his sword to the side and gathered her in his arms, searching for her heartbeat. When his fingers found the pulse in her throat, he let out a shaky breath.

"Jennet, can you hear me? Hey, wake up." He smoothed the hair back from her face. *Please, open your eyes. Be all right.*

For a long moment there was no response. Fear

stuttered in his chest. Then her eyelids fluttered open.

"Tam?" Her voice was almost a whisper.

He tried not to squeeze her too tightly. "You scared me."

It was a weak word for the panic that had consumed him. Damn it. When had Jennet become so important? *When she saved your life?* a voice inside him suggested. Or maybe when he'd saved hers.

"Did the knights appear?" she asked, trying to sit up. "Did we beat the goblins?"

He leaned back, giving her some space, but kept one arm around her for support.

"Yeah," he said. "A bunch of knights came out of nowhere and kicked their goblin asses. Just in time, too."

"It worked!" She managed a wavering smile. "That's so sparked. I created them with my Kitsune illusion powers, when I saw the fight was getting grim."

"They were great—but Jennet," he gave her a tiny shake, "it doesn't do any good to summon an army to help us, if it kills you in the process."

"I wasn't expecting the illusion to take so much out of me." She frowned. "I created a hawk, when I was in-game with Roy, and that only made me a little tired."

"An army of mounted knights riding to the rescue is a bit more complicated than a bird."

"Yeah." She blew out her breath. "But they saved your butt. That was no easy-level fight."

For a second, his body clenched with the memory of those deadly spears aimed right at him.

"Maybe the game doesn't want us to find a quest-giver."

"We're not that easy to stop." She sat forward. "I'm feeling a little better. I think this illusion thing is like when we summon items in-game."

He nodded. "That makes sense. Something can't be created from nothing—and the bigger the stuff, the more it takes out of you."

"I wonder if…" she raised her arms.

"Jennet, stop." He caught her hands. "Don't drain your energy."

"But when there's another fight—"

"Stick with the bow for now," he said. "You're a decent shot. We can figure this illusion-casting out later."

"All right." She leaned back against him. "I have to say, we make a great team."

Their hands were still clasped. Tam dipped his head and brushed his lips over the top of her hair. So lightly, she couldn't feel it—a stolen glimpse of happiness. She smelled like flowers.

"We should get going," she said after a minute.

"You sure you're ready?"

"Yeah. Help me stand."

Tam got to his feet and pulled her up. She swayed a second, then caught her balance.

"Makes me wish I had my mage staff," she said.

"You can lean on me." *Always.*

"I don't want to get in the way of your sword." She took a few steps, then gave him a pale smile. "Good as new. Let's go."

He kept a close eye on her, ready to catch her if she stumbled, but she did seem to be recovered. The long grasses around them moved in the breeze, and the sky was a perfect blue overhead, but Tam didn't let down his guard.

They headed toward the place he'd seen earlier, where the hills opened up. Sometimes it seemed close, and then they would crest a rise and the meadow would stretch onward, like they'd made no progress at all. Finally, he glimpsed the structure up ahead. It was grey and rocky, covered with swatches of moss, as though it had grown out of the ground.

"Look," Jennet said. "You were right—there's something there."

"It doesn't look like a building." He squinted, trying to make sense of the shape. "Any ideas?"

She tilted her head. "It's a dolmen."

"A what?"

"Two standing stones with a capstone laid over the top. You know, like an ancient gravesite."

He didn't know, but as they approached there was something primally familiar about the shape. The massive granite stones formed a shape like a doorway. His nerves tightened.

"Stop." He gestured for Jennet to stay back, then pulled his sword and squinted into the shadows. "There's something in there."

CHAPTER THIRTEEN

Jennet grabbed her bow, her heartbeat echoing in her ears. She was barely recovered from the last fight—her weapon felt heavy in her hands, and she just wanted to sit down in the sweetly scented grass and take a rest. But there was no napping in Feyland.

Holding his sword at the ready, Tam approached the dark opening of the dolmen. She reached for an arrow and quietly nocked it to her bow. The wind ruffled the grasses, but inside the stones everything was still. She wanted to call out for him to be careful, but held her tongue. Tam knew what he was doing.

The silence stretched, shadows gathering thickly in the hollow of stones. Then a *thunk* issued from the opening.

"Come out," Tam said.

For a moment, there was no answer. Then a figure moved forward into the light—a man with ancient, weary eyes and gray-brown hair. He had a guitar slung across his back.

All her fear left her in a rush. "Thomas!"

She dropped her bow and sprinted toward him, tears prickling the back of her eyes. He held out his arms, and she went straight into his hug.

"There you are, Jennet," he said in his warm, raspy voice. "And Tamlin as well. I have been waiting for you, though I had hoped our meeting would not come so soon."

Tam slid his sword back into its sheath, metal hissing on metal.

"What do you mean, waiting for us?" he asked. "How long have you been here?"

"How long? I cannot say. Time has a different meaning in Feyland. Long enough, it seems." Thomas let go of Jennet and stepped back, looking her over. "You have taken a new form. I pray it serves you well on the path fate has laid for you."

"Fate?" she asked.

He nodded. "It is always at work, but here in the Realm one can feel fate clearly, weaving the threads of lives. Come—place your hands against the stone."

Thomas moved to the dolmen and laid his palm on the granite. Jennet followed, though she wasn't sure she believed in destiny or whatever. The stone was rough and sun-warmed under her hand. After a moment, Tam did the same, a skeptical look in his green eyes.

"Now," Thomas said, "close your eyes. Do you feel the power, the magic and intent of the land?"

She did—a vibration thrumming through the stone, like a note too low to hear, but felt in her chest, in her bones. The skin of her palm throbbed, then suddenly flared up, as though she had passed her hand over a flame.

"Ow!" She snatched it away and stared at her palm.

The red scar burned into her hand was glowing, so bright it was almost white-hot. As she watched, the light faded, along with the searing sensation, until the mark left by the Dark Queen was just a faint trace on her skin.

"Are you ok?" Tam stood in front of her.

"Yeah." Her voice wobbled. "Look—my right hand is almost completely healed."

She held out her hands, palms up, and he took them gently, comparing the two. "Wow. Can the stone fix the other one, too?"

"Worth a try."

She put her left palm to the granite—but there was no humming within the rock, no flare of energy. When she took her hand away, it was unchanged.

Tam frowned. "It didn't work."

"I suspected it would not," Thomas said. "The magic of this place never moves in the same way twice. It is beautiful, and confusing, and dangerous, as you both well know. More dangerous by the day, as the power of the Realm stirs. It wants to flow into the human world like a wave, washing everything before it and changing the mortal realm beyond recognition."

Jennet shivered, fear seeping into her like an icy mist. "So... my version of Feyland isn't just a fluke? The game really is dangerous?"

"It is perilous beyond words." Thomas slung his guitar off his back and began to play a mournful melody.

"We must speak of it quietly. Better not to draw the attention of the powers that rule the Realm."

"Where are we, anyway?" Tam asked. "This doesn't seem like the way to the Dark Court, not exactly."

"We are on the fringes of Feyland. A place where possibilities overlap. Where things are, and are not, at the same time."

Thomas always spoke in half-riddles. He'd been poetical when he was alive, and becoming the queen's Bard had only made it worse. Of course, when he was alive, he had also talked about baseball and tech stuff and movies—things that didn't exist in the Realm of Faerie.

She had the uncomfortable thought that his humanity was beginning to fade, diluted by dwelling among the fey folk. If only she could get him out somehow—but he had refused to leave Feyland, saying he no longer had a body to return to. She supposed he was right, but the thought of him stuck here forever with the Dark Queen made her want to weep.

"Now what?" Tam asked. "We just stand here and listen to you give a concert?"

Jennet gave him a warning glance. He was always so impatient with Thomas.

"Have you heard of another mortal coming here recently?" she asked. "There's a guy in our school who has some kind of weird powers. He's played Feyland. And he talked about a king."

"Ah." Thomas's fingers moved to shape a minor chord. "There have been no mortals in the Dark Court since you defeated the queen. She was greatly angered—it is best if you never return to her court. But there is another place this human boy might have traveled."

Tam leaned forward. "So we're right—there is a Seelie court?"

"In this land, at this time, it is called the Bright Court," Thomas said. "Heed the power of names, Tamlin."

"Is it ruled by a king?" Jennet asked.

Her nerves tingled with anticipation. Finally, they were getting the answers they needed. Even if those answers were grim—like knowing Feyland truly *was* a threat.

"Indeed," Thomas said. "The Bright King is gathering his power. If you wish to keep your mortal world safe, you must find a way to stop him."

"Defeat him in battle?" Tam asked.

"Perhaps." Thomas played another curl of melody. "Defeat can come in many forms."

"But you can help us," she said. "Like you did with the queen."

"Alas, I cannot."

Her throat went dry with disappointment "Why not? Thomas, we need you."

"It is impossible for me to enter the Bright Court. I am bound to the Dark Queen, and thus barred from the halls of the Seelie."

"Can't you do anything?" She couldn't help the pleading note in her voice. How could he just abandon them?

"I may only give you counsel." Thomas looked at her with his sad eyes. "But it does not mean that others cannot assist you."

"Who?" she asked. "Puck?"

"Like his *help* is so helpful," Tam said.

She turned to him. "If Thomas can't help us, we need everything we can get. And Puck got us out of some rough places last time, remember?"

"Yeah, but—"

"Children, be still." Thomas played a quick run of notes. "My time here grows short, but I have one last piece of advice. Use the strengths that gained you victory once, and you will triumph in the end."

Jennet could see the outline of the stones behind him—his presence was starting to fade.

"Which strengths?" Jennet asked, her voice thick with sorrow. "Wait—Thomas…"

"Do not cry, Jennet. We must go where fate sends us, and do our best. Even if we do not understand the purpose, or feel strong or wise enough to play our part. Now listen—yonder lies the boundary of the lands claimed by the Bright Court." He pointed to a tall, gray rock poking up from the horizon. "You must reach the standing stone marking the border. Do not tarry here overlong."

"But…"

She lifted her hand toward him, but he was disappearing before her eyes. There was almost nothing left but a dim outline against the granite, an echo of notes hanging in the air.

"Trust one another." The words were a whisper.

Then Thomas was gone, and there were only empty shadows beneath the dolmen. Jennet swallowed past the tightness of tears. Why did he always have to *leave*?

"Come on," Tam said, taking her hand. "I'm worried that standing stone is going to disappear. It wasn't there before."

She let him pull her away from the dolmen and in the direction Thomas had indicated. The standing stone ahead of them looked solid and unmoving, but she picked up her pace to match Tam's strides.

"At least we know our theory about the Bright Court was right," he said.

"And we don't have to fight the queen." Or, hopefully, ever see her again.

"Yeah. But the king could be worse."

Jennet bit her lip. "Roy seemed ok. He wasn't being drained of his essence or anything. This is the Bright Court, after all."

"Remember that old book of yours?" Tam said. "Just because the Seelie faeries aren't evil, doesn't make them *good*."

Unfortunately, she knew he was right.

Another minute of fast walking brought them to the gray bulk of the standing stone. It stood about ten feet tall, and was patched with orange lichen. A path ran from it, into the lands Thomas said belonged to the Bright

Court. Jennet stepped onto the path, bracing herself for a shock that didn't come.

"It doesn't feel like we've crossed any boundary," she said.

"No." Tam turned in a circle. "I guess we just follow the path."

Together, they started down it. The grassy hills in front of them looked exactly the same as the ones they had left behind.

"There's something ahead," she said after they'd gone a short distance. "It looks like…"

"Another standing stone." He glanced behind them. "Or maybe the same one—since it's not back there any more."

They hurried up to the stone. Jennet touched it, ready to snatch her hand away if it started humming at her.

"I can't tell," she said. "It looks the same."

Tam folded his arms. "Why do I get the feeling we're going in circles?"

"Because," a high voice piped, "you are! Oh, well riddled, Bold Tamlin."

Jennet glanced up, to see a spritely figure sitting cross-legged on top of the stone. He was dressed in gossamer tatters, and had an impudent twinkle in his brown eyes.

"Puck!"

She couldn't help but smile at him, despite the emptiness Thomas had left. Puck had a way of cheering her up.

Tam dropped his hand to his sword hilt. "How long have you been there?"

"Long enough, Bold Tamlin."

The sprite leaped to his feet. He made a jaunty somersault, landed on Tam's shoulder, and tweaked his ear.

"Hey!"

Tam batted at Puck, but the sprite had jumped nimbly back to his perch atop the stone. His bell-like laughter chimed through the air.

"I give you nothing you do not deserve, knight. Now listen, listen well." The sprite's voice grew serious. "Do you brave adventurers desire to continue further into the realm?"

Jennet nodded, then recalled Thomas's words. The power of names, he had said.

"We wish to reach the Bright Court," she said. "Just so there's no confusion."

Tam sent her a quick glance of approval, sending warmth through her. They were such good partners in-game. Why did things have to be so much harder in real life?

"Well spoken." Puck nodded, his spiky hair standing up in tufts. "Then I have a quest for you. Will you accept it?"

"Yes," Tam said, stepping forward.

A basket woven of twigs appeared on Puck's arm. He jumped off the stone, then hovered before them and held the basket out to Tam.

"The two of you must bring me a basket of berries from yonder wood." Puck gestured to the path, which now led into a dark, piney forest. "Once you return with it, I will grant you passage to the next level."

"All right," Jennet said.

Tam gave a single nod, then turned and headed toward the woods. Jennet followed. When she glanced back over her shoulder, the sprite was gone.

CHAPTER FOURTEEN

Jennet let out a low breath as they entered the shadow of the trees. The dark evergreens rose around them, the aroma of needles filling the air like expensive incense. Low-growing purple flowers edged the path, and there were no birds calling, only the hush of wind through the pines. Shafts of sunlight pierced the forest, beams that looked nearly solid in their brightness.

"Do you see any berries?" She glanced around. There were some bushes with shiny dark leaves, a few sprays of ferns, but no obvious berries.

"It won't be that easy," Tam said. "This is a faerie quest, remember? We probably have to go deep into the forest, where the monsters dwell."

"I know. I was just… hoping."

Things were never that simple in Feyland. Every tale she'd read in her old book, every quest Feyland had given them, had a twist. There was no way to prepare. Even though she knew things would go wrong, it was always in some chaotic, unexpected way.

Still, there was a long way between not-simple and life-threatening. The further in-game they went, the more danger they would face. And whether it was from the

Dark Court or the Bright, things wouldn't be easy.

She followed Tam, the quiet of the forest giving her a moment to think. Not being able to count on Thomas had been a blow. At least Puck had shown up. No matter how Tam felt about the sprite, he had never yet done them harm, or led them astray.

Ahead, a beam of light slanted down into a small clearing, pricking bright glints of red from among the leafy plants growing there. She peered into the shadows.

"I think we found our berries," she said.

Tam handed her the basket, then drew his sword. "You do the picking. I'll stand guard."

She paused at the edge of the clearing, the back of her neck tightening as she scanned for danger. The forest was still, nothing stirring in its shadowy reaches. The berries shone like crimson jewels—rubies and garnets scattered on the bushes. She plucked one. It was round and smooth under her fingers, a succulent gem of fruit. She held her breath and dropped it into the basket.

The forest remained quiet. Unchanging.

She glanced over at Tam. His armor glinted silver and his green eyes held a fierce determination.

"Keep picking," he said, his voice low.

It didn't take long before the basket was nearly filled. With each berry she dropped in, she kept expecting an attack, until her nerves were stretched taut. Tam seemed steady, outwardly calm, but she could see his tension in the way he gripped his sword hilt. His knees were bent, like he was ready to leap in any direction to defend her.

Another berry. Another. Her fingers trembled.

A long, screeching wail sounded through the forest, and Jennet almost dropped the basket.

"Quick," Tam said, beckoning. "Something's moving under the trees."

She hurried to join him, taking care not to spill the berries, then tucked the basket between the roots of a nearby tree. If they were about to fight, she needed her hands free.

On the far side of the clearing, a figure appeared—a woman shrouded in a black cloak.

"Who picks my berries?" she said in a high, wavering voice. "Who steals my bounty?"

"We didn't know the berries were yours," Jennet said. Though the woman didn't look dangerous, there was something about her that made the back of Jennet's neck prickle with fear. "There's no fence—they look like they're growing wild."

"They are mine. Mine!"

As she spoke, the bent figure began to grow taller. She moved into one of the shafts of sunlight and her cloak blew back to reveal a pale, tattered gown. Her dark hair fell about her in waves, her mouth was a red wound, and her eyes were black as a moonless night.

"What is she?" Tam whispered. He shifted into a battle stance and his shield appeared, strapped to his left arm.

The woman opened her mouth and wailed. It was the sound of bone scraping ice, the sound of death waiting nearby, honing a rusty scythe. Her cry sliced through the clearing, and Jennet flinched. Forcing her hands steady, despite the pounding of her heart, she pulled her bow off her back and nocked an arrow.

"Banshee," she said.

The woman drifted toward them, her gown fluttering, and stretched out her hands. "Give me the berries, and you shall leave here unscathed."

"I don't think so." Tam lifted his sword.

"Then," the banshee screeched, "I shall take them!"

She flew directly at Jennet, her hands turning into claws. Jennet dodged back, a second too late. Wicked nails scratched her cheek, she stumbled and fell—and then Tam was between her and the creature. He slammed the banshee with his shield, forcing her away. The creature tried to dart around him, but he aimed a blow at her heart. He was forcing her to stay and fight him instead of going after Jennet.

Taking advantage of the banshee's distraction, Jennet scrambled to her feet. She raised her bow, trying to get a clear shot. Tam stepped back, and she let an arrow fly, the twang of her bowstring buzzing the air. It was a good shot—but the arrow went right through the banshee and lodged in the tree behind her.

Jennet let a frustrated breath hiss out between her teeth. Tam was stabbing and slicing, but his sword passed harmlessly through the banshee's body.

The creature was almost impossible to fight—but they had to do something. Jennet lowered her bow.

Maybe she should cast an illusion… but what? She shook her head, trying to think as Tam battled the banshee. Nothing came to her except a sense of bone-deep weariness, as though her energy wasn't replenished enough for that particular magic.

The banshee laughed and stretched out her clawed hands. Tam bashed her with his shield, and she staggered back a pace.

Jennet's cheek still stung. She touched her face, then studied the thin line of blood left on her fingers. Of course! Their enemy was insubstantial now—but mist couldn't inflict damage. In order to hurt them, she had to take on a more fleshly form.

Quickly, Jennet set her bow down and drew her dagger. It was short, but finely honed on both edges. Gripping the hilt, she moved forward, looking for her chance.

Tam was moving fluidly, blocking the banshee at every pass, but his expression was grim. No fun to fight an enemy that slid away like mist.

The banshee laughed, a sound like a deranged cat. Her face was transforming, the features of a woman becoming haggard, the slash of her mouth widening. Jennet moved closer, until she was just behind Tam.

"Here I am," she taunted. "The berry stealer. Come get me."

"Jennet—get back," Tam said.

She stayed where she was, holding her breath. This had to work.

With a caterwaul, the creature sprang forward, her nasty claws swiping. Jennet raised her dagger and stabbed the banshee in the palm. Tam, quick as ever, brought his sword down, hard.

Dark blood spurted from the banshee's severed wrist. She let out an agonized howl, so loud Jennet's ears rang from it. The woods reverberated, throwing the screech back at them. From a far distance, black crows erupted into the sky, cawing harshly.

Cradling her injured arm, the banshee screamed once more. Then, like a nightmare, she dissolved into the air. All that remained were the tatters of her gown, and the last echoes of her wail.

A moment later, the clearing was empty. Beams of sunlight slanted down as though nothing had happened—but there was a smoking hole in the moss at Jennet's feet, where the banshee's blood had spattered.

Tam took her arm and pulled her to the edge of the trees.

"Washcloth," he said. A second later, a damp cloth appeared in his hand. He brought it up to her face, dabbing lightly. "Does that hurt?"

"No. Is it bad?"

"It won't leave a scar, if that's what you're asking. Make sure you disinfect it when we get out." Unhappiness shaded his green eyes, and she could guess why.

"Tam—I had to get into the fight in order to defeat the banshee."

"I know. That doesn't mean I have to like it."

"Look." She grabbed his wrist. "You put yourself into danger for me all the time."

"That's different. I'm the Knight—it's my job." He met her gaze.

"We're a team. It's *my* job to contribute everything I can. Ok?"

He didn't say anything for a moment. Their eyes locked, held. Her heart did a somersault and suddenly she could barely breathe.

The raucous cry of crows filled the air, their dark forms flashing overhead, and the moment was broken.

"Here." Tam stepped back and handed her the washcloth. "Hold it against your cheek. I'll carry the basket."

Her throat was tight with longing. Why did he have to be so cautious?

He picked up the basket of berries. Without saying anything, they headed down the path leading out of the forest. Tam kept glancing at her, then away, as if he wanted to say something but didn't know how.

"At least we won," she said, to break the silence.

"Yeah."

She frowned. She hated this version of Tam—so withdrawn and self-contained.

"Are you ok?" She couldn't help asking, though she knew she wouldn't get any real answer from him.

"Just… thinking."

There wasn't anything she could say to that. Her

cheek stopped hurting. Jennet handed Tam the washcloth and he vanished it.

Despite the heavy silence, it seemed to take half the time to return, and soon they were in front of the standing stone.

Puck was there, swinging from what looked like precarious handholds in the rock.

"Greetings, Puck," she said, giving him the proper quest-giver words.

"Well, well," he said. "Fair Jennet, Bold Tamlin. You return—though not unscathed. Have you completed the quest I set you?"

"Here are your berries." Tam thrust the basket at the sprite. "You could have warned us about the banshee."

"Had I warned you about her, another creature would have appeared instead." Puck took the basket, then popped a berry in his mouth. "Delicious! Did you not taste of them?"

"Are they safe?" Jennet asked.

"Where's the fun in *safe*?" The sprite gave them a sly look. "Mortals are nothing but fools, denying themselves of sweetness. Here." He held a berry out to Tam.

Tam shot a look at Jennet. They both knew it wasn't wise to refuse the faerie's gifts and risk angering Puck—especially when he was acting helpful. But they also knew that it was dangerous to eat or drink anything in-game. Doing so could trap a person in the Realm indefinitely. The faerie lore was pretty clear on that point.

"Take it." There was an undercurrent of darkness in

Puck's tone.

"Alright." Tam plucked the berry from the sprite's palm. "Doesn't Jennet get one, too?"

"She has no need of it," Puck said.

Was that a good thing? She exchanged another look with Tam. Then he glanced down at the berry, his face uncertain.

"Um," Tam said. "Can I save it for later?"

The sprite laughed. "Always so careful, Tamlin. Take care that you do not wait too long, or the fruit will wither into bitterness."

Jennet had the uncomfortable feeling Puck was talking about more than just a berry.

"I made a promise, once," Tam said, "not to eat or drink anything in-game."

She let out a breath, and smiled at him. "Yes, you did."

"Sometimes you mortals are too cautious for your own good." Puck wrinkled his face into a scowl, then flipped into a handstand. Upside-down, it looked like he was smiling.

Tam dropped the berry back into the twig basket. "Are we done, here?"

"Indeed." The sprite vaulted back onto his feet. "You have completed the quest, and won passage to the second circle. Prepare yourselves."

Without thinking, Jennet reached for Tam's hand. He was there, his clasp warm and steady. A golden glow surrounded them, and she caught one last glimpse of

Puck. The sprite winked at her. Then the world spun in a vortex of glittering light, replacing the standing stone and whirling the dark forest away.

A moment later, the spinning stopped. Jennet glanced around, to see that they were again in the center of a fairy ring. This time the clearing was surrounded by majestic oak trees.

"Looks good," Tam said. He let go of her hand and gestured. "Red mushrooms. We're on our way to the Bright Court. Should we keep going?"

"Next time. I bet it's getting late."

Time could get funny, in-game, rush and flow and slip away almost unnoticeably. Dad would be coming home at some point, and she and Tam would be in serious trouble if he caught them using the Full-D systems.

"Alright then," Tam said. "See you out there."

His character faded, leaving Jennet alone in the clearing. She cast a glance at the path leading between the oaks. That direction lay the Bright Court, she felt it, like a compass tugging in her chest. The Bright Court—and a powerful king they would, somehow, have to defeat.

CHAPTER FIFTEEN

Tam stripped off the gaming gloves and ran his hands through his hair. A minute later, Jennet emerged from the game and removed her sim helmet. He studied her cheek, where a long red scratch marred the pale perfection of her skin.

"Don't forget," he said. "Disinfectant."

"Right." She got up and turned the jamming switch off. "HANA, let George know that Tam is about ready to go."

"Of course, Miss Carter."

She went to the wall and pushed a hidden button, revealing a cupboard where medical supplies were stored. It wasn't the first time she and Tam had left Feyland with injuries. They'd found out the hard way that the damage they took in battle transferred out of the game.

He glanced toward Jennet's hands. She'd nearly ruined them while saving his life. The only thing that made the knowledge bearable was the fact that he'd saved her first.

He couldn't quite believe that today, the game had healed her hand. Had it carried over?

"How's your right hand?" he asked.

She flexed it a few times, then held it up. Only a faint redness showed on her palm—in contrast to the dark burn that still marred her left hand.

"It feels good," she said.

"Show your dad. Maybe that will convince him the game has real-world consequences."

"I'll try. But he's good at explaining things away. I mean—magic? It's hard to believe." She swabbed her face with a disinfectant pad. "Ow—that stings."

"Here." Tam held out his hand. "I'll spray the plas-skin on for you."

She hesitated a second, then handed him the bottle. Was she that skittish at the idea of him touching her? Well, and he was just as bad—one minute wanting to kiss her, the next beating himself up for even thinking it. But at least he could help her with this.

He was close enough to smell her hair again—close enough that his faded T-shirt brushed the designer fabric of her blouse.

"Shut your eyes and hold still," he said.

Her lashes fluttered closed, hiding her intelligent blue eyes. Her lips were so soft-looking. The pounding of his heart filled him up, until his whole body was a drum. Surely she could hear it. He put one hand under her chin, his thumb a little too close to her mouth. Moving it would just make it more obvious he was almost touching her lips. He tried to ignore the warm wash of her breath across his skin.

Puck's teasing words echoed in his mind. *Mortals are*

nothing but fools, denying themselves of sweetness. Take care that you do not wait too long, or the fruit will wither into bitterness. He knew exactly what the sprite had been talking about. But did he have the courage to follow through?

Forcing his other hand steady, he brought the bottle up to her face and sprayed a thin layer over her cut. The chemical odor of plas-skin masked the distracting scent of her.

She opened her eyes, and the look in them nearly stopped his breath.

"Tam," she whispered.

Goosebumps chased across his whole body. She stared at him, then, slowly, closed her eyes again. Heart bumping crazily in his chest, Tam leaned forward.

This was it—the kiss that had haunted his sleeping, and waking, for weeks. The dream? memory? of kissing Jennet had been one of the only things that kept him sane through the long, tedious hours of recovery in the hospital.

Now.

The brush of a kiss, as light as a whisper. He barely dared more. Her lips were even softer than her hair, but warm. Warm as sunshine. Sparks flew through him. He pressed a little more, letting their mouths meld. Her arms came around him, and with a huge thump, his heart settled. It felt like floating—like an even deeper magic than the mysteries of Feyland.

"Miss Carter." HANA's crisp tone echoed in the little room.

Tam jumped back, feeling as if he'd just touched fire. He stared down at the carpet. Half of him felt like the worst idiot ever, but half of him was still flying. It was a giddy mix of embarrassment and elation.

"Yes?" Jennet said to the house.

"George is waiting with the car."

"Um, ok. Great." She cleared her throat. "Tell him Tam will meet him outside in a minute."

"Very good. I have notified him."

Silence fell. Tam could feel Jennet's gaze, but couldn't quite bring himself to meet it.

"Tam. Look at me."

Reluctantly, he raised his eyes. She didn't seem upset, though her cheeks were pinker than usual.

"I'm sorr—"

"Shut it." She put her hands on her hips. "Don't you dare apologize to me for that kiss, Tam Linn. I've wanted it to happen for ages."

He supposed he'd known. It wasn't like he was totally oblivious to the signals. But still, she was a thousand miles above him.

"Yeah. Well—I'm still not so sure... Jennet, you could do a lot better than spoilage from the Exe."

"You idiot." She grabbed his hands and pulled him toward her. "Weren't you listening, earlier? You're the one I want."

"I'm hardly perfect, Jennet. I mean, I know I'm a good gamer, but the rest..."

"Yes, you're a prime gamer. Yes, you have a family

that half the time is falling apart at the seams. We're not even going to talk about the Exe. But all of those things make you who you are, Tam. As yourself, you're flawless."

The sincerity in her voice made him start to unravel. It was all too much. He pulled his hands free, then had to jam them in his pockets to keep from reaching for her.

He wanted to kiss her, again and again. He wanted to turn and run, far away from the idea she had of him—an image of himself he was deathly afraid he couldn't live up to.

"I… I'm not sure I can do this," he said.

He could hand her some cheap psych-babble about how everyone he'd ever loved had ended up leaving him, or argue that their friendship was too important to screw up over a short-lived infatuation. But none of that would change the way he felt when he looked into her eyes.

Her face softened, just a little. "Just think about it, Tam. No rush." Her mouth gave a wry twist. "After all, I've waited *this* long."

"Alright." His voice came out thicker than he wanted. "See you tomorrow."

It was lame, but he really didn't know what else to say. His thoughts were whirling, spinning sickeningly, like he'd been dropped back into Feyland.

She set her hand on his arm. "I wish you'd stop running away from me."

"It's not you, Jennet." He scuffed at the carpet with his shoe. "I'm running away from *me*."

Too bad there was never any escape from the person inside his own skin.

He turned and walked down the hall, feeling her eyes on him. The cameras watched his every move, no doubt monitored by hawk-eyed Marie. He trudged down the stairs, let HANA open the door for him, and went out alone into the cold gray evening.

The drive down into the Exe was quiet. George was a man comfortable with silence, and Tam was glad. He stared out the window, counting streetlights until they ran out, the bulbs shattered, the wiring torn away.

"Here we are," the driver said, bringing the grav-car to a smooth stop in front of Tam's place.

"Thanks." Tam slid out of the back seat and headed for the rickety stairs running up the side of the building.

The car quietly pulled away. He could feel people watching from the boarded-up place down the street, their hostile curiosity pricking the back of his neck. Even though he lived on the outskirts of the Exe, it wasn't safe. Next time, he needed to convince George to drop him off in regular Crestview. Being chauffeured home like this made him too conspicuous.

How long until the smoke drifters decided Tam's family had something worth stealing? Not that they did, but confrontations like that could end badly. Really badly. He shivered and drew in a breath of rot-flavored air.

The seventh tread gave under his foot and the railing wobbled precariously as he sprinted up the last few steps.

Just another reminder of how drastically things were falling apart.

He had his key-ring out and ready when he got to the front door, jingling as he undid the multiple locks. Nothing could beat old-fashioned tech. Chips and scanners could be jacked too easily, and only fools used them in the Exe.

"Tam!" his mom said as he opened the door. "You're just in time for dinner."

He slung off his backpack and did up the deadbolts again, then turned to greet her. She stood in their kitchen alcove, wearing a faded yellow apron and holding a spatula. Canned synthi-meat sizzled in the pan in front of her.

It was weird, having her home so much. And so cheerful. He didn't trust it. How long until she decided her meds were 'getting in the way of her true self' again, and stopped taking them? The shock of him almost dying was beginning to wear off—he could see it in the corners of her eyes. There was a wildness starting there, a low-grade panic that was going to eventually boil over. Then he and the Bug would be fending for themselves. Again.

"Tam, Tam." His little brother bounced up off the couch. "We got a present today, and you're gonna be so sparked when you see it! The men brought it, and it's flawless. Come on, let me show you." He grabbed Tam's hand and yanked him toward the door.

"Hold on, Bug." He pulled free from his brother's

sticky grasp. "Mom. What men? What's going on?"

"Oh Tam." She smiled, like the sun had risen for the first time ever. "The big tech company sent some representatives over this afternoon. Everything's going to be fine."

He tensed. "What? VirtuMax people came *here*? What did they want?"

"They brought you a brand new Slix sim-system!" The Bug danced around him, all excitement. "Now I don't have to fix the old one I broke. It's downstairs—come on."

Not that his little brother was getting very far with the repairs. But a new system, so Tam could play at home again.... Something deep inside him released, a tension he hadn't realized was coiled there.

The relief was short-lived, though. Mom was still smiling at him, something expectant in her face.

"What else?" he asked.

She brought her hands together, the spatula clasped between them. "They gave us money, Tam." Her voice was low. "Lots of money."

His stomach clenched. "And did they ask you to sign anything?"

"It was just a formality. A little release form, a promise that we wouldn't blame them for what happened, or say anything about it. And then they gave us thousands. Thousands."

"In cash?"

She nodded, and he felt sick.

Damn the arrogant company, thinking they could buy their way out of trouble. Bringing cash here, to the Exe, along with a fancy new sim-system. Relying on his family's poverty to buy their silence. He swallowed back bile. Damn *him* for not being here when they arrived.

"We have to give it back." The words scraped his throat. "That's blood money, Mom. VirtuMax knows their game almost killed me. They're buying us off so we can't take legal action."

Or warn anyone about how dangerous the company's new game really was. He wanted to kick something.

His mom's smile wilted. "But, honey, we couldn't do that anyway. It's better just to take the cash."

"We could find someone to help us. There are programs—"

"Do you really think the Crestview prosecutor would defend us, against the biggest corporate donor in the state?" She shook her head. "It was the right choice—the only choice. You're all better now, and we have some money to take care of things."

"And a flawless new sim-system!" the Bug chimed in.

Tam closed his eyes, tasting lead. It was too late— Mom had signed the paperwork, taken the money. The new system was downstairs in the gutted auto-shop, probably already hooked in. There was nothing he could do except grit his teeth and accept it. He swallowed sour defeat and looked at his mom.

"We need to at least get the cash into a bank or something. It's not safe here." He wasn't going to ask her the amount, not with the Bug watching, wide-eyed and big-eared.

He'd take part of the money, too, and put it in his own safekeeping. If-and-when Mom went off the rails, he and the Bug would need some insurance.

"Fire!" his little brother yelled, voice gleeful.

Mom whirled to face the kitchen, and Tam sprinted past her. He grabbed the ragged dishtowel, picked up the pan of now-flaming meat, and dumped it in the sink. The nasty smell of charred food filled the house as he doused the flames with cold water.

"Ew." The Bug made a face. "We don't have to eat that anyway, do we? Can we go out for burgers instead? Please?"

"All right." Mom squeezed his shoulder, then glanced up at Tam. "Don't be mad, honey. Things are going to work out for the best."

Yeah. He stared at the steaming ruins of dinner in the sink. His life just got better and better all the time.

Marny caught him in the halls the next morning between second and third period.

"Hey, Tam. You look like hell." Seemed she was back to her usual blunt self. "My uncle Zeg wants to know when you're coming around again. There's some new content about to release that he thinks will spark you."

Coldness squeezed the back of Tam's neck. He sure hoped the 'new content' wasn't Feyland.

"I have a replacement system now, so I'm not sure how much I'll be at the sim-café."

"You do, huh?" She raised a brow. "That rich girlfriend of yours set you up with some leet gear?"

"No. And she's not my girlfriend."

Marny rolled her eyes. "Get over yourself already, Tam. You're not as toxic as you think."

"Anyway." He ignored her comment. "The equip came from VirtuMax. A 'gift' – strings fully attached. They did everything possible to buy my family off."

"Whoa, really? I'm sorry."

He shrugged. There wasn't anything more to say about it. So far he'd avoided going down into the shop, despite his brother's pleas. As soon as he did, he'd want to play. The new Slix would be great, he knew it— though not as good as the Full-D. Still, he'd love simming on it. And then hate himself for enjoying it.

As if an expensive bribe could make up for him nearly dying. Playing on the new system would be like forgiving VirtuMax, saying everything was fixed now. But things were still severely broken.

"Jeez." Marny glanced down the crowded hallway. "Did I say you look bad? I take it back. *She* looks like hell warmed over."

Tam followed her gaze to where Keeli, the black-haired girl from the View, leaned against the wall. She looked wan and weary, with dark circles under her eyes. As he watched, she took a breath and straightened, then moved carefully into the throng of students. The way she walked, as if she felt fragile as glass, was eerily familiar. She reminded him of… of… The thought teased Tam's mind, but he couldn't quite catch hold of it.

"I guess being Lassiter's girlfriend doesn't agree with her," he said. The second the words were out of his mouth, alarms went off in his head.

Damn—that was it. Keeli moved the way Jennet had, back when the Dark Queen was draining her energy. Like someone breakable and exhausted. He knew the feeling, himself, and it came from one place.

Feyland.

CHAPTER SIXTEEN

The corner of Jennet's tablet lit up with a private message—from Tam. Her heart kicked, and she sent a quick glance to the front of the classroom, where the Lit teacher was droning on about poetic forms. Holding her tablet low, she opened the message.

Keep an eye on Keeli. Remind you of anyone?

Hm, that was cryptic.

She set the tablet back on her desk. Keeli shared this class with her, though she hadn't gotten to know the other Viewer girl that well. What had Tam meant? Jennet leaned forward and glanced down the row to where the black-haired girl sat.

Wow. Keeli looked pale as milk. Her skin seemed almost translucent, and her eyes were shadowed. As Jennet watched, the girl brought a trembling hand up to her throat and swallowed.

Keeli looked like… she looked…

"Mr. Clark?" Jennet didn't wait for the teacher to acknowledge her. "I think Keeli's about to faint."

"Miss Carter, you're disrupting—"

"Catch her!"

Jennet was out of her chair and at the other girl's

side just in time to keep her from tumbling to the floor. Geez, she was heavier than she looked.

Jennet wasn't the only student to get there, though. Roy Lassiter crouched beside her and gathered Keeli up in his arms. A strange look, almost of regret, crossed his face.

"I'll take her down to the nurse," he said.

"Is she still breathing?" Jennet couldn't tell.

"Yes." A spark of annoyance flashed in Roy's eyes. "Move, please."

She backed up, and Roy got to his feet, carrying Keeli. Jennet started after him, but Mr. Clark held up his hand.

"Take your seat please, Miss Carter. I'm sure Mr. Lassiter has everything under control."

The door closed behind Roy and his burden, and the room fell uncomfortably silent. Jennet slowly went back to her desk, feeling the prickle of everyone watching her, though it was hardly her fault Keeli had collapsed.

But was it Roy's?

At lunch, the cafeteria was filled with the buzz of speculation. Every student had a theory about what had happened to Keeli, and the babble of voices was loud in Jennet's ears.

"You're late," Marny said as Jennet set her tray down at their usual table.

Tam gave her a long, level look. His green eyes were serious. "Did you see my message?"

"Yes." Jennet said. "I stopped by the nurse's office—I wanted find out how Keeli is doing."

"And?" Tam asked.

"They took her to Central Hospital for testing."

He leaned forward, tense. "She's that bad?"

"She's not in a coma, if that's what you mean. The nurse said she's going to be all right. They thought Keeli was dehydrated."

"Dehydrated. Right." His voice was flat.

Marny glanced between the two of them, her bobbed black hair swinging across her shoulders. "What are you guys saying? Did Keeli game on some flawed equip, like what happened to Tam last month?"

"Maybe," Jennet said. "Though Keeli doesn't sim. In fact, from what I know, she pretty much despises gaming."

When she'd first arrived at Crestview High, Jennet had desperately needed to find a prime simmer. She'd tried the Viewers, first, with no luck. Had Keeli changed her mind, under Roy's influence? The thought made her cold.

"We do know *someone* who's been playing," Tam said. "Roy Lassiter."

Jennet met his gaze, seeing her suspicions mirrored in his eyes. Something, or someone, had drained Keeli's energy to the point she had collapsed.

"Come on—you're trying to pin this on Roy?"

Marny snorted. "That's taking the jealousy a bit far, don't you think?"

"Hey," said a voice behind them. "Talking about me?"

Jennet pivoted to see Roy Lassiter himself standing there. An easy smile lay on his face, but his eyes were cold.

"Hi, Roy," Marny said, her voice suddenly all soft and gooey.

Jennet wanted to give her a sharp elbow to the ribs.

"Mind if I join you?" He didn't wait for an answer, just set his tray down on the other side of Marny.

"Actually, we do," Tam said.

"Funny." Roy shook his head. "You crack me up, Exie. So, Marns, how's it going?"

"Really good," Marny said, "now that you're here."

Jennet nearly choked on her water. She set it down and blinked at the other girl.

"Are you serious?" she asked.

"Relax." Roy turned to look at her. There was an odd glow in his eyes. "Everything's fine. I thought it would be nice to spend a little time with Marny. She's sturdy—just how I like my women."

Marny giggled. Giggled! A sick feeling washed over Jennet.

"Stop it." Tam shoved his tray away and glared at Roy. "Your girlfriend just collapsed, and now you're putting the moves on Marny? That's seriously flawed."

"Piss off, Tam," Marny said, a hint of vigor back in

her voice. "You think Roy's too good for me? Well, not everyone shares your warped social views. Just because you're so screwed up over Jennet, doesn't mean I can't appreciate a good thing."

"Whoa." Tam held up his hands. "This isn't about you—it's about him."

"That's what I'm saying." Marny stood up. "Come on, Roy. I'm sure we can find someplace more hospitable."

"She's got spirit," Roy said, standing too. "I like that."

He laid his arm across Marny's shoulders, and she glowed, happiness practically rolling off her in waves.

"Wait," Jennet said, holding out her hand. "You two can stay here."

She didn't want to let Roy out of her sight, and the way Marny was acting was just… wrong. The whole situation was so freaky it made her skin itch.

"I don't think so." Marny tossed her head. "Let's go."

Roy kept his arm around her as they walked away. Across the table, Tam looked as stunned as Jennet felt.

"This is grim," she said. "What are we going to do?"

"First thing, we need to get Marny away from him." He set his hands on the table, then balled them into fists. "Keeli looked the way you did, when the Dark Queen was sucking your energy."

She nodded. "But Keeli isn't a sim player. Even with Roy helping her, there's no way she could have gone that deep in-game already."

"Maybe she didn't have to. Remember what Thomas told us before, about how the Realm of Faerie is starting to die?"

"Yes—he said there's not enough contact with the mortal world. You think this is the Bright Court's solution?" She glanced to the front of the cafeteria where Roy sat with his adoring fans. And Marny.

"I do." Tam narrowed his eyes. "Somehow Lassiter is taking people's energy, then transferring it in-game for the faeries to feed off. He's probably giving it directly to the Bright King."

Cold comprehension crept down her bones. "I guess we don't need to warn Roy about the tithe—not when he's taking other people's energy to pay it. I wonder how many others he's harmed."

"He's not getting Marny." Tam's voice was hard.

"Agreed—but how do we get her away from him? She's convinced he's wonderful."

He swiped a hand through his hair, then let it fall back over his eyes. "I bet that's another thing we can thank the faeries for. Lassiter's amazing ability to influence people. All that false charm and handsomeness."

His words rang an echo of recognition deep inside her. Handsome looks. False charm…

"Faerie glamour!" She leaned forward. "Tam, that's it."

"Faerie what?"

"Glamour. It's one of the fey magics described in my book. Here."

She rummaged in her satchel and pulled out the green-bound copy of *Tales of Folk and Faerie* – the old book Thomas had given her, before he died.

It had given her the answer for how to save Tam, and she'd kept it with her ever since. She paged through, looking for the stories about faerie glamour. There, starting on page 238.

"Faerie glamour," she said. "Confusing the senses and enchanting human perception in order to change the appearance of a thing."

"Like making a regular-looking guy seem irresistible?"

"Exactly. Read this." She slid the book over to Tam.

He scanned the pages, then frowned. "So what's this ointment they talk about, that lets mortals see through the enchantment?"

"Faerie ointment. Here." She set her finger on the opposite page and read aloud. "*Wylde Thyme, Marygold Flowers, A Four-Leaved Clover, Budds from a Younge Hazelnut, and Grass of a Faerie Throne.*"

"Nice. Grass of a faerie throne. Unless you know of some faerie throne sitting around in the real world, we're going to have to go in-game for that."

"Yes, but I think I know where I can buy most of rest of the ingredients—the herbs and stuff, anyway."

He lifted one brow. "Does your upscale market sell four-leaf clovers?"

"Um..."

"Don't worry—I was kidding. I know where to find some clover, even this time of year. I can go this afternoon."

The harsh tone of the bell cut through the cafeteria babble, signaling the end of lunch. Jennet closed the book, but something made her hesitate. Instead of tucking it back in her satchel, she slid it across the table.

"Here," she said. "You keep this for a while. Catch up on your reading."

"Are you sure?" He picked it up, the gilt-edged pages glinting in the light.

"Yes." She didn't know why, but it felt right that Tam take the book. "I'll hit the View market today, and get what ingredients I can. The sooner we make the ointment, the better."

CHAPTER SEVENTEEN

The halls were crowded at the end of the school day. Still, Jennet could always find Tam, no matter how many other students were around. She hurried up to where he stood, one hand on his locker. His lips were set in a worried line, and following his gaze, she knew why. Roy Lassiter was walking down the hall, his arm draped around Marny.

"Oh, no," she said. "You don't think he's going to take Marny home with him?"

"That's exactly what I think." He sounded grim.

"We can't let that happen! We've got to keep her out of his clutches."

She hurried after them, Tam right behind her. They caught up to the couple outside school. Roy was leading Marny over to the parking lot, where his red grav-car waited.

"Hey, Marny, hold up!" Jennet called, waving.

Marny scowled, but at least she stopped. "What do you want?"

Tam stepped forward. "I thought we could go to Zeg's today. You know, do some gaming. All together."

"I don't think so, Exie," Roy said. "You lost your

chance at that, a while back. No, Marns is coming over to my place to check out my gaming systems. They're pretty sparked. Just like me." He winked.

Jennet drew in a quick breath. They had to do something—Marny was in peril, whether she knew it or not. Thinking fast, only one solution came to her. Too bad Tam was going to hate it.

"Sweet!" Jennet said, trying to sound excited. "I'd love to come over and game, too. Let me drop my stuff off at home, and I'll meet up with you two at Roy's."

Tam shot her a glance—but what else could she do? She *had* to invite herself along, and cross her fingers Roy would agree.

"What about your low-level boyfriend?" Roy asked. "Leaving him in the dirt, where he belongs?"

"Tam's not dirt," Marny said, some of the star-struck glow fading from her eyes.

"Don't be so literal, babe." Roy squeezed her shoulders.

"Anyway," Marny said, narrowing her eyes at Jennet, "You're not invited. What is it with you, fancy-girl? You have to try and steal every guy in my life?"

Jennet forced out a laugh. "You can have Roy—believe me. But he's asked me to come play on his systems too, right?"

She glanced at Roy. He looked amused and indulgent, as if he were used to girls fighting for his attention.

"Chill, Marns," he said. "Jennet can come along. If

she wants an excuse to ditch Exie-boy, why would I stop her?"

Tam's face was set, his hands jammed in his pockets. "Well," he said in a voice like stone, "you three enjoy your afternoon."

"Oh, we will." Roy swung Marny back toward his grav-car, then glanced over his shoulder. "Come on by anytime, Jen."

Marny frowned, but it was clear she wasn't going to argue with golden-boy Roy.

"Great," Jennet called. "I'll see you guys over there. Can hardly wait."

As soon as they were out of earshot, Tam turned to her. His green eyes sparked.

"What the hell are you doing?" he asked.

"Look—it's not like you can follow them around. One sight of you, and Roy would call View Security to throw you out. I have to go—we can't let Marny be alone with him."

"No way." Tam shook his hair out of his eyes. "It's too risky."

"I know you don't like it, but at least I understand what I'm dealing with. Marny has no idea."

He regarded her a moment longer, the anger in his expression slowly fading. She was right, and he knew it.

"I hate you putting yourself in danger," he said.

"I know, Tam. I'll be on my guard."

"You better."

He stepped forward unexpectedly, and wrapped his

arms around her. Surprise zinged through her. She leaned into him and returned his embrace, closing her eyes to better memorize the warmth of his body against hers. His breath brushed her temple, and she felt their pulses settle and match, their heartbeats echoing together. Time seemed to stop for a long, golden moment.

Then Tam released her, and she reluctantly stepped back.

"Alright," he said, clearing his throat. "Go watch out for Marny—and yourself."

"I will."

"And be careful. We don't know what Lassiter is capable of—but he's severely dangerous."

Tam dodged through the graffiti-etched alleys of the Exe, senses alert. He hated having to let Jennet go back into the lion's den, alone. Given a choice, he'd like to stab that particular lion through the heart, and drag both Jennet and Marny to safety. Too bad it didn't work that way in real life.

Jennet. Her name was a bright flame inside him. A flame he feared would suddenly blow out, leaving him in darkness. Though he knew she'd had to play along, he was bruised by the idea she was dropping him for Lassiter. She wasn't—he knew that in his head. But Lassiter's ugly words still ricocheted through him, sharp-edged.

He exhaled, trying not to taste the smell of rot that clung to everything in the Exe.

At least he had something to do, to dispel the anxious energy pulsing through him. Find a four-leaf clover. He'd take the Bug, too, for added distraction. Plus, the Bug could help him look—after all, the kid was closer to the ground.

Tam made it home without any trouble. When he got the locks undone and pushed the door open, he was surprised to see his mom sitting on the couch. Her face was wet with tears, and she held a faded paper photograph he'd seen hundreds of times—a picture of herself as a girl, wearing a red dress and smiling. A past that nobody could return to.

Damn. Weepiness was a sign she was heading for one of her downturns.

"Hi, Mom," he said, closing the door and doing up the locks behind him.

"Tam—you're home early, honey." She tried giving him a smile, though it wobbled weakly at the corners.

"Not really. Can I make you a cup of coffee or something?"

He set his backpack down beside the roll of his sleeping bag. What he really wanted to know was if she'd taken her meds, though the answer was obvious. Anyway, she'd lie like she always did, and tell him everything was just fine.

Not for the first time, he considered doing something sneaky like grinding up her pills and putting them in her food. Except that if she *was* taking her mood stabilizers, a double-dose might end up making her severely tweaked.

"Oh, coffee would be nice," she said. She surreptitiously dabbed eyes with her sleeve, then tucked the photo away.

Tam went into their tiny kitchen, put the water on to boil, then pulled down the jar of powdered coffee. His hands were steady, calm, as if they weren't attached to the same body that was tensing with anxiety. Should he message Mom's new state-mandated counselor? Or could the family just ride this one through, as they had so many times in the past?

He glanced over to where she sat on the couch, looking pale and a touch wild-eyed. Not too over the edge though, not yet. Ok, he'd send a message. Maybe the counselor would be able to do something.

Right, a voice inside him whispered. *Like they've ever helped before.*

"So," he said, keeping his hands busy with mugs and spoons, "I thought I'd get Peter from school today and take him down to the park."

"Isn't it a little... cold for that?" She glanced out their wire-webbed window. "It's a sweet idea, honey, but what if it snows?"

"Mom, it hasn't snowed in Crestview for years."

No, it just threatened to. Every winter he could remember was hard and bare, with nothing soft and white to redeem it.

"It used to snow." Her voice went wistful. "We'd go sledding down the big hill outside of town."

That hill was now The View, and certainly not outside town any more. But Mom didn't need to hear either of those things—not when she was fragile like this.

The battered kettle began its creaking whistle. Tam grabbed it off the stove and fixed two cups of coffee, putting lots of sugar and creamer into her cup. He took them over to the couch and handed her the less-chipped mug, careful not to spill.

"Thanks." She pulled in a deep breath. "Some days it's just... I want more for you and Peter than this."

She waved a hand, encompassing the living room with its ramshackle bookcases and piles of clothes. The only bedroom he and the Bug had ever had. He sat next to her and slid an arm around her shoulders.

"Hey, Mom, it's ok. We're doing better than some."

Like the squatters down the block, who half the time were so smoke-drifted they didn't know they were half-starved and freezing. Still, that reminded him. He needed to take part of the cash VirtuMax had paid them off with—the blood money—and stick it downstairs in his own secret stash.

Especially if Mom was going unstable again. He took a long swallow of coffee, trying to dissolve the cold knot of fear in his belly.

"Shouldn't you go, if you're meeting Peter?" she asked.

"Yeah." He gave her shoulders a quick squeeze.

Rising, he gulped the rest of his coffee, though it was too hot. He set the mug by the sink, then pulled on his coat. More threads hung down inside, where the lining was coming off, but for now the coat was hanging together. Sort of like his life.

He paused with the door open. "We'll be home around dark."

"Take care of your brother. I love you, honey."

"Me too," he said.

The door thudded closed behind him, the keys cold in his hand. The old, familiar worry clenched through him. When he came home, would Mom still be there?

CHAPTER EIGHTEEN

Jennet made herself hurry to Roy's after George drove her home. She hummed along on her g-board over the empty streets, leaning forward to increase her speed until she arrived at Lassiter Palace. Her skin chilled from the winter air, she tucked her cold hands in her pockets and waited for the house to let her in.

The door slid open. Roy stood in the entryway, but she couldn't see Marny. Fear snagged in her throat. Was her friend all right?

"Hey," he said. "You made good time over here. Couldn't wait to see me, hm?"

She stepped into the house and propped her g-board by the door. "Where's Mar—"

"You came over." Marny said, appearing in a nearby doorway. "Can't you give it a rest?"

"Nice to see you too, Marny." She actually meant it, though the other girl wouldn't take it that way.

Roy smiled. "You two are cute. Come on in and have something to drink. House," he raised his voice, "three mochas in the sitting room."

"Right away, sir," the network said in its tinny tones.

Jennet saw Marny looking around, locating the

speakers and cameras tucked up in the corners. It must seem weird to her. On second thought, it *was* kind of strange, living in a house that tracked your every move.

Marny lifted her hand and fingered the guest pass clipped to her shirt. Did she feel as out-of-place here as Tam had the first time he'd come up to The View—or did Roy's glamour smooth over her reactions?

"Come along, ladies," Roy said, waving them forward.

"Fine," Marny said. She pivoted and stalked back down the hall.

After a second, Jennet followed. She could feel Roy right behind her. This was so awkward—but who knew what he would do to Marny, if she wasn't there?

The sitting room was all done up in blue velvet, like some prince's antechamber. Which it probably was—at least in Roy's mind. Jennet wanted to take one of the chairs clustered around the low, ornate table, but instead she sat on the couch next to Marny. Now there wouldn't be enough room for Roy.

Marny made a face and leaned away, but at least she stayed on the couch. Ignoring their little interplay, Roy went to the wall and slid aside a panel. He returned carrying a tray with three gold-rimmed china mugs on it.

"Don't you have staff?" Jennet asked.

She had finally figured out what made the Lassiter's so eerie. It seemed empty of life. Even this plush room had an air of disused silence.

"Yeah," Roy said, "but not, you know, in-your-face

maids. Though I guess some people like that kind of overdone service." There was a mocking twist to his words.

"At least I talk to more than just my house when I'm at home," she said.

There was Marie, and George, and the chef, and a couple of maids named Tish and Trixie. Whom, she had to admit, she mixed up about half the time. Of course, they had only been hired a few months ago, whereas the house manager and chauffeur had been on staff for years.

"You Viewers are like aliens," Marny said. "There's an extreme unreality effect up here. Maybe it's in the air or something."

"Or the water." Roy gave her a sly look. "How do you like your mocha?"

Marny rolled her eyes and took a big sip. Then she smiled—the first genuine smile Jennet had seen on her face since she'd gone off with Roy at lunch.

"That's seriously delicious," Marny said, "but don't expect me to believe there's any water in it."

"Probably not." Roy lifted his own mug and downed his drink in four long swallows. "Finish up, and we can get to some gaming."

Jennet wrapped her hands around her mocha, letting it warm her fingers. The beverage *was* delicious, but she was wary of it all the same. She took a small sip, then set her mug aside.

"Mind if I bring this with me?" Marny asked. "It's too good to waste." She cast a scornful look at Jennet.

"I thought you didn't sim," Jennet said. She'd seen Marny play other games though, and the girl was good.

"I don't."

"Yet," Roy grinned at Marny. "I have this amazing game you have to see. You'll love it. I'll show you everything you need to know."

Obviously Roy wanted to get Marny into Feyland. Jennet let out quiet breath, glad that she'd trusted her instincts and forced herself to come along. The thought of the other girl in Feyland, at Roy's mercy, made her shudder.

An odd expression crossed Marny's face—half pleasure, half fear. It was like her essential nature was trying to fight Roy's glamour. She was strong-willed, but that wouldn't be enough to save her.

"Jennet, you want to play Feyland again, right?" Roy rose and smiled his toothy grin at her.

"It was interesting," she said, "but can't we play something else this time?"

His smile dimmed. "If you don't want to go into Feyland, you can always go home."

"Oh, I'll come." She swallowed. "I just thought, maybe a change…"

Marny let out an impatient huff. "Are you two done? Let's go."

Roy held out his arm to her, in a move that looked more calculated than courtly. "My lady," he said, "the theater awaits."

Marny let him escort her down the hall, carrying her

mug in her free hand. Jennet trailed after them. Short of breaking the sim equipment, she couldn't stop this proposed jaunt into Feyland—which meant she needed to think strategy.

Should she make a Knight? What kind of character would Marny create to go in-game? Would Roy try anything tricky, or was Jennet's presence enough to keep him in line?

When they stepped into the theater, Marny halted. She glanced from side to side, her eyebrows raised.

"This is… big," she said. "You Viewers sure like your expensive toys."

"A lot of it is VirtuMax prototypes," Roy said. "You know—nothing you'd actually be able to buy."

"Right." Marny sipped her mocha again. "Nothing but hand-me downs. So sad. Well, why don't you show me your pathetic sim-systems."

Jennet stifled a laugh. Either Roy's glamour was starting to slip, or nothing could keep the real Marny down.

Roy frowned and strode over to the partitioned-off area. He waved his hand, and the frosted glass panels slid open. The three Full-D systems shone in the soft illumination. Beside her, Jennet heard Marny draw in a breath.

"The throne room, huh?" Marny said. Somehow she didn't sound quite so sarcastic.

"Come on in," Roy said. "We'll get you geared up."

"Actually…" She took a step back. "Just looking is

fine by me. I'm more of a screenie, myself. You know—playing without being enclosed in all that equipment."

She gave a little shudder, and suspicion bloomed through Jennet. Was Marny claustrophobic? That would explain her distaste for simming.

Roy set his hand on Marny's arm. "It's perfectly safe. You'll have fun, I promise. Nothing to worry about."

There was a crooning, hypnotic edge to his voice. Even Jennet took a step toward the Full-D systems, and she wasn't the focus of Roy's charm. She shook herself and made her voice sharp.

"Hey, Marny doesn't feel like simming. Don't make her."

"It's ok," the other girl said. "I guess I do want to."

Jennet put her hand on Marny's shoulder. "Really. You don't have to sim. There are lots of other games here."

Without a word, Marny shrugged off her touch and moved toward the sim-systems. Roy gave her a triumphant smile.

"Sit here," he said, patting the Full-D on the right. "I'll help you gear up."

Marny nodded, and Jennet wanted to scream.

"Marny." She leaned forward, keeping her voice low. "Remember what happened to Tam? Going into Feyland isn't a good idea. Let's go play a screen game."

"I want to play Feyland," Marny said, though the words had almost no inflection.

"I know you do," Roy said.

He helped Marny settle into the sim chair and pull on the gloves. Jennet caught a glimpse of her face—pale and set—before he lowered the helmet onto her head.

"Stop it," Jennet said. "She doesn't want to do this."

"You're getting annoying, Jen." He looked at her, and something in his eyes flared. "If you don't want to game with us, go do something else. Like you said, there are plenty of other options."

"Fine. I'll play."

There was no winning this one. She snatched up the gloves for the Full-D system in the middle. She couldn't let Marny go into Feyland alone with Roy.

"What do I do now?" Marny asked, a slight tremble in her voice.

"Choose the *F* icon, then make a character," Roy said. "You'd be a good healer-type. Just stand in the back and let me handle the fights, then fix me up afterward."

Marny made a noise in the back of her throat. It didn't sound like agreement. Maybe a healing priest wasn't going to be showing up in the faerie ring, after all. Maybe Marny could still fight the glamour, in her own way.

At least, Jennet hoped so.

CHAPTER NINETEEN

The Bug came running up to Tam, where he stood waiting in the school yard after last bell. His brother's eyes were bright under the shapeless knit hat he insisted on wearing every day. At least the thing was colorful—a garish mismatch of rainbow stripes.

"Tam! What're we doing?"

"Give me your backpack. I'm taking you to the park."

"Prime! Can we get ice cream?"

"Yeah." Good thing he'd brought some money. He smiled and slung his brother's pack up on one shoulder. "Though why you'd want ice cream on a day like today…"

"'Cause if we have something cold, then it will snow," the Bug said, with the perfect logic of an eight-year-old.

The Bug tilted his face up to the sky, giving the dirty, low-hanging clouds careful consideration. His hat started slipping, and he clutched it to the back of his head.

"Maybe," Tam said. "But if it snows, our quest will be harder."

"Quest?" His brother gave him a wary look. "Do we

have to go camp out in the Exe again?"

"No." Hopefully, never again. "We're on a special mission to find a magical plant."

"A magic plant? Will Puck help us?"

Tam's breath hissed out between his teeth. "Uh, you haven't mentioned Puck to anyone else, have you?"

The last thing they needed was his brother in psych eval for believing in faeries. Even if they *were* real. He'd given up trying to talk the Bug into thinking his glimpse of Puck had just been a dream.

"Course not," the Bug said. "Who'd believe me?"

The kid was pretty insightful. Or cynical. For a fleeting moment, Tam wished his brother didn't have to grow up this way.

A flash of muddy orange caught his eye—the drab color Crestview had chosen for its public transportation. Probably the paint had been on sale.

"There's the downtown bus," he said. "Race you!"

The Bug took off, laughing, and they made it to the stop right on time. During the long ride down to the park, Tam listened to his brother prattle on about school with half his attention. The other half picked at the tangles in his life—Jennet, faerie ointment, Lassiter, Marny's infatuation. The possibility that Mom wasn't fixed, after all.

The one good thing was that he was feeling better, at least physically. The lingering effects of being in a coma seemed pretty much gone. Had going back in-game helped with that? It made sense, in a weird, backwards kind of way.

"Can I pull it, Tam?" his brother asked.

Tam looked up, to see the silhouette of bare branches outside. They were at the park.

"Sure," he said, and the Bug knelt up on the seat and yanked the wire, signaling their stop.

As soon as they were out on the mostly-brown grass, his little brother started dancing around. Damn, the kid had too much energy.

"What does it look like, the magic plant?" the Bug asked. "Is it bright purple? Will it shock me when I touch it? Where is it?"

"Over this way—but its magic is a secret. You have to look closely in order to see it."

"Oh." The Bug frowned. "I thought it would be, like, *magical*. Floating in the air or all lit up."

Time for a bribe. "We'll look for a little while, then get an ice cream, ok?"

His brother brightened right up, and didn't even complain when they got to the scrubby clover patch and started searching.

"Is this it?" the Bug asked after a minute. He held up a limp clover in one grubby hand.

Tam leaned closer, his heart rushing with quick hope. Could it be that easy? The anticipation died as he inspected his brother's find.

"No—that one has three leaves."

"It does not! There's four, right there."

"Peter. Tearing one of the leaves in half does *not*

make it a four-leaf clover. Keep looking."

"This is boring." His brother folded his arms and plopped himself down, right in the middle of the patch.

"Hey, you're squishing them. Get off."

"I want my treat."

"We're going to try one more place, ok? And *then* you can have ice cream—as soon as we find one."

The Bug gave him a transparently calculating look. "If I find one, can I get two ice creams?"

"Maybe—but it has to be a real four-leaf clover. No faking."

"Ok! Let's go *now*." His brother stood up and took off across the flat, brown grass.

"Hey," Tam called, "go over by the fountain."

The Bug veered in that direction, and Tam broke into a jog to keep up. Hopefully the kid would tire out enough to settle down and be helpful.

When they got to the fountain, his brother made a disappointed noise. "They turned the water off. Why'd they do that?"

"Probably because it's getting too cold. Fountains don't like the winter."

Tam squinted up at the sky. The clouds were thicker, and there was a definite bite in the air. The sun was a pale disc somewhere behind all that smudge. He pulled the Bug's hat down over his ears, then led his brother to the leafless trees.

Last summer he'd come here, when Mom was around to look after the Bug. He'd lie in the shade and work out game strategies, or read on his battered tablet—chewing clover stems for the bite and sweetness. The patch was smaller, and shriveled, but this was the last, best option.

Without prompting, his brother squatted and began running his fingers over the cold plants. Tam hunkered down beside him. He was going to be dreaming of small green leaves all night, he just knew it. In silence, the two of them worked over about half of the patch. Tam bottled his mounting anxiety. There was a four-leaf clover here, somewhere. There had to be.

"Look!" the Bug cried, pointing to a spot in front of him.

"Did you find one?" Tam's breath caught, and he crawled over.

"No, it's snowing! Really it is—the ice cream plan worked!"

Tam followed his brother's finger, to see a white speck on top of a clover. A clover that… *no way*. Holding his breath, he leaned over and counted the leaves. *One, two, three. Four. Yes!*

Keeping his eyes fixed on it, he carefully snapped the stem—then held the clover up and counted again, just to make sure.

"Hey, you ruined my snowflake," the Bug said.

Tam laughed. Trust his little brother to see the first tiny snowflake, but totally miss that it landed on the four-leaf clover they'd been searching for.

"Don't worry," he said, "I saw it. Double ice cream

will be yours."

The Bug spread his arms out and whirled around, full of snowy ice cream joy. Bits of white flecked his colorful hat. Still smiling, Tam pulled a crumpled plastic bag out of his pocket and carefully tucked the clover inside.

Quest complete.

❧❧❧

The dizzying, golden light of Feyland enfolded Jennet. As soon as it cleared, she glanced around. Red-speckled mushrooms—check. She drew in a breath of relief. Around her towered the dark pines she remembered from reaching the second level of the game, last time she played with Roy.

His character appeared beside her, and she blinked, shocked once again at how good-looking he was in-game.

"Hey, foxy lady," he said, then laughed. "Get it? Your character is—"

"Yeah. I get it." She had half a mind to put an arrow through him. "Marny, can you hear us?"

"Of course I can." Her voice came clearly through the helmet speakers, even though she wasn't in-game yet.

"Need me to explain the interface again?" Roy asked. "What you want to do is select *Healer* from the list of various classes, and then—"

"I got it." Marny sounded annoyed.

Maybe playing Feyland with Roy was a good idea,

after all. Would his hold over Marny be less strong inside Feyland? Jennet would have to watch and see.

"So, we're not in the starting area again?" she asked. "I thought that with a brand-new character, we'd need to go in from the beginning."

"I've played Feyland long enough to know some shortcuts." Roy winked at her. "Don't worry—there's nothing in here I can't handle."

There might not be any monsters the size of his ego, that was for sure. But she bet the game had some nasty surprises waiting for them.

"What's the hold-up, Marns?" he called. "Are you coming?"

"Yeah—just a second."

Roy hopped out of the faerie ring, then drew his two-handed sword and went through some moves—sidestepping imaginary opponents and cutting wide swaths through the air. Probably trying to look good for Marny, as soon as her character materialized. Jennet rolled her eyes. It wasn't like their avatars needed to warm up before battle.

On the other hand, it wouldn't hurt to look over her own gear.

She was checking her arrows when Marny's avatar appeared in the ring. She was clad all in black, with a headband cinching back her dark hair. She had a set of long, slim blades, one on each hip, and there was a dagger sheathed in her boot. A wicked-looking morning star mace hung from her belt, and she probably had hidden knives strapped to her arms. She looked big—and deadly.

Jennet smiled. Oh yeah—so much for Roy's 'you should be a healer' suggestions.

"What are you?" Marny asked, looking her over. "One of those fox things?"

"Kitsune," Jennet said. Maybe she'd try turning into a fox for real, this time, depending on what the game threw at them.

"Whoa." Roy sheathed his sword, then gave Marny a disbelieving look. "Why didn't you roll a healer? You are a noob, aren't you? Assassin classes are one of the hardest—"

"Shut it, Roy," Marny said. Then she vanished.

CHAPTER TWENTY

"Hey!" Roy jumped back into the mushroom-bounded ring. "Come on, Marny, show yourself. This isn't the time to be messing around. Marns?"

Jennet took a couple steps away, giving the other girl room. Maybe it was her fox-senses, but she had a vague impression of where Marny was, despite her invisibility. Oh, this was seriously good. Roy was about to be taken down a peg—and she didn't know anyone who deserved it more.

"Looking for me?" Marny asked, suddenly visible again.

She had ghosted around behind Roy, and had one of her blades across his throat.

"Alright, alright. Careful with that!" Roy sounded a little panicked, and she couldn't blame him.

Marny didn't know that in-game injuries carried over to the real world. A slice from her dagger could have serious consequences.

"Never underestimate a rogue," Marny said. She stepped back and sheathed her blade.

Roy swallowed. "Ok, point taken. Just—watch your step in here. This is a complicated game."

Ha. Marny was a rogue in every sense. It was clear she made her own rules. Who knew what she'd do to disrupt the world of Feyland? Or what it would do to her, in return? Jennet was glad to be along, whatever happened.

If she and Tam and Marny went in-game together at some point… now *that* would be prime. She could just imagine the possibilities. Of course, neither she nor Tam had the ability to force Marny into simming. Somehow, she didn't think there would be many repeats of this afternoon's venture.

"Ok, ladies. Follow me." Roy's cocky assurance had returned. He jumped out of the faerie-ring and started down the path winding between the dark pines. His bright hair shone like polished copper.

"Hey." Jennet touched Marny's shoulder. "Nice job. You really got the hang of that character right away."

"I hate being told who to be," Marny said. "That's what took me so long. I had to study the invisibility talent until I really understood it, you know?"

"I'd say you did." Jennet grinned. "The look on Roy's face was priceless."

"Good." Marny glanced up the path. "He's kind of a jerk, in-game."

And out. Jennet bit her tongue. If she and Tam could make the ointment, Marny would see that soon enough.

"By the way," Jennet said, "Roy doesn't know how much Tam and I played Feyland. So if you could, um, not mention it, that would be good."

Marny raised an eyebrow, but she nodded. "All right. But some day soon you're going to have to spill your secrets, fancy-girl."

That was becoming clear. Marny was involved in the magic of Feyland now, whether she knew it or not.

"I will," Jennet said. "I promise."

The air shimmered at her words, like a far-distant bell had been rung. The vibrations lapped the air around them, making invisible ripples.

"What was that?" Marny asked.

"The sign of a true pledge." Jennet swallowed. She hadn't anticipated that. "Unexpected things have power here. Words. Blades."

The other girl narrowed her eyes thoughtfully. She was smart. It wouldn't take her long to realize there was something skewed about Feyland.

"In fact..." Jennet lowered her voice. "It sounds crazy, but if you get hurt in-game, the injury carries over into the real world. So be extra careful."

Marny's eyes widened, but she nodded.

"What's taking you two so long?" Roy called. "Come on!"

Jennet leaped over the red-speckled mushrooms and headed down the path, with Marny right behind her. Overhead, the wind sighed in the branches of the pines, then tickled her cheek with cool strands of breeze.

The trees were thinning out by the time they caught up to Roy, who was waiting for them by the edge of the forest. The path widened to a dusty road leading into a village—a collection of buildings with multi-paned windows and thatched roofs.

"Grendel Village," he said. "Lots of quest possibilities here, but I want to show Marns some excitement. Follow me."

The three of them strode into the village. There were a fair number of human-looking NPCs around—kids running and laughing, an old woman working her garden, and groups of citizens standing and talking. They looked serious, and Jennet could guess where this particular set-up was going to lead.

In the center of the village was a paved square, with a few carts selling vegetables and a crowd of people milling around. As she, Roy, and Marny arrived, a man in a blue coat stepped up onto a makeshift stage. He banged a stick on a large pan to get people's attention, and the computer-controlled characters around them quieted.

"Hear ye, hear ye," the man announced. "As you know, the vile creature that has been threatening our village is growing bolder. The council will reward anyone brave enough to fight this monster and defeat it."

"How much?" someone called.

"Fifty gold pieces!"

The crowd burst into excited babbles.

"Quiet!" The man clanged his pan again. "Who is bold enough to accept this offer?"

A sudden hush covered the square, as if someone

had thrown a sodden blanket over the gathering. Everyone stilled, not quite meeting one another's eyes.

"That's our cue," Roy said.

He strode to the platform and leapt up beside the blue-coated man, then beckoned for Jennet and Marny to join him. When Jennet stepped up onto the stage, she caught a glimpse of a blackened, smoking field at the village's edge. What were they getting into here?

"We accept the challenge," Roy said.

"Royal one," the man said with a slight bow. "We are honored by your presence. You bring the Lady Jennet, and... another companion to aid you on your quest."

"This is Lady Mar—"

"Just Marny," the big girl said. "I don't need a fancy title, like *some* people."

"Whatever." Roy turned back to the quest-giver. "Where shall we find this monster?"

"By yonder lakeshore." The man waved to where the road led out of the village.

Jennet squinted in that direction. She could make out a silvery sheen that might be water. Not too far, then.

"If you prove victorious," the man continued, "return here with the creature's head, that we may know your quest is complete and the village saved. Then we shall bestow upon you our thanks."

"And the reward," Roy said.

"Indeed. Good luck, bold adventurers!"

The crowd cheered as the three of them stepped off

the platform and headed out of the square. Nobody followed, however. Roy set a quick pace, and it didn't take long for them to leave the last thatched cottage behind.

"So," Jennet said. "What kind of creature are we facing here?"

"Depends," Roy said. "But don't worry. Whatever it is, I can take care of it."

"Depends on what?" Marny came up on Roy's other side, the three of them striding abreast down the road.

"I think fire is involved," Jennet said. "Look at that field over there. Scorched."

Roy nodded. "When I've soloed this quest, it's mostly been a big wolf, and once a troll. But now that there's three of us, it's going to be something more... complex."

"Do we have anything that can repel flames?" she asked.

For a second, she wished she were playing her mage. She could probably have figured out some kind of magical protection. Somehow, she didn't think an illusory shield would do much against real fire.

"We'll just have to rush it, whatever it is." Roy said.

"Nice strategy," Marny said. "Glad to be in here with such 'leet players."

Roy shot her a look. "Relax. I told you—I can protect you from anything Feyland throws at us."

"Heh." Marny shook her head. "Guess we'll see about that."

They were at the lakeshore sooner than Jennet wanted. Silvery waves lapped the bank and the sun sparkled on the water. It looked deceptively peaceful—until she caught sight of the swath of blackened grass on the right-hand side of the lake.

"Look." She pointed to the scorched area. "I'd say that's our direction."

Roy shaded his eyes with one hand. "I think there's a cave in the rocks over there."

"Typical," Marny said. "Of course all scary monsters lurk in caves."

"Well, it could also come up out of the water," Jennet said.

She eyed the lake, making sure to keep well back from the shore. She'd had more than enough encounters with nasty water creatures in Feyland.

"It's not in the lake if fire is one of its weapons," Roy said. "Ok, here's the plan. We'll sneak up to the cave, then I'll lure it out. Marny, you'll want to go invisible. Jennet, stay back and use your arrows. Quiet, now."

She shared a quick, exasperated glance with Marny. Roy was the master of stating the obvious as though it were some brilliance on his part.

Slowly, the three of them moved around the lake, skirting the dead grass. An acrid smell rose from the scorched earth, and Jennet swallowed hard, trying not to cough. Marny drew a black kerchief up over her nose and mouth, which made her look even stealthier.

Roy was right—there was a cave in the tumble of rocks, an opening that grew larger the closer they got. Finally they were within a stone's throw of the place. It stank—a foul mix of burnt grass combined with something rotten. Jennet drew shallow breaths through her mouth, trying not to taste the oily residue.

Roy signaled them to stay where they were, then drew his sword. It made a faint hissing sound as it left the scabbard. A heartbeat later, Marny disappeared. Time to find cover. Jennet sidled over to a nearby outcropping of stone. Whatever was about to emerge from that cave, she didn't want to be in its direct line of sight.

"Hey!" Roy shouted. "Come out and meet your death!"

A little theatrical, but then, that was Roy.

For a moment, nothing happened. Then something stirred in the back of the cave.

CHAPTER TWENTY-ONE

A flicker of heat lit the inside of the cave. Jennet saw something outlined in the orange afterglow—something big, with wings and talons and horns. She felt air stir as the creature drew in a breath. Heat tingled through her, a premonition…

"Roy," she cried, "look out!"

A huge gout of flame exploded from the darkness. Roy leapt out of the way, spinning nimbly to the edge of the entrance while a stream of red fire poured past. The instant the fire ended, the creature appeared.

It was fifteen feet tall, and covered in brownish-yellow fur. Bat-like wings rose from its back, but the worst thing about it was its two heads. Jennet shivered. The left head was a lion with curved horns, smoke still curling around its wicked teeth. Beside it was an evil-looking goat head, green spittle dripping from its mouth. Great—fire and poison, and aerial abilities on top of that.

Jennet nocked an arrow. Things were about to get way ugly.

"Over here," Roy shouted.

He swung at the creature's foreleg, slicing a red gash through the fur. It screeched and, with a mighty flap, rose into the air. The goat-head veered around, spraying vile green mist through the air. Roy ducked back into the cave, and Jennet bit her lip. Hopefully Marny would stay clear of the poison.

Breathing slowly to keep her hands steady, Jennet sighted on the creature. It was hovering, obviously searching for Roy, its wings sending drafts of dust back and forth. She aimed at the leathery juncture of one wing.

The arrow flew true, burying itself in the creature's body. The monster cried out and landed, then turned on Jennet, quick as a striking snake. She stumbled back and saw it draw another deep breath.

Fear sizzled down her bones. There was no way she could run fast enough to escape the flames building between the lion-head's jaws. This was it. She'd finally find out what happened when her character died in-game—and she had a feeling it wasn't going to be a good experience. In fact, it might be truly lethal.

Her skin burned, her bones shrieked, and her eyes blurred—but the creature was still drawing in its breath. She wasn't on fire.

What? Her view was oddly flattened, the colors washed out while the details of the ground before her grew razor-sharp. Moving on instinct, she dashed forward, her paws placed unerringly to give her the burst of speed she so desperately needed. Heat scorched her tail and she yelped, but kept running until she was directly beneath the hovering monster. Safe, for the moment.

She panted, her tongue lolling out from between her teeth, but she continued circling, staying under the creature's belly. Out of reach—for now.

Behind the creature, Marny materialized. She swung her morning-star, bashing the creature's leg and distracting it from Jennet. The beast howled out of both its mouths and spun, wickedly fast—but Marny had already somersaulted out of the way. An eye-blink later, she'd disappeared again.

"Over here!" Roy yelled, waving his sword as he darted out of the cave.

The goat-head spit at him, but he moved faster. This time he took a clue from her, and ran right at the creature, sword raised. The tip of it cut a bleeding line in the monster's chest. With another screech of pain, it flapped into the air again.

"Come on," Roy said. "Into the cave. We need to get the chimera back on the ground."

She gave a yip of agreement, and the two of them dashed for the cave mouth. Fire scored a dark line at their heels, but they made it. In the deeper shadows, Roy took a long breath.

"It's coming down," he said. "Can you turn back into a girl now?"

Was she a girl? She couldn't quite remember.

"Jennet? Hurry. You can't fight in that form."

Girl. Jennet. Concentrate.

Pain seized her. She doubled-over, clutching her belly, while tears streamed down her face. But she was human again.

"That… was severe," she managed.

"Not as severe as getting torched by a chimera," Roy said. "Get ready to run again."

She took a deep breath and squinted out into the light. The monster was folding its wings, malice in its two sets of eyes.

Suddenly, in a flurry of black cloth, Marny was on its back. She slung the chain of her mace around the goat-head's neck and pulled tight. The lion-head roared, but it couldn't flame her without scorching itself.

Jennet reached for her bow, glad to find that her weapons stayed with her during the transformations. Pulling her bow off her back, she fitted another arrow to the string and aimed for one of the lion's evil yellow eyes.

She released the shot—and missed. The arrow clattered uselessly against the rocks.

Roy sprinted forward and swiped at the chimera's leg as it bucked and lunged, trying to dislodge Marny. She was hanging on, her face grimly determined, her chain still wrapped around the goat's head. Green froth bubbled from the creature's lips, and a few drops landed on Marny's arm. Jennet saw her wince, but she didn't let go.

Roy made another pass, this time leaping up at the lion's head and scoring a cut along its jaw. Embers glowed deep in its throat.

Last chance. Jennet notched another arrow and pulled the bow back until it creaked from the strain. This time, the arrow flew straight and true, entering the lion's right eye with a nasty squelch.

The monster shrieked, a horrible sound like metal and glass crashing together. Flames flickered between its teeth, then died. The goat-head gave a final thrash, and the chimera collapsed. Its leathery wings folded in, the body shuddered, and then it was over.

Marny slowly unwound her chain and clambered down from the creature. Her hair had come loose and was hanging around her face. There were five red blisters the size of coins on her forearm—souvenirs of the chimera's poison.

"Hey," Roy said. "Nice job, there."

Jennet nodded. They couldn't have won this without the three of them working together.

"I hate sim games," Marny said. "This one's worse than most. Can we log off now?"

"Almost," Roy said. "Have to complete the quest, or the whole level will reset and we'll be back at the beginning again. I don't know about you two, but I'd rather not have to repeat this fight."

He turned, and with two swift strokes detached the chimera's heads from its body. There was no blood, though the eyes remained open, glassy and staring.

Marny took a step away. "I'm not carrying either of those. I had my up-close time already."

"I'll take the goat," Jennet said.

Luckily, it wasn't too heavy, despite its size. Nothing like game mechanics to skew physics. She held it by one horn, making sure to keep the mouth away from her body. Even though the chimera was dead, the poison could still be active.

When they reached the road, they were met by a throng of cheering villagers.

"Brave heroes!" the blue-coated man said. "You have slain the evil beast. Now receive your reward."

Roy set the lion-head down, and Jennet carefully lowered her own burden to the ground. The villagers could take it from there. A pace behind them, Marny folded her arms and watched.

"Fifty gold pieces." The headman pulled out a bag and handed it to Roy. "And now, prepare for the next stage of your adventure."

Roy stepped back beside Marny. "He's going to transport us to the third level of the game," he murmured. "Hold on."

"We're ready," Jennet said, falling back to Marny's other side.

The man raised his hands. "Farewell, bold adventurers!"

Golden light swirled around their feet, rising in a cone until it blocked out the headman and villagers, the severed heads, the sparkling lake—everything. Jennet set her hand on Marny's shoulder as the usual wave of dizziness hit her. It was like being tumbled in space—no sense of down or up, only the whirling glow and a faint, high humming.

Jennet's feet hit the ground, and she swallowed back

her discomfort. The three of them stood in the center of a faerie ring. But instead of the Dark Court's moon-pale mushrooms or the familiar red and white ones, this ring was formed of thin-stalked mushrooms that shed an eerie, purplish glow.

A chill gripped the back of Jennet's neck and shivered into her body.

"Come on, guys," Marny said. "Where's the escape button?"

"Relax, Marns," Roy said, though his voice was tight. "We're leaving Feyland. Right... now."

CHAPTER TWENTY-TWO

Jennet pulled off the sim helmet, and took a deep breath. That had been even freakier than usual. She thought Roy was off-balance, too, not that he would ever admit it.

"Ok, I'm done," Marny said, slapping her e-gloves down across the leather seat. She had gotten her gear off in record time, and now stood beside the sim-system, looking as if she'd eaten something nasty. "If I play with you again, it'll be a screen game."

"You didn't like Feyland?" Roy asked. Master of the obvious.

She shook her head vigorously. "I hate having to gear up. And I *really* hate being pulled into a game like that—one where you can't just put the controls down and walk away."

"Next time, it will be fun. I promise."

"There won't be a next time." Marny turned away from the sim-systems, and winced. "Ow. Do you have some kind of poisonous bugs in here, Roy?"

She pushed her sleeve up and looked at her arm.

"Let me see." Roy hopped out of his sim chair then froze for a half-second.

Jennet sidled over. When she saw what they were looking at, her breath caught. There were five red marks on Marny's skin—blisters from the chimera's poison.

"Uh. Oh, those." Roy's voice had a sudden, scared edge. He gripped the side of the sim chair, so hard his knuckles were white.

Was he worried about Marny making the connection, or had he never seen an injury carry over from the game? Jennet bit her lip and studied him. That flash of fear across his face—she guessed he'd never been hurt in-game, whether through luck, or the Bright King's protection. Which made sense, when she considered his insistence about how safe Feyland was.

"They kind of burn," Marny said, raising her arm.

"Right—they burn." Roy relaxed a fraction, and that spooky glow started in his eyes. "That's because you spilled your mocha on yourself earlier. Don't you remember?"

"I…" Marny looked up at him. The sharpness left her expression, and her eyes were going dreamy again.

"I bumped you, Marns, and your cup sloshed," Roy said. "Come on, we'll get the house to spit out some meds for you, and it'll be fine."

"Okay, Roy," Marny said. The adoring look was firmly back on her face.

"Stop it!" Jennet set her hands to her hips. "Tell the truth, Roy—those marks are carryover, from the game. We both know it wasn't the mocha."

His lips twisted into a scowl. "I have no idea what

you're talking about. A computer game can't affect the real world. You're tweaked, Jennet. I'd say it's time for you to go home."

He strode to the glass panels and opened them with a wave of his hand. Marny just stood there, a blank look on her face.

"Come on, Marny," Jennet said, ignoring Roy. "We need to get your arm fixed up. And then we're *both* out of here."

She'd get George to take Marny home. No way was she leaving her friend alone with Roy—not for another second.

"You like to spoil people's fun, don't you?" he said.

"Whatever. Where are your med supplies?"

"Follow me." Roy pivoted and stalked down the hall.

Back in the sitting room, Jennet settled a too-quiet Marny on the couch. She could hardly wait to get her friend out of here—away from Roy's creepy, toxic influence. The house delivered a medi-pack to the slot in the wall. Roy grabbed it and sat next to Marny.

"You'll be fixed up in no time," he said, dabbing plas-skin on her arm. "How's that feel?"

"Great." She smiled up at him.

Jennet stood behind one of the chairs, scraping her fingernails over the blue-velvet upholstery. Roy was lying to her. Could she force him to tell the truth, or was he lying to himself, too?

"Done yet?" she asked, stepping around the chair.

Marny had her eyes half-closed, as if she was falling asleep. Roy's hands were wrapped around her bare forearm, above the blisters. His eyes were intent—and his hands were glowing.

"Hey!" Jennet rushed forward and shoved his shoulders, pushing him away from Marny.

The moment she touched him, a weird spark arced between them, like rogue static. He fell back on his elbows, letting go of Marny's arm. Two glowing handprints were etched on her skin, fading even as Jennet watched.

"Whoa—feeling drastic?" Roy sat up and glared at her. "If you want to play nurse, just say so. Here." He thrust the medi-pack at her.

"You were doing a lot more than that. Stay away from Marny."

A sick shakiness rose up in her stomach. That had been the magic of Feyland—no question. Roy was harvesting people's energy, just as she and Tam had suspected. She glanced at Marny, who still slumped against the cushions, looking half-asleep.

"Look, Roy," she said. "Whatever the Bright King promised you, it's not worth it. Mortals and fey magic don't mix." She locked eyes with him. "Admit it—you know as well as I do that the power of Feyland is real."

He narrowed his gaze and stared back at her. Jennet wanted to punch him—but she also didn't want to touch him again. What if any contact enabled him to do the energy-suck thing? She shivered.

"You're one freaky girl," he finally said, his voice flat. "I think you should leave now. And don't bother coming back."

"I'm not going anywhere without Marny."

As if she'd heard her name. Marny moaned and sat up. "My head hurts."

"Can you stand?" Jennet asked, turning to her and holding out one hand. "I'm taking you home."

"You are?" Marny shot a confused look at Roy.

"Yes," Jennet said. "Come on."

Pointedly ignoring Roy, she helped Marny to her feet.

"Hey, Marns," he said. "Go ahead and stay. We don't need Jennet around—she was just leaving."

"I…" Marny seemed dazed, like she wasn't sure what to do.

Taking advantage of her confusion, Jennet linked arms with her friend and towed her to the hallway. They had to get out of there without Roy touching either of them. Almost running, she hauled Marny toward the front door. Roy stalked after them, his eyes furious. Would he think to tell the house to lock the door before they got there? Jennet's heart pounded in her throat.

"Why the hurry?" Marny protested. "I want to talk to Roy."

"Trust me," Jennet said. "We have to leave. Now."

They reached the entryway, and she scooped up her g-board, not pausing. The wide front doors swung open, as she'd hoped. Thank goodness for the Lassiter's overprogrammed house-network.

"Go," she said, pushing Marny out the door. "Head for the street."

Jennet shot a look over her shoulder. Roy stood in the hall, arms folded. Maybe pursuing them was beneath him—or maybe he knew he'd be able to get Marny under his spell again, at school. Jennet swallowed back the sour taste of fear. She and Tam had to get the faerie ointment made, as soon as possible.

What then? a voice inside her whispered. Save Marny—and Roy still had the whole school to pick from, while the Bright King got stronger and stronger. How soon until he was powerful enough to reach between the realms without a human intermediary?

"We're not done, Jennet Carter," Roy called, his voice full of menace.

"I'm counting on it," she said, trying to sound bold.

But inside, panic clawed at her ribs. They were running out of time, even faster than she'd expected.

She backed out the door, not wanting to take her eyes off Roy. When she got to the sidewalk, she hopped on her g-board and skimmed fast, not stopping until she reached Marny waiting by the gate.

"What is this?" Marny asked.

Jennet pressed her lips together. How much would her friend believe? She'd shoot for the truth, anyway.

"Roy was using magic on you."

Marny gave a snort. "Right. I can't believe I let you invite yourself along on my date—and then push me out of there before I could spend any quality time with Roy."

She squared her shoulders, like she was going to march back into the Lassiter's mansion.

"Wait! We had to get you out there because... of your allergy."

Marny gave her a suspicious look. "I don't have an allergy, fancy-girl. Though if I did, it would be to you."

"Your arm—don't you remember?"

If Marny didn't believe her about Roy, she sure wouldn't believe that her injuries came from a computer game. At least, not until the ointment had done its work.

Marny glanced down at her arm, her brows drawing together. "I thought... didn't I burn myself?"

"On a mocha you'd mostly finished drinking? I don't think so. Roy just told you that to make you stay. There's something in his house that doesn't agree with you."

Like him.

"Come on," Jennet continued, glancing up at the evening sky. "It's getting late. I'll have George drive you home."

Too late to visit Tam—but she'd message him, ask him to meet her tomorrow before school. Reception in the Exe was spotty. She'd just have to hope her message got through.

CHAPTER TWENTY-THREE

Tam stood on the sidewalk in front of Crestview High, waiting for Jennet. The early-morning clouds hung low, still shadowed with the memory of night. It was cold—a dry frigidity in the air that chafed his lungs. He shivered and shoved his hands in his pockets.

He'd only waited five minutes before her sleek black grav-car pulled up. The door slid open and Jennet hopped out, looking warm in a coat lined with fur. Probably real. He hunched his shoulders against the sharp chill.

She gestured to George, slung her bag over her shoulder, and hurried over to where he stood.

"Hi, Tam." Her words left little puffs of white in their wake. "Glad you could meet me so early."

"Yeah, well, Mom mostly takes care of the Bug now, so…" He shrugged, hiding the fact that he'd meet Jennet anywhere, anytime. "How'd it go, yesterday? You didn't say much in your message."

She pressed her lips together. "It was freaky—and frightening. I wanted to tell you in person."

"Let's get out of the wind."

He jerked his head toward the side of the building. It

wasn't much cover, but at least they wouldn't be quite as exposed. This was a somewhat decent neighborhood, but a lifetime of caution had kept him alive. So far.

Once they reached the shelter of the wall, Jennet described going in-game with Roy and Marny. She told him about killing the chimera, and the blisters on Marny's arm that had carried over to the real world.

"And then…" She wrapped her arms around herself. "Then, Roy did something to Marny. Some kind of energy suck."

"What—like he went vampire on her? Right there, with you watching?"

His throat went dry with fear. A deep, restless part of him wanted to grab Jennet and pull her into his arms. Hold her tight, keep her safe, no matter what.

"Yeah," Jennet said, shivering. "He wrapped his hands around her arm and they started to glow. Marny slumped back with her eyes closed. It was like she wasn't there."

"Damn. That's grim." Tam turned one shoulder to the wall, blocking the worst of the wind from Jennet. "Did he do anything else? Chant or, I don't know, say an incantation?"

"No. Just the touch. And his eyes were doing that freaky thing."

"So—he's pulling energy from people, just by touching them. First Keeli, now Marny. I wonder how much he needs. How much he can hold."

"Maybe he stores it in a talisman of some kind,"

Jennet said. "Like how the Dark Queen kept my energy in a glass sphere. I'll have to go back over to his house and look."

"No." He reached out and caught her by the shoulder. "You're not going to Lassiter's, ever again."

"Funny," she gave him a crooked smile. "Roy said the same thing, after I accused him of using fey magic."

"And did he admit it?"

She shook her head, the dawn light gleaming on her pale hair. "He acted as if I was insane, but he was lying. I could see it in his eyes. Tam, we have to get Marny away from him."

"Of course. Today, we make the faerie ointment. I got the clover." He patted his coat pocket.

"I bought the herbs and things, last night. So all we need now is grass from a faerie throne. I wonder what the Bright King's throne looks like."

"Me too."

For a moment, he was caught up in memory—a clearing where grotesque and graceful figures danced around a strangely purple bonfire. On the far side stood a throne made of vines and shadows. And sitting upon that throne, the Dark Queen. Midnight stars were tangled in her black hair, her gossamer dress was made of stolen moonlight, and her fathomless eyes held secrets no mortal should know.

She smiled at him.

Tam's breath left his lungs—but who needed breath when *she* was there? Shadowy promises brushed through him, tingling his senses, bright, winged sparks that flashed by like shooting stars.

"Tam?" Jennet's voice pierced the vision, calling him back to the present. "Are you all right? Tam…" Her breath was warm against his cheek.

He blinked, to find her concerned eyes staring into his, her hand wrapped tightly around his arm. Behind her was only the dingy wall of Crestview High—no mysterious clearing, no bonfire with dancing fey folk. No Dark Queen. He exhaled, from lungs that felt too tight.

"I, um… yeah. Just thinking."

Her brow still furrowed with worry, Jennet let go of his arm. He wished she hadn't—her touch had been warm and solid, anchoring him. He glanced down, letting his hair fall across his face. Why was he suddenly thinking of the queen, when he had a perfect, human girl right in front him?

"How are we going to get the grass out of Feyland?" he asked, breaking the silence before it veered into awkward.

She frowned. "If Roy really does have a talisman from the Bright King, then it must be possible to move stuff from Feyland into the real world."

"We've brought back plenty of injuries," he said. "That has to count for something."

The squeak of brakes interrupted him—the first of the buses arriving. In another few minutes, Crestview High would be full of talking, jostling students.

"Come on," Jennet said. "We need to go back to my

house, right now. Dad's at work, and I don't care if the staff says anything—as long as we get the ointment done."

She headed toward the curb, where George still waited with the grav-car. Either she'd told him to stay, or he was keeping an eye on her.

"Are you sure?" He didn't mind cutting school, but she could get in serious trouble.

"Yes. If everything goes right in-game, we can get back before school ends. Even if we can't save everyone, we can at least save Marny."

Tam paused beside the open car door. "Do you think we can make it all the way to the Bright Court?"

"We don't have any other choice."

CHAPTER TWENTY-FOUR

Jennet selected her Kitsune character and gave the command to enter game. Urgency pulsing through her, she closed her eyes and concentrated. *Take us to the Bright Court.*

She and Tam had to get there—had to find the Bright King's throne, and figure out how to harvest its grass. If it meant fighting the king himself... well, she was ready to do whatever it took.

The queasy sensation of entering the game twisted her stomach. When the feeling faded, she opened her eyes.

White-dotted scarlet mushrooms encircled her, and tall oak trees lifted high branches above. The air was quiet and warm. The path between the trees beckoned, and once again, she felt the tug of the Bright Court. Relief swept through her like a sudden gust of wind, making her sway in place.

A moment later, Tam appeared in the faerie-ring. He shot a quick glance around, his clear, green gaze coming to settle on her.

"Looks like we're in the right place. Let's go."

She nodded, and together they stepped out of the

ring and headed down the path. Emerald moss cushioned their footsteps as they wound between the trees. Ahead, vivid spots of color resolved to orange and blue-winged butterflies, flitting in and out of a shaft of sunlight.

"This is beautiful," she said.

It reminded her of the first time she'd entered Feyland—a bright veil of magic stitching over the landscape, the smell of herbs sweet in the air, the chiming laughter of the pixies overhead. She sent a wary glance into the tree tops.

Tam looked up, too, at the glimmering silver flashes. "Didn't you say the pixies attacked you, when you were playing with Roy?"

"Yeah. Kamikaze pixies—always a nice surprise."

A grin flickered across his lips—the lighthearted side of Tam that she so rarely saw outside the game.

"I'll hold them off with my shield if they attack," he said. "They'll just bounce off."

It made an amusing picture, but… "I'd rather not test it out. It was kind of unnerving, having them diving at me that time."

"They seem to be keeping their distance." He looked up again. "Is it getting brighter?"

It was. The trunks of the trees glowed almost silver, and the beams of sunlight were a piercing white.

"Makes sense," she said. "Remember, as we got closer to the Dark Court it got more and more midnight."

"You think we're near the Bright Court now, since it's so light? But don't we have a quest to do, first?"

She shook her head. "I don't know. I guess we keep going forward, and see what happens." Sort of like life, really.

The path widened, the moss now spangled with white flowers. It looked idyllic, but the back of her neck prickled.

Without warning, two gnarled brown creatures leaped out from behind the trees. Tam drew his sword and Jennet grabbed her bow off her back. Was the first fight upon them so quickly?

Rather than attacking, the figures, took up positions on either side of the path and blocked it with their crossed spears. Jennet let her arrow slide back down into the quiver, but she still kept her bow to hand.

"What business do you have with the Bright Court?" the taller one rasped, regarding them with bright, beady eyes.

Its fingers were long and twiggy, but it looked strong enough to use its sharp-pointed spear convincingly.

"We seek an audience with the Bright King," Tam said. "Let us pass."

"Mortals," the second guard said. Its voice sounded like dry branches rubbing together—an odd contrast to the liquid birdsong filling the woods. "Give us a reason for it."

She glanced at Tam, and he gave her a look that said it was up to her. All right then. She'd try to be as vague as possible. Somehow she didn't think the fey-folk would be happy about their plan to take a bit of Feyland back into the real world. Even if it was only a handful of grass.

"We come to..." She cleared her throat. "To beg a boon of your most gracious king."

"A boon?" The taller guard let out a cackle. "Tricksy mortals. The king will untangle your words well enough—and he does not grant wishes lightly."

The other creature leaned forward with a creaking sound. "Be careful what you ask for, knight and lady. Everything carries a price."

Didn't she know it. For a second, her palms tingled with the aftermath of scorching heat, the searing memory of when she'd saved Tam from the queen.

He looked at her as though he could read her thoughts, his green eyes serious. They had both paid, in the court of the Dark Queen. What new sacrifice awaited them at the Bright Court?

The taller guard cocked his head, as if listening to something they couldn't hear.

"Pass," he said after a moment. "The king has granted his leave to attend the Bright Court—provided you mortals can find your way there." He gave his cackling laugh again, then pulled his spear back, opening the path.

The second creature nodded and did the same, and Tam slid his sword back into its scabbard. Trying to ignore a shiver of worry, Jennet slung her bow across her back. She followed Tam down the path, glancing at the gnarled creatures as she went past. More like them—and stranger—would probably fill the Bright Court.

Once they left the guards behind, she glanced at Tam. "It sounds like they're expecting us to get lost along the way."

"Then we'll just have to disappoint them. We're reaching the court, no matter what."

He sounded so determined—but there was no way of knowing what Feyland was going to throw their way. No use speculating, either, until it was upon them.

The trees thinned, the light growing stronger as they went forward, until they stood at the edge of a meadow. Purple and gold flowers scattered among the low grasses, and the sweet smell of summer tickled her nose. Overhead, the sky was a clear and flawless blue.

The path, however, was gone. Nothing marked the meadow, not even a faint track through the knee-high grass.

"Straight ahead?" Tam asked.

"Makes sense."

They set off across the meadow. After a minute, Jennet looked over her shoulder, checking the edge of the forest to make sure they were still going in a straight line. Her breath tightened. Only grass stretched out around them, in all directions.

"Tam? I can't see the trees anymore."

He whirled, his hand going to his sword. "Damn. I guess they *do* want us to get lost. We could end up going in circles for hours."

"We'd know." She tried to keep her voice confident. "Look, the grass behind us is trampled."

Not that she'd be surprised if Feyland regenerated the meadow when they weren't looking, making the grasses spring back up and erasing all signs of their passage. But that kind of thinking would start fear hammering through her blood, and she was not going there. Not yet, anyway.

After a few more minutes of unchanging landscape, Tam paused. "If we do end up wandering around in here for too long, we can log off."

"We should keep going. There's no guarantee we'd get back to this level again, or even this close to the Bright Court. You know that Feyland is tricky that way."

"Yeah," he said, tromping forward. "Onward, it is."

As if their conversation itself had been a turning point, the meadow began to change. The grasses on either side of them rose, until they were waist-high. Bright scarlet poppies dotted the fields, and a swallow swooped high overhead.

There was something ahead, too, cutting across the landscape. Another minute of walking brought them to it—a tall wooden fence, blocking their view of whatever lay beyond.

"Do we just climb over?" Jennet asked, studying the fence. "We could use those knotholes for hand and footholds."

"There's a break or something, down there." Tam tipped his head to the left. "Let's try that, first."

He was right. The fence dipped, straddled by a tall, ladder-like construction.

"A stile," she said, when they reached it. "Never thought I'd see one of those, let alone clamber over it."

Tam began to climb. The stile seemed sturdy enough, even for a knight in armor. When he got to the top, he paused and shaded his eyes with his hand.

"What do you see?" she called up to him.

"More field. And some kind of creatures out there— horses maybe. I can't tell if they're dangerous or not at this distance."

Jennet nodded. Anything in Feyland could be perilous. Or not.

Tam stepped across the top of the stile and started down the other side, and she began climbing. She'd gotten to the third rung, when a high, cheerful voice called out.

"Fair Jennet, Bold Tamlin! Well met again, brave adventurers."

"Puck!" She'd know that voice anywhere.

She looked up to see the sprite sitting, cross-legged, atop the stile. On the other side of the fence, she could just see the top of Tam's head.

"I have but little time in this between place," Puck said. "Listen, and listen well. The answers you seek lie ahead. Do not be afraid to battle fiercely for them."

"Great," Tam said. "More flawless advice from the little guy."

Puck stuck out his tongue. "Better prepared you are,

Bold Tamlin. But do not thank me for it."

"Right," Tam said.

The fey-folk didn't like to be thanked directly—she knew that much from the tales in her old book. She was glad Tam remembered, too.

"Farewell," the sprite said, giving a jaunty wave as Jennet gained the top of the stile.

"Wait…" she said, but it was too late.

Tam's foot touched earth on the other side, and Puck was gone, leaving only his chiming laughter behind. That faded quickly, too, and she sighed.

"At least his advice is better than nothing."

"Maybe." Tam reached up a steadying hand as she began to descend. "With Puck, I'm never so sure. He's mischievous."

"It's part of his charm."

She jumped down, skipping the last couple rungs, then drew in a deep breath of the grass-scented air, the ground solid under her feet. Not that virtual reality *or* the Realm of Faerie were particularly solid to begin with. Reluctantly, she let go of Tam's hand.

At least they knew Puck could reach them, even within the lands of the Bright King. She took comfort in the thought, although Tam obviously didn't.

A sharp whinny broke the warm air, followed by the pound of hooves. A moment later, a herd of silvery horses streamed into view—heading straight toward them. They weren't at all friendly-looking. White fire flickered at their feet, and their eyes were glowing, as though lit by coals.

Jennet's heartbeat notched up, echoing the thudding hooves. She snatched her bow off her back, then shot a quick glance over her shoulder, judging the distance to the fence. They could make it over the stile to safety, if they sprinted hard.

"Run for it?" she asked.

"No." Tam pulled his sword in one smooth move. "Remember what Puck said? We stay—and fight."

CHAPTER TWENTY-FIVE

Jennet nocked an arrow to her bow and waited, barely breathing. Were the horses going to trample them to death? Just when she was poised to turn and run, the herd pulled up short.

They were even more frightening, up close. The dark hollows of their eyes were filled with flame, and their flickering hooves looked razor-sharp. The horses stood eerily silent—no milling about, no snorting and whinnying. Then a figure emerged from the middle of the herd, a young man, clad in a silvery robe the same color as the horse's hides. He had white hair, and eyes black as night.

She blinked. Where had he come from?

"Halt!" he called, his voice deep and resonant. "Who trespasses on the lands of the Bright King? Turn back, turn back, else a reckoning is upon thee."

"Reckon away," Tam said, and raised his sword.

Clearly he'd taken Puck's advice to heart.

"Ah," the man breathed. A thin, sharp blade appeared in either hand. "Impetuous mortals."

Tam rushed forward, but the white-haired man danced nimbly away. Biting her lip, Jennet lifted her bow and sighted down the arrow. Drat it. She didn't have a clear shot. If she missed, she'd hit one of the horses, and that didn't seem like a good idea. Maybe they'd *all* transform into enemies with knives. She started circling around, looking for a better angle.

Tam and his opponent clashed blades, parted, then came together again. The sun glinted brightly on his armor, shone on the robes and white hair of the other fighter, until she had to squint against the glare. They seemed evenly matched as fighters—but that wouldn't be enough for her and Tam to win their way forward.

She finally found a position to shoot from. Now the trick would be avoiding Tam. She lifted her bow again, then lowered it with a growl of frustration. He was too close to his opponent. Her aim was decent now, but not flawless enough to take those kinds of chances.

Maybe an archer/warrior combo in-game wasn't so great after all. She could use her Kitsune flame powers, but again, that risked injury to Tam.

Tam and the white-haired man fought on, moving almost as if they were dancing. There was a hypnotic beauty to it—the push and parry, spin and turn. Jennet shook herself, pulling her eyes away from the graceful flashing of silver blades under the sun. Time to end this.

"Tam, jump back!" she yelled, keeping her arrow trained on the white-haired guy.

Without looking at her, Tam threw himself backward. Jennet released, and with a zinging noise, her arrow flew true. It hit the enemy's arm with a meaty thunk, and he let out a cry that sounded almost like a neigh.

Tam sprang forward again and held the edge of his blade to their enemy's throat. Jennet wasted no time in nocking another arrow to her string.

"Do you yield?" Tam asked.

The man blew his breath out through his nose, nostrils flaring. His fingers were clenched around the shaft of the arrow stuck in his arm. A thin trickle of blood ran down toward his wrist.

"Very well," he said, his voice tight with pain. "You and the lady have won victory—and further passage."

Tam gave a single nod and lowered his sword.

Jennet hurried over to the man. He winced as she approached.

"Let me help you," she said. After all, it was *her* arrow sticking out of him.

His black eyes considered her. "I did not expect injury. Your aid would be welcome."

"Hold still." She grasped the arrow, and, before she could think too hard about it, pulled straight back. The man gasped as the point came free, making blood spurt freely.

"Here." Tam handed her a thick gauze pad he'd summoned.

"Thanks—good idea."

She slapped the gauze over the man's injury, and he shuddered beneath her hands as she pressed firmly against the arrow hole.

"I shall transform," he said. "This wound will close of itself when my flesh changes shape."

"Transform… into a horse?" she asked.

"Aye. When I do, take your place upon my back, and I shall carry you as far as I may."

"Do you swear no harm will come to us?" Tam asked.

The man nodded. "I promise to carry your lady safely."

"Hey," Tam said. "What about me?"

The man's laugh was a high whinny. "Have no fear, brave Knight. Another of my herd shall bear you, with the same promise. Now, stand away."

Jennet stepped back, holding the bloody gauze. Before them, the man shimmered, as if the air around him was suddenly molten. Between one heartbeat and the next, he was gone—as was the cloth she'd been holding. Now a silvery steed stood before them, with white fire at its feet and glowing coals for eyes. The horse bobbed its head and, extending one foreleg, bent low.

A minute later, she and Tam were mounted and riding through the tall grasses. It was surprisingly easy to stay on the horse, and the loping canter made it feel as though she were flying. Her fingers twined in his silvery mane, and his wide back was warm and secure beneath her legs. It was like the very best of a good dream.

The rest of the herd spread out to either side, their manes and tails frothing like water. Jennet laughed, letting the wind snatch mirth from her lips. For a precious span of time, nothing else existed—only the rhythmic beat of hooves, the scarlet poppies under the sun, the bright air against her face. And Tam, riding beside her.

At last, the herd slowed. Ahead of them, she saw another fence, this one bisected with a gate. When they reached it, her mount stopped and gave a brief whinny, and Jennet slid off. The air shimmered and the horse disappeared, replaced by the white-haired man.

"I leave you here," he said. "Your path lies beyond this gate. Fare well, mortals."

"Fair running to you," Jennet said, bowing. Beside her, Tam did the same, the sunlight glinting off his armor.

The man gave a nod, his dark eyes watchful as she and Tam went up to the gate. It was secured by a silver latch, and opened easily. Tam strode through, but she paused to wave one last time at the horse-man. He lifted his hand in return. Then the gate swung closed, blocking her view. She could hear the quiet thunder of hooves, racing away over the bright fields. For a heart-twisting moment, she wished she could go with them.

Instead, she let out a sigh and turned to see what new adventure awaited.

"Another field?" she said. "This is getting a little old."

"Guess we're seeing the full tour of Feyland." Tam strode forward, through grasses dotted with vivid blue blossoms. "At least the flowers here are a different color."

She paused to look at one—it had a deep blue center, with ruffled petals at the edge. Pretty, but she had no idea what it was called.

This was a noisier field than the last one. The hum of insects droned through the lazy air. It would be so nice to sit down in the grasses and feel the sun, warm on her face. Just for a minute—a short rest...

"Jennet!" Tam was kneeling beside her, shaking her shoulder. "Hey, wake up—this is no time for napping."

She blinked up at him, feeling as though she was wrapped in mist, stumbling toward a faint light.

"What?" She rubbed her eyes, and looked around.

Oh, right. Field. Flowers. Feyland.

"Come on." Tam held out his hand and helped pull her to her feet. "Stay close, ok?"

She nodded, a last bit of haziness still clinging to her senses. Walking seemed to help, and a few minutes later she finally felt like she was awake.

"How come you're not tired?" she asked.

"Oh, I am." His voice held an edge. "But that's normal for me."

"What, you're an insomniac?"

He hitched up one shoulder. "Nah—but sometimes life is way too complicated to sleep."

What kinds of things kept him awake deep into the night? She was about to ask, when they crested a slight rise. Below them was another herd of animals, with long, wickedly-pointed horns.

"Cows?" she guessed.

"And bulls," Tam said. "I wouldn't want to be on the wrong side of those horns."

"Then it's pretty much guaranteed we will be. Look, one's heading over."

The largest of the shaggy black beasts had turned and was ambling up the rise toward them. It had the same glowing, eldritch eyes as the horses.

"There's something on its back," she said, catching sight of a small brown figure perched just behind the bull's head. "It's not Puck, is it?"

"Doesn't look like. Maybe one of his relatives."

The big animal halted a few feet away, and the figure riding it stood, holding one horn for balance. It *was* a sprite of some kind—it had the same crooked grin and ramshackle clothing, the same jaunty bearing as Puck. But this one seemed to be a girl, judging by the wild tangle of hair and tattered skirts.

"Greetings, bold adventurers," she said, her voice high and clear. "What brings you to the king's pastures?"

"We seek the Bright Court," Tam said. "Can you tell us in which direction it lies?"

The sprite laughed. "Indeed, I cannot."

Tam frowned, and turned to Jennet. "Any thoughts?"

She stepped forward and addressed the sprite. "You cannot tell us freely, but may we *win* this information from you?"

"That you may." The creature cocked her head and

regarded them with bright eyes. "What manner of contest do you choose?"

"Um..." Jennet folded her arms. "What are our options?"

"Riddle, rhyme, or rending—those three choices I lay before you."

Riddle—no. She'd lost her fight against the Dark Queen, in part because of a riddle. Rhyme? Maybe. But Puck had said to battle fiercely. Which left...

"Rending," Tam said, and pulled his blade.

CHAPTER TWENTY-SIX

The sprite laughed and pointed one finger at Tam.

"Brave Knight - so be it." She stood and vaulted off the bull's back, leaving the animal facing him squarely.

Before him, the bull's eyes glowed brighter. It lowered its head and swung it side-to-side, the sharp tips of its horns glinting wickedly. Tam's throat went dry. Slowly, he circled to the left, turning the animal away from Jennet and giving himself room to fight. The bull followed, pivoting to keep those eerie eyes focused on him.

The bunching of enormous muscles was his only warning. The beast charged, an explosion of deadliness hurtling right at Tam. He threw himself into a tumbling roll, trying not to stab himself on his naked blade as sharp hooves flashed by. Jennet gasped, but he couldn't spare her a glance.

He took his sword in both hands and swung, scoring a deep gash along the animal's flank. It bellowed and turned, nicking Tam's arm with its horn. The sharp tip punctured his armor, tearing a rent in the silvery plate. He felt the sting of blood, beneath. This was not good. So far, his armor had proven impervious to anything

Feyland threw at him. Why did it have to fail him now?

"Get *off!*" he heard Jennet cry, behind him.

No time to turn and see what was going on - the fiery-eyed beast was preparing to charge him again. The bull pawed the ground, once, then rushed forward. Damn, that thing was fast.

Tam darted to the side, and heard the swish of air by his ear as the horn narrowly missed gouging him. He made another quick stab with his sword, but the beast was getting smarter now. The next pass, or the next, Tam wouldn't be able to jump clear in time.

Brute force wasn't the answer. He was way overmatched in that arena. So, what did he have? Brains and agility - and high time he started using them. As the animal gathered itself to charge him once more, Tam sheathed his sword and slipped his shield from his arm.

"Tam - what are you doing?" Jennet called, fear sharpening her voice.

There wasn't time to reassure her. He held the shield out to one side, as far from his body as he could, and waved it up and down.

"Come on," he murmured. "Go for the shiny."

The beast snorted and plunged forward - but this time it aimed for the shield. Tam waited, heartbeat crashing in his ears. At the last second, he dropped the decoy and leaped as the animal rushed past. His outstretched hands touched hide and horn, and he scrabbled desperately for a handhold.

His right hand closed over the bull's horn, but he

only had a moment more to get himself up, away from those deadly hooves. With a harsh grunt, he flung his leg up, feeling like his back was about to break from the angle. For a sickening second he dangled there, half-suspended on the side of the bull. Then he managed to grab a tuft of hair, enough to keep him from sliding off. The beast swung its head, trying to find him, and the motion was enough to propel him onto its back.

Tam pulled himself upright and clamped his legs around the animal, hard. He only had a heartbeat before it figured out he was aboard. Praying he wouldn't be bucked off, he slid his sword out of its scabbard. He grasped the hilt in both hands, took a deep breath, and poised the blade, point-down, right above the beast's spine.

"Halt!" the sprite cried. She rose into the air, tattered clothing whirling about her, and flung her arms wide.

Tam felt his muscles lock. Beneath him, the bull went still as a stone. To one side, Jennet stood frozen, too, her hands outstretched.

"Sword, speed away," the sprite said.

With a twitch of her fingers, Tam's blade spun from his grasp. It fell harmlessly into the grasses, gleaming among the blue flowers.

"Knight, dismount."

Another twitch, and Tam was sent tumbling to the ground. At least his paralysis was broken. He hastily stood, grabbed his sword, then hurried over to Jennet.

"Release her," he said.

The sprite wrinkled her nose, then slowly lowered her arms, and Jennet pulled in a gasping breath. Tam was glad to see that the bull was still under the sprite's spell.

"We won," Jennet said. She turned to the sprite, who still hovered in mid-air. "Admit it - we won."

"Yon Knight carried the day," the sprite said. "I concede the victory to you, mortals."

She snapped her fingers, and the bull shook, as though dislodging flies. It let out a low moo, but didn't look like it was going to charge. Still, Tam wasn't putting his sword away.

"Your shield." Jennet went and retrieved the trampled metal.

She held it up and examined the deep dents. Tam suppressed a shiver. Good thing it had been the shield, not him under those hooves.

The sprite snapped her fingers again, and in an eye-blink the shield was smooth and unmarred. Without a word, Jennet handed it over. He strapped it on, then turned to the sprite.

"Tell us," he said, "Which way to the Bright King's court?"

The creature cartwheeled through empty air and landed on the bull's back, then sent them a jaunty smile.

"Through the gate, of course."

"Which gate?" Jennet sounded exasperated.

"Why, that one." The sprite pointed past their shoulders. "Farewell, brave adventurers."

She gave a shrill whistle, and the fire-eyed bull

lumbered away, back down the hill. Tam was glad to have those horns headed in the opposite direction.

"Annoying little thing," Jennet said. "At least she wasn't lying about the gate."

Tam turned, to discover another fence had materialized right behind them. He and Jennet stood before a gate that looked identical to the last one they had passed through—except this one was secured by a golden latch.

"Ready?" he asked.

She nodded, and he lifted the latch and pushed the gate open.

Beyond lay an orchard in full flower, rows of trees planted in orderly lines, with emerald grass between. White drifts of petals scattered over the ground, and a sweet smell filled the air. It seemed a little too peaceful.

"A nice change from the fields," Jennet said.

"It still doesn't look like the Bright Court." He stepped forward, one wary hand on his sword.

"Things usually come in threes in the Realm of Faerie," she said. "This should be the last test."

He glanced around, eyeing the insects buzzing among the blooms. "So, what is it this time? Killer bees?"

"I hope not." She cast a suspicious look at the bees. "Are their eyes glowing?"

He stepped over to the nearest tree and drew down a bough, inspecting the insects. After a moment he shook his head.

"They seem ordinary," he said, gently releasing the

branch. Dislodged blossoms fell around him like snow.

She grinned at him. "You've got petals in your hair."

So did she—bright stars of flowers that crowned her like a princess.

"My new look," he said. "It accents my warrior-like qualities. Besides, I'm not the only one with tree litter on me."

She glanced down, then brushed at her vest. Not that it would help—petals drifted all around them, eddying in the slight breeze.

"You're not allergic, I hope," he said, starting down the row.

"Luckily, no. A sneezing fit would really mess with my aim." He could hear the smile in her voice. "Tam— you totally won that last fight. I was trying to help, and that dumb sprite kept jumping on me and pulling my hair. I couldn't even get my bow out. Nice job."

"Hey, I'm a Knight. It's what I do." He shrugged, though her words kindled a glow inside him.

"You know—"

"Hold up." He lifted one hand. "Do you hear something?"

Faint clucking and chirping sounds filtered through the drowsy hum of the bees.

"Yeah." She cocked her head. "Birds, maybe?"

"This way," he said, ducking under the trees to their right.

Jennet followed, matching his quiet footsteps. Three rows over, they found the source of the noise. A flock of speckled chickens browsed on the green grass, with a few white pigeons mixed in. The birds seemed oblivious to their presence—though they had the same freaky glowing eyes as the horses and cows.

"Now what?" she said at his shoulder. "We battle a flock of birds? This could get messy."

Something moved beside the trunk of a nearby tree. Tam whirled, to see an old woman in a gray cloak step forward.

"Is it battle you seek?" she asked, her voice low and raspy.

"Actually," Jennet said, "we seek the court of the Bright King."

"It lies ahead—but you may not pass."

"I think we *will* pass." Tam set his hand to his sword.

"A foolish choice," the old woman said with a sigh. "Not unexpected, when dealing with mortals."

She reached beneath her cloak and drew out a handful of something, then scattered it with one quick move. Golden seeds sparkled in the sun, settling like bright sequins on the grass. The fowl hurried over to peck furiously at their feed. A moment later, they erupted into flight—heading straight for Tam and Jennet.

He stepped forward and pulled his sword, feeling a little absurd. How was he supposed to fight a flock of chickens? All sense of humor fled, however, as the birds buffeted him. Their sharp claws were outstretched, scratching along his armor. One chicken flew right for his face, and he hoisted his shield, battering the bird down.

He swept his blade in wide arcs, and feathers scattered in the warm air. The birds squawked loudly, but were surprisingly good at avoiding his sword. From the corner of his eye, he caught a flash of dusty red leaping into the air. A fox! Or... was that Jennet?

There wasn't time to be sure—the birds were coming at him even faster. He hit them with his shield, ducking away from their vicious claws and beaks. The fox was darting and jumping, leaving a growing pile of limp feathered bodies in her wake.

"Enough!" the old woman cried.

She held up her hands, and the remaining flock flapped back to her feet. Tam lowered his sword. Beside him, the fox stretched and grew, and was suddenly Jennet. She was breathing hard, but smiling.

"Nice trick," he said.

"Instinct—though I have to say, chicken blood doesn't taste all that great, in human form." She scrunched up her nose in distaste.

"Water," he said, summoning a glass, then handing it to her.

Creating little things like that in-game was easy—it was the bigger stuff that was dangerously draining.

Jennet drank the water, then handed him the glass back, and he vanished it.

"Now, hen-wife," Tam said, "which way to the Bright Court?"

The old woman nodded. "Well may you ask, brave

adventurers—and you have won the right to know. Go on a little farther, and you will see a round green hill rising against the sky. The hill will have three terraces ringing it, from bottom to top. Go once widdershins round the bottom terrace, saying, *Open from within, let us in, let us in.*"

Tam leaned toward Jennet. "What's widdershins?"

"Counter-clockwise," she said.

"Go twice widdershins around the middle terrace," the old woman continued, "saying, *Open wide, open wide, let us inside.*"

Tam repeated the words to himself, committing both the first and second rhyme to memory. He knew Jennet was doing the same.

The woman paused, glancing up into the sky. Then she closed her eyes, as if ready to take a short nap with the sun on her face.

"And the third terrace?" he prompted.

"Always so impatient, you mortal blood," the hen-wife snapped, opening her eyes. "Very well. At the top terrace, go widdershins thrice around, saying, *Open fast, open fast, let us in at last.* And the door in the hill will open, giving passage to the Bright Court. Now, go. I am weary."

She closed her eyes again, clearly done with them. Jennet traded a quick look with Tam, and together they slipped past the drowsing hen-wife. The birds pecking around her feet paid them no mind, though their eyes still glowed with eldritch fire.

"Glad that's over," Jennet said, once they put some distance between themselves and the hen-wife.

He frowned. "We still haven't made it to the Bright Court."

"We will. Look, the trees are thinning out."

The orchard ended suddenly, and before them, as the old woman had promised, a round green hill rose against the sky.

They stepped up to the first terrace. Tam drew his sword and stuck it, point first, into the earth. It swayed, a silver sentinel bright against the green grass.

"What's that for?" Jennet asked.

"So we know when we've gone once around."

She nodded, then reached over and caught his hand. The clasp of their fingers felt right.

"Ready?" she asked, giving his hand a little squeeze.

"Always."

CHAPTER TWENTY-SEVEN

Jennet turned to her right. Widdershins. Hand-in-hand, she and Tam paced around the first terrace, saying the words the hen-wife had given them. The rhyme didn't seem at all childish or silly, as she had feared. Instead, the syllables hung in the air. Clouds began to gather at the horizon, a dark line that made her shiver.

She was glad when they reached Tam's sword. That had been a smart idea, if a little dramatic. Then again, Feyland was a dramatic place.

"Round two," he said, yanking the blade free.

It was a steeper climb, ascending to the second terrace. When they gained the flat section, Jennet took a deep breath. The orchard spread below them, the tops of the trees like fluffy pillows. Beyond the orchard, she could see the fence, and the meadow dotted with grazing cattle.

Again, Tam drove his sword into the earth, and they took hands, facing widdershins. The words of the rhyme tolled out like a bell. As they walked, the wind began to rise, pulling strands of Jennet's hair free to whip about her face. They passed the sword. Clouds were piling up in the sky, a dark bruise reaching for the sun.

"Hurry," she breathed when they reached his sword the second time.

Tam yanked it out of the ground and they scrambled up to the final terrace, grabbing onto tufts of grass to keep their balance. Tam took her hand and hauled her up the last few feet, then pushed the tip of his blade into the earth. From here, she could see the far meadow, where a silvery herd of horses raced under the darkening sky—and beyond, the edge of a wood.

Clasping hands again, even tighter, they went around the top terrace, faster and faster. The words of the rhyme fell from her lips, echoed on his, until the very air seemed to be vibrating.

"*Open fast, open fast, let us in at last.*"

Past the sword once. Twice.

The clouds devoured the sun, the air suddenly cold and clammy against her skin. The wind grew even fiercer, snatching the syllables from her mouth almost before she said them. Tam raced ahead, pulling her by the hand. Ahead, the silver blade of his sword glowed, as if lit from within.

She reached the blade a second behind Tam. As she did, the air was rent by a clap of thunder that brought them both to their knees. He stood and wrenched his sword free, and a sudden stillness fell over the land.

"Look," he whispered.

Above them, at the very summit, a seam opened in the side of the hill. The grasses shimmered and melted away, revealing a wooden door. Slowly, it swung open—a shadow-mouth leading someplace unimaginable. Cold air breathed out, scented with age and long-forgotten things buried in the earth. Two tall, hooded figures swathed in mist-colored cloaks stood guard on either side.

Jennet swallowed, fear a sharp tang in her mouth.

"That doesn't look very... bright," she said in a low voice. Whatever she'd been expecting, it wasn't this—a gaping passage leading into a dark hill.

Tam slid his arm around her shoulders and pulled her in for a quick, comforting hug. It worked—probably because it was so unexpected. She blinked at him, and he gave her a half-smile.

"Come on," he said.

He stepped away from her and led the way up the last bit of rise. Despite his confident bearing, she could see that his fingers were tight on the handle of his sword.

As they approached, Jennet peered at the doorway, trying to catch a glimpse of what lay beyond the threshold. She couldn't see anything, just a swirling, heavy mist.

"Bold Tam Linn and Lady Jennet," the cloaked figures said, their voices chiming in eerie unison. "The door into the hill stands open, and our king awaits. Enter."

Her heartbeat galloping like the silvery horses, she moved up beside Tam. Shoulder-to-shoulder, they walked forward into the pale mist.

Instead of darkness, it was as luminous as the dawn clouds catching the first glow of sunshine. Their footsteps were muffled, and the air around them was strangely warm. Just visible through the mist, she could see the shapes of arches on either side of them. They were made of quartz crystal, the pale material nearly the same color as the swirling air.

"I don't think this is the Bright Court," she said, her voice muted by the mist.

"Me either," Tam said. "Do we try one of these side passages?"

"Maybe." She squinted. "What's that up ahead?"

"I'll go see." Tam lengthened his stride. "Another door."

She hurried to catch up, then caught her breath as the mist swirled up around them. A second later it faded away, revealing a tall crystalline arch closed with two richly decorated golden doors. She leaned forward for a closer look at the sinuous designs—foliage and flowers and capering fey-folk.

"Watch out," Tam said, taking her elbow and pulling her back as the doors began to open.

Radiance spilled from the widening crack, so bright that she lifted her arm to shield her eyes.

"Hello?" she called.

There was no answer, just the doors opening wide until they stopped, spread open like shining wings.

"All right," she said, dropping her arm and trying not to squint. "I'd say we've finally reached the Bright Court."

With a deep breath, she stepped over the threshold.

They were there—she felt it in her bones.

Past the doors, the light was as bright as day, gleaming on tall pillars carved of gold and silver. She tipped her face up to see the roof—but there were only waving branches overhead. Branches that glimmered and gleamed, with emerald leaves and brightly jeweled flowers winking between. She looked again at the pillars. No, not pillars—they were the trunks of those fantastical gemmed trees. Underfoot, moss as lush as green velvet cushioned their footsteps.

She glanced at Tam, to see his eyes were wide.

"I don't think we're still under the hill," she said.

"Oh, but you are," a high, familiar voice piped. "In and in, and deeper in, to the very halls of the Bright Court you have come."

"Puck?" Tam turned a full circle, and they were rewarded with the sprite's laughter.

"Can't you show yourself?" Jennet asked. "I thought you were free to move between the courts."

"That I am!" The sprite leapt from behind an ornately carved trunk, did a handspring, and landed lightly in front of them. His eyes were bright with mischief and merriment. "I shall escort you to the feet of the Bright King himself."

"Are you sure you aren't going to just disappear at a crucial moment?" Tam asked

Jennet gave him a look. "Come on—we have to trust Puck. I'd hate to lose our way, after getting so close."

"Make haste," Puck said. "The king's patience only extends so far."

The sprite pursed his lips and let out a shrill whistle. An answering *skree* came echoing from the metallic trees. A moment later, an owl with a pale, heart-shaped face and dun feathers swooped low over their heads and landed beside Puck.

He jumped up onto its back and grabbed a leather strap attached between the bird's wings. With a flurry of feathers, the owl launched itself back into the air and began winging away.

"Follow us," Puck called from his perch. "Quickly!"

"Classic," Tam said. "At this rate, we'll get lost, anyway."

She didn't bother answering, just strode out, trying to keep the pale shape of the owl in sight. They dipped and twisted between the trees, and it was all she and Tam could do to keep up. Ahead, Puck and the owl went into a dive, then straightened up into a smooth glide. She wouldn't be surprised to see the sprite pilot the bird upside-down, like a trick g-boarder. Though probably his ride wouldn't be much amused.

The light grew brighter still, not quite sunlight, but nearly. She shaded her eyes and peered at the roof— though it felt more like the sky. Something was glowing up there, and they were getting closer to it with every step. The vaulted trees shimmered and clinked, and the warm air wafted the scent of roses.

"Almost there" she murmured.

She looked up again, at a break in the trees, and saw an enormous, luminous pearl suspended high overhead on a silver chain. The white radiance was mixed with touches of scarlet, as though a live coal—or stolen bits of the sun—smoldered in the heart of that brightness.

"That's a serious light fixture," Tam said.

Puck brought his owl to earth in a smooth swoop, then dismounted. The owl leaped back into flight, winging away between the glimmering trees.

"Attend," the sprite said. "Yonder clearing is the center of the Bright King's court."

He gestured, and Jennet bit her lip. So close. At least nothing had challenged them to mortal combat—yet. Slowly, she walked forward, Tam right beside her.

As they approached the clearing, she could make out glimmering figures, hear their sparkling laughter. In the very center rose a dais with a throne upon it. And on that throne sat a figure, shining so brightly she could hardly look.

Three more steps brought them into the clearing. They had reached the Bright Court of Feyland.

CHAPTER TWENTY-EIGHT

Pixies flew back and forth, stitching the air with brightness. Beneath one of the trees a long-limbed dryad sat, plucking the strings of a harp. The sweet, yearning melody pierced through Jennet like the echo of some precious thing, lost.

On either side of the throne, fey-folk reclined on couches fashioned of velvet and silk. Ethereal-winged women, more of the gnarled creatures who had guarded the path, a capering gnome—all watched them with curious eyes. Curious, but not unwelcoming, unlike the denizens of the Dark Court.

Then a voice spoke from the dais, deep and rich, like sandalwood and gold. "What bogles do you bring before me, Puck?"

The glow surrounding the throne began to fade, and Jennet risked a peek at the king. He was tall, his pale hair swept back by a circlet of pure gold. Piercing silver eyes surveyed them from above sharp cheekbones. His face held strength, and an otherworldly beauty that made her shiver.

She dropped her gaze to the throne, then let out a relieved breath to see that it was made of the metallic foliage. Plus, the whole dais was covered with glimmering grasses. The ingredient they needed for the fairy ointment.

"Your highness." Puck swept an improbably elegant bow. "I bring two mortals who would ask a boon of you. They have passed many tests to stand before you, and I pray you grant them what they seek."

"Come closer," the king said, beckoning to Jennet and Tam.

Puck moved to the side, making a place for himself on one of the velvet couches, between two of the faerie maidens.

When they reached the foot of the dais, Tam made a slight bow and Jennet dipped her knees in a passable curtsey. They weren't here to fight the king—at least, she hoped not.

"Ah," the king said, an amused note in his tone. "Mortals, yes. And familiar with the Realm, if I am not mistaken. Tell me, how fares my shadow-sister, the Dark Queen?"

Jennet swallowed. "Um... well enough."

If you didn't count the fact that she and Tam had ruined the queen's plans to open a gateway into the mortal world.

"Step closer, human girl," the Bright King said.

Almost against her will, she stepped up onto the dais. The king's gaze was warm upon her, his eyes deep wells of sparkling magic. She took another step. Her heart hammered her ribs, excitement and fear blending into a dizzy rush through her blood.

"Quite fair, indeed," the king said. "Maiden, would you grace my halls?"

"Hey!" Tam cried. "Leave her alone!"

She felt a wrench on her arm as Tam pulled her away. She stumbled off the dais, but Tam steadied her, his hands solid on her shoulders.

"You ok?" he asked with a worried tilt to his mouth.

"I... yeah." She glanced up at the king, who was watching them impassively. "Are you sure that was a good idea? I mean, we need his help."

Tam's face shuttered. "Not at that price."

The Bright King let out a long breath, and the gemmed trees on either side of the clearing swayed. Behind him, the pixies hovered—poised to attack? Jennet fingered the leather wrappings on the handle of her dagger. No, if it came to a fight, she'd use her illusion power again. But she had a feeling they had to find another solution here.

"Tam, he doesn't even know what we want," she said.

The king leaned forward. "Of course I do," he said in his deep voice. "You want what every mortal entering the Realm wants. Magic. Power. And you may have it— for a price."

"Actually," Tam said, "we only want a handful of grass from your throne."

The king raised his elegant brows. "Anything taken from the Bright Court is imbued with both magic and power. Your request is no different from all the others."

"What others?" Jennet asked. "What did you give the Royal one?"

Names had power, and she knew better than to tell the king Roy's real-life name.

The king smiled, something sly in his eyes. The pixies laughed, a sound both sweet and unsettling, like chiming bells that were slightly out-of-tune.

"The Realm holds its secrets," he said. "But if you come and dwell with me for a year and a day, Fair Jennet, I will tell you anything you would like to know. Anything."

Tam's hand went to his sword and he made a low noise in his throat.

"No thanks," Jennet said. "We'll just bargain for the grass, ok?"

"A pity."

The king beckoned to one of his fey handmaidens, who rose, light as a breath, and winged up to the throne. She bent her head close as he whispered something to her, then laughed and made him a bow.

"As my liege wills," she said, her voice clear as mountain water. "I shall return, anon."

She took a handful of bright air, pulling it around herself like a cloak. Between one heartbeat and the next, she was gone.

"Neat trick," Tam said.

The king waved his hand, and a golden platter appeared at his elbow. Upon it was a basin of white liquid and a loaf of bread.

"Would you take refreshment, while we wait?" he asked.

"No," Jennet said quickly.

Her old book held tales of mortals trapped in the Realm of Faerie after they ate a morsel of food or sipped a drop of drink. She glanced at Tam.

He nodded at her, then looked up at the king. "We're not hungry."

"What?" The king's expression darkened. "Do you spurn my hospitality?"

Overhead, the pearl light sent out a spray of reddish sparks. Puck scrambled to his feet and leaped over to stand with Jennet and Tam.

"Your majesty," the sprite said, "they are but mortals—young and foolish. Surely you cannot take offense at their oddities."

The king folded his arms, his face severe. "I am no longer amused at your presence, Bold Tamlin and Fair Jennet. You have told me what you seek. Now I will offer my bargain in turn. For a handful of golden grass from my throne, you will give me something of equal weight and measure."

"Um..." Tam said. "I don't think we have anything like that."

"Wait a sec," she said. "It's a riddle. We have to solve it in order to make the trade."

Puck nodded at her, his eyes bright, but he remained silent. At least she was on the right track.

Tam leaned closer to her. "Great. So what do we have that's of 'equal weight and measure' to some magical grass? I don't trust this. It feels like a setup."

"All of Feyland is a setup, Tam, but we need to make this work. Marny's safety depends on it." She pressed her lips together. "So, start thinking."

The fletching of her arrows? Maybe if she unraveled part of her clothing?

"Right." His brown hair fell in front of his eyes as he dipped his head. "I'm not wearing anything remotely close to grass-like—and my armor doesn't have pockets. Maybe we can summon something."

"I don't think so—the king wouldn't accept anything made in Feyland."

"Jen." Frustration seeped through Tam's voice. "*Everything* here is made in Feyland—we're just controlling avatars that are created from the pixels of this place."

"Are you sure about that?" She turned to face him. "Remember when you first made your character. Did you choose the eye and hair color, the body type? Did you pick out a name?"

"Yeah—the usual character creation."

"Except that it's not. Somehow I don't think you chose the name Bold Tamlin. And I bet you didn't select green eyes, either. I know a lot has happened to us in-game, but tell me if I'm wrong."

There was a stark look in his eyes now, as though he'd been able to forget the dark power of Feyland while they played. But she'd just ripped that illusion away.

"Ok. You're right." He drew in a long breath. "I still don't see how that changes anything."

"Well…" She was thinking through it as she spoke. "The queen was able to take a part of me, using my avatar. And we both know about injuries carrying over. So, our characters have a connection to our real-world bodies." She tugged on a strand of her hair. The answer was so close—she could almost taste it.

He stilled, his eyes on her hand. "That's it. Our hair. We can trade our hair for the grass."

"Oh, well puzzled," Puck said. He made a quick cartwheel, then leaped onto the king's dais. "Have the mortals riddled it out well enough, your majesty?"

"Nearly so," the king said.

His expression no longer held the tint of anger. The dark clouds had rolled away, the imminence of the storm dissolved.

With a gust of rose-scented breeze, the king's handmaiden appeared beside the throne. She held a pair of silver scissors in one hand, and in the other, two finely-worked golden boxes.

"Alright," Tam said. "I agree to trade a handful of my hair for the grass from your throne. Your majesty." He bowed.

The king laughed, like sparks of sunlight reflected on the water. "Very courtly of you, brave knight. But no. Your dun tresses will not satisfy. I will only trade gold for gold."

"But—"

"It's ok," Jennet said. She stepped forward and dipped her knees again in a half-curtsey. "I will offer a lock of my hair in exchange for some grass from your throne."

"Jen," Tam hissed at her. "It's too dangerous. You can't leave a part of yourself in Feyland again."

"He won't take *your* hair, Tam, much as you want him to. We have to make the ointment for Marny. This is the only way."

Puck nodded vigorously at her words, then jabbed Tam in the leg with a sharp finger. "Quiet now," he said. "The Bright King speaks."

The king rose, his silken robes glimmering as though made of liquid light. He fixed his deep eyes on Jennet and she felt giddy, as if she'd sipped something extra-bubbly and dizzy-making.

"Bear witness, Bright Court of the fey," he said, his voice rolling through the clearing. "These two mortals offer a bargain—a lock of Fair Jennet's golden hair in trade for a handful of golden grass from my throne. It is a fair trade. I agree to it."

Tam's eyes were full of worried questions, but before he could say anything, the king continued.

"Puck, prove your use on this instance and bear the vessels of this bargain."

The sprite nodded, then leaped into the air. Hovering beside the faerie maiden, he took the golden boxes, one in each narrow hand. The maiden smiled—

like the sun seen through mist—and opened the ornate lids.

Music flurried through the clearing—the harper was now playing a lively jig. The watching fey-folk leaned forward, or took to the air for a better view, competing with the bright fire of the pixies.

Puck and the king's handmaiden descended to stand, or hover in Puck's case, just before Jennet and Tam. The tempo of the music increased, the harper now joined by a flute player weaving silvery sprays of notes into the tune.

"All is in readiness," the king said. "Bold Tamlin, pluck you a handful of grass. Peaseblossom, shear you a lock of Fair Jennet's hair. Mortals, prepare yourselves."

Tam shot her a worried look. Yeah, she wasn't too thrilled about it either, but it had to be done. She tried to ignore the wild beating of her heart.

"Ready," she said.

The faerie maiden lifted a strand of Jennet's hair with pale, delicate fingers. Tam went down on one knee and took hold of a tuft of grass. Snip—the silver shears cut effortlessly. There was a brief tearing sound, and Tam stood, brightness cupped in his palm.

"Together, now," Puck said, holding up the boxes. "Place them inside, one to each."

Human hand and fey deposited their treasures. There was a flash of bright light, a sudden quietude, and Jennet blinked. The boxes were both closed, their contents hidden, but she had no doubt the king would keep his word.

"It is a powerful binding," Puck said, sounding subdued. "Use what you have won, posthaste, else you will find naught but a collection of dry leaves. Fairy gold will not last the night."

He handed Jennet the box containing the faerie grass. The lid was closed, and she didn't think it would be a good idea to open it just yet. Soon though—once they got back to the real world. The faerie maiden took the other container and returned to the king's side.

"A fine bargain," the king said, taking the box from his handmaiden. He stroked it with his fingers and gave Jennet a look she couldn't decipher. "Now, mortals, farewell."

The pearly light flared again, then deepened to a swirl of gold. Dizziness clenched Jennet's stomach and the world tipped.

CHAPTER TWENTY-NINE

Tam swallowed hard as the queasy light surrounded him. The king was kicking them back into the real world, and he couldn't say he was sorry. If he never entered another faerie court again, it would be too soon.

After a moment, the whirling stopped, and he could see Jennet's gaming room through the tinted screen of his sim helmet. In the chair beside him, Jennet stirred. He sat upright and pulled off his helmet.

"Are you all right?" he asked.

He hadn't liked the way she acted around the Bright King. It reminded him of his own fascination with the midnight beauty of the Dark Queen—an enthrallment that had almost been his downfall. No way was he going to let Jennet succumb to the same thing, even if he had to hold her down and smear fairy ointment all over her eyelids.

"More than all right." She thrust out her hand. "Look!"

There, in her palm, was the golden box holding the grass from the faerie king's throne. It looked rich and strange, even in the opulence of the Carter's fancy house. Knotwork designs scrolled around the edges, and the metal had a soft sheen that seemed completely out of place in the modern world.

"It looks like it should be in a museum," he said.

"I know." Still holding the box, she took her helmet off. Her shorn piece of hair just brushed her cheek. "Should we open it?"

"Let's get everything together for the ointment, first."

He fished in his pocket and pulled out the plastic bag, which was a little crumpled from riding around with him all morning. Inside, the four-leaf clover lay, limp as a dead thing. But it would still work—it had to.

Jennet gave the wilted clover a doubtful look. "All right. I have everything else in my bathroom. We can make the ointment in there."

He glanced at the clock in the corner, hoping the day hadn't flown while they were in-game. He'd hate to have to explain to Jennet's dad why he was locked in the bathroom with her.

He blinked at the readout, then turned to Jennet. "Is your clock set right?"

"Of course." She looked over to it, and her eyes widened. "Really? All of that only took an hour?"

"Time's funny in-game, we both know that." Though this was severely weirder than usual.

She let out a breath. "We have plenty of time to make the ointment and get back to Marny before school's out. Come on."

She led the way down the hall, the plush carpet

muffling their footsteps. Halfway to the main stairs, she turned left and opened the first door.

"It's a little messy," she said. "Hold on a sec."

Tam trailed her into a bathroom that was as big as his living room-slash-bedroom at home. Dark-veined marble floors were softened with fancy patterned rugs, and there was a long countertop with two sinks. The counter was cluttered with girly stuff—mysterious bottles of pink and orange liquids, hair bands and barrettes, tubes of who-knew-what. The air smelled of soap, and flowers. Two hairbrushes and a comb lay next to one of the sinks, which seemed like more than enough.

He looked at her fine, pale hair for a moment. Well, maybe she needed two hairbrushes and a comb—what did he know? No question she had the prettiest hair he'd ever seen. The Bright King had certainly thought it a fair trade for magical faerie grass. The thought made him scowl.

"Don't worry," she said, her anxious smile reflected in the mirror. "I'll get this cleared away."

"It's fine," he said. "I was just thinking about something else."

Like how he'd wanted to charge at the king with his sword drawn. Probably not the best move, but it would have been momentarily satisfying.

Jennet swept a bunch of her stuff into the drawers beside the sink. She swiped the counter with a fluffy white towel, then pulled open a cabinet concealed by one of the mirrors. Taking out a few items, she lined them up on the counter—a jar of tiny green leaves, another full of curly orange petals, and a container of knobby nuts.

"Our ingredients. Thyme, marigold, and hazelnut." Carefully, she set the golden box beside them. "And grass from a faerie throne."

Hard won, too. Was it worth the cost?

Tam laid his four-leaf clover bag on the counter. "That's everything," he said. "Now what?"

"Now, we get creative."

She pushed her sleeves up, then opened the bottom drawer and pulled out a white bowl and a weird stick, both made out of marble. She handed the items to him.

"What are they?" He picked up the stick thing—it was heavy, and rounded on one end.

"A mortar and pestle, silly. You use them to grind up herbs. Here." She shook some of the thyme leaves into the bowl. "Grind."

"Are you sure this is going to work?" He set the rounded end in the bowl and rocked it back and forth, trying to break up the tiny green herbs. A pungent smell tickled his nostrils.

"I'm not sure of anything, but we have to try. Now, the marigold."

She added a handful of the orange petals, and a different tang joined the mix as he crushed them into the thyme. A greenish-brown paste was beginning to form in the bottom of the bowl, but it barely looked smearable. He bit his tongue on more questions. Clearly, Jennet had some idea of what they were doing.

"Hm." She pressed her lips together, lifted the bag of nuts, then set it back down. "What's next, hazelnuts or the clover?"

"Nuts? Since we only have one clover." He didn't know why that made sense, but it did.

She nodded and dropped three nuts in. They were harder to grind. One flew into the sink with a clack, and Jennet fished it out. She put it back in the bowl, and frowned at the mess of broken nuts and half-crushed herbs inside.

"Do you have a blender?" he asked. "That might be a lot easier."

"Easier, maybe, but does using electricity for this feel right to you? Besides, I don't want to be in the kitchen, where Marie could see us and ask questions."

"Fair enough." Anything that kept him away from Marie was fine by him.

He pounded for a while longer, then took a look at their handiwork. "It's not very ointmenty."

"I know." She stared at their concoction for a minute, a frown bending her eyebrows. "We need something else. Something to help it stick together."

Tam glanced around the bathroom. "Soap? Lotion? Um, shampoo?"

"Not pure enough. Wait! I know. Stay here—I'll be right back."

Like he was going anywhere. He nodded, but Jennet was already out of the room. Ok then—back to mortaring, or pestleing, or whatever the verb was.

She returned a few minutes later, carrying a bottle of something golden and viscous.

"Olive oil." She held it up with a smile. "This should totally work."

"If you think so," he said. "Let's do the other stuff, and add the oil at the end. A little at a time, until it's the right consistency."

"Good idea." She set the bottle on the counter. "Clover's next."

She opened the bag and coaxed out the four-leaf clover. It mushed pretty well into the mixture, though the bits of nuts were still kind of coarse.

"Faerie grass?" he said.

She took a deep breath. "All right. Here we go."

Slowly, she lifted the lid of the golden box. A soft glow illuminated her face, shimmered over her pale hair. He peeked over her shoulder, aware of the heat of her body, the soft smell of flowers rising from her hair.

Inside the box, the handful of grass shone, strands of spun gold. Like something from an old fairy tale with a goblin and a princess. Hard to believe, but they were *in* a faerie tale—though this was no story he'd ever heard of.

Jennet picked up the grass and put it into the bowl. It glimmered, looking strange and magical against the glop.

"Do I grind it?" he asked.

"I don't think so." She stared at the mortar and pestle a second, her blue eyes intent. "Just a guess, but I think we try the oil now."

"So far, your guesses have turned out pretty good."

He held out the bowl, keeping his hands steady as she tipped the bottle. She poured a small dollop of olive oil into the mixture. As soon as the liquid touched the faerie grass, it began to dissolve, imbuing the oil with a faint but unmistakable golden glow. Then the herb and nut mixture began to change, the greenish-grey paste turning a rich jade color. The oil seeped down, gold on green. Tam felt a faint breath of warm wind against his neck and the sweet scent of the Bright Court swirled about them.

Jennet pulled a spoon out of her back pocket—something way fancier than any of the battered utensils Tam used at home. Probably pure silver, or maybe even platinum. She dipped it into the bowl, stirring once, twice, three times. Widdershins, he noticed. The mixture flared, and he swore he heard the faint, chiming laughter of pixies.

"I think we did it," Jennet said. Her voice trembled a little. "That was… magic."

"Right here in your bathroom." He studied the ointment, now a smooth, emerald-green concoction. "It looks good."

She pulled a jar from one of the drawers, wiped it inside with a tissue, then held it out. "Pour it in here."

He nodded and tipped the bowl. The contents flowed slowly down into the jar, leaving only a slight residue behind. He lifted the glass jar. The ointment glittered, jade green, with flecks of golden dust suspended in the light.

"One jar of faerie ointment," he said.

"Whew. That was a little more complicated than I thought it would be."

She leaned back against the counter and tucked a strand of hair behind her ear. It was the piece the faerie maiden had cut, so a second later it swung free again, brushing her cheek. She pushed it irritably away again.

"Hold still," he said.

He opened the top drawer she'd dumped her stuff in earlier and fished out a blue barrette. Without thinking too much about it—otherwise he'd completely lose his nerve—he gathered up the loose strand of her hair and secured it with the barrette. Damn, her hair was the softest thing he'd ever felt.

She smiled at him, then set her hands on his waist and drew him close, closer, until their bodies were touching. Heart thumping, he bent his head and brushed his lips over hers. He could feel the shape of her smile. He pressed his mouth more firmly against hers, and she sighed.

This was even better than their first kiss, though his nerves still trembled at the fact that he was holding her, Jennet Carter, in his arms. Her breath was warm across his mouth. He deepened the kiss, and her hands tightened around his back.

Sparks flew through him, like the golden flecks scattered in the ointment they had just made. He could stay here forever, in the safety of her bathroom, kissing.

But they had the little matter of the world to save.

After another long, perfect moment, he drew back. "We should go."

"Yeah." She sounded breathless, and he knew the feeling. "Let's go out the back. I convinced George this was a one-time emergency, but Marie won't be so easy. I'd rather not run into her."

"Me either." He could just imagine the scene, if the house manager caught them. At least the chauffeur didn't seem to mind keeping their secrets.

Jennet leaned forward and kissed the tip of his nose, then let go of him and grabbed the jar of ointment. "Too bad the hardest part is still to come."

Tam raised his brows. Seemed like winning their way to the Bright Court, bargaining with the king, and then figuring out how to make the ointment had been more than enough.

"What's that?" he asked.

She made a face. "Getting the faerie ointment on Marny."

CHAPTER THIRTY

Jennet waited for Marny outside the science room door after third bell. The jar of faerie ointment was tucked in her satchel, practically vibrating with importance. She hadn't been joking when she told Tam this was going to be the hardest part. She'd rather face a dozen more fiery-eyed creatures than try to apply the faerie ointment to Marny.

Too bad it had to be put on the eyelids. She'd thought of mixing it with eye-shadow and giving Marny a make-over, but that was so not the big girl's style. And explaining? Marny wouldn't believe them, and then she'd be far too wary.

Jennet curled her fingers into her palms and scanned the passing students. It would have to be plan B, and she'd only get one chance to make this work. She spotted Marny, walking behind a clump of noisy seniors. Jennet waited for them to pass, then stepped out and grabbed her friend's arm.

"Hey, Jennet," Marny said, sounding surprised. "What are you doing?"

"Ahh, my stomach," Jennet gasped, hunching over. "Help me to the bathroom. Please."

Marny slung an arm around her, supporting her. "Don't you think you ought to go to the nurse?"

Maybe she was overdoing it. Jennet straightened up a little. "No—it's only, uh, cramps. I just need a hand getting down the hall."

Marny raised her eyebrows, but helped guide Jennet to the girl's bathroom at the end of the corridor. Once inside, Jennet leaned against the wall and opened her satchel.

"Could you get me a drink of water?" she asked, handing Marny her water bottle. "I've got some pain meds in here that will help."

Marny took the bottle and turned away. While she was at the sink, Jennet surreptitiously opened the jar of faerie ointment and dipped her finger in.

"Here." Marny returned and held out the water.

"Great." Jennet gave her a weak smile. "Hey, what's that by your eye?"

"What?" The other girl rubbed her hand over her face. "Which eye?"

"Close your eye and let me get it."

When Marny obediently leaned forward, Jennet took her ointmented finger and swiped it across her friend's left eyelid.

"Hey!" Marny leaped back. "What the hell? It's all greasy—what'd you do that for?"

"Let me do your other eye, too," Jennet said. "And then I'll explain."

Marny scowled and shook her head. "I don't think

so, Fancy-girl. How about you just explain."

She pulled a handful of paper towels out of the dispenser and rubbed her eye.

"Wait—don't rub it all off!"

"You're insane." Marny crumpled the towels and threw them in the trash. "Now, talk."

Jennet pressed her lips together. Had she put enough on? Would the ointment work on only one eye, or did it have to be both?

"It's about Roy Lassiter—"

"I knew it." Marny crossed her arms. "This is some Viewer prank of yours, isn't it? Tell me, does my eye turn all black in a few minutes? Maybe red dye starts running down my face? Nice try, Jennet. You and your weak tricks." She made a simpering face, and pitched her voice high. "Oh, help me to the bathroom, oh I'm feeling sick. Pfft. Stay away from me, rich girl."

She pushed past Jennet's outstretched hand and stalked out.

"Marny! Wait…"

Great. That had gone tweaked, and Jennet hadn't even explained what the ointment was for. With a deep sigh, she screwed the lid of the jar closed. The next bell blared through the bathroom, a harsh, metallic sound like the caw of an iron raven.

On top of everything else, she was late for her next class.

"Well?" Tam leaned across the cafeteria table, impatience in every line of his body. "Did it work? Is Marny cured?"

"I don't know." Jennet set her tray down with a clunk.

Too bad the school didn't allow people to bring their own lunch, since the food here was pretty much inedible.

"What do you mean, you don't know?"

"Look, Tam, I tried. I got the ointment onto one of her eyes, but she stormed off before I could explain anything."

"Huh." He sat back. "When was this?"

"Right before last period. I hoped we'd see her at lunch, and...well, find out."

"There she is," Tam said in a low voice. "Walking into the cafeteria with Team Lassiter."

Jennet looked over. Sure enough, a besotted-looking Marny was among Roy's usual gaggle of girls. Though, while Jennet watched, Marny rubbed her left eye, and for a second her expression of Roy-worship wavered.

Maybe the ointment was working, after all—though there was no guarantee. They'd done their best, but some of the ingredients had been sketchy. What would they do if the ointment failed?

Jennet chewed her food, but paid no attention to what she was eating.

"Look," she said to Tam. "Marny's rubbing her eye again. Now watch her face."

Tam half-turned. "Yeah—something's getting through. Come on, Marny, you can do it." He swiveled back to Jennet. "I bet if you got some on her other eye—"

"Let's give it a little more time." She really didn't relish a repeat of the scene in the bathroom. Besides, Marny would never fall for that trick again. "Stop turning around. Come sit by me so you can see."

"Alright." He slid around the corner of the table and leaned his arm companionably close to hers.

The contact shouldn't have made her so happy, but it did. Little waves of delight washed through her. Tam had issues, but they were figuring things out. Patience, that was the key. And maybe more kisses...

"Jennet," he said, "stop looking at me. We're supposed to be watching Marny."

"Um, yeah." She felt heat flush into her cheeks as she turned her attention to Roy's table.

Marny was watching Roy with an odd expression. She tilted her head and closed her left eye, then opened both eyes wide. Then she closed her right eye, leaving only the ointment-smeared one open. Her eyebrows rose and a frown slid across her lips.

"Score," Tam whispered.

As if she'd heard him, Marny's gaze went directly to their table. She saw them watching, and her scowl deepened. Still with one eye closed, she tapped Roy on the shoulder, said a few words, then got up and left. He watched her go, a perplexed look on his face. Then the perky blond girl on his other side tugged at his arm, and he turned to her, smiling.

"So." Marny's voice was hard. She stood at the end of their table, hands fisted on her hips. "How about that explanation."

"Sit down," Tam said. "And you can open your other eye, by the way. I promise Jennet and I will look exactly the same."

Marny took the spot across from them. "I'm waiting."

"It's complicated," Jennet said.

"How about this," Tam said. "Tell us what you see out of your left eye, as opposed to your right. Then we'll know what to explain."

Marny's lips twisted. "Ok. Before now, Roy Lassiter was the most gorgeous guy I had ever seen. I mean *ever*. Not only that, he was special. He made me feel amazing, just being around him. Somehow, Jennet ruined that."

"Yeah, by making you see what's *really* going on," Tam said.

"What if it's the reverse?" Marny's eyes narrowed. "What if you guys are the ones playing tricks?"

Jennet let out a low breath. Trust Marny to never blindly accept—though she had been blind where Roy was concerned.

"Believe us or not," she said. "But here's the truth. Roy's been using...well, the best explanation is *magic*, to enchant the people around him. What I put on your eyelid was a special ointment that let you see past the glamour he cast."

"I liked the way things were." Marny still sounded pissed, though there was an edge of uncertainty in her voice.

"Come on, Marny," Tam said. "You always prefer the truth, no matter how pretty the lie is."

Marny frowned and glanced at the front table. She chewed on her bottom lip, and Jennet could see her wrestling with the idea. Slowly, she closed her right eye, and her shoulders slumped.

"Fine," she said. "You guys win. Roy Lassiter is nothing special."

Jennet laid her hand on her friend's arm in silent sympathy.

"It gets worse," Tam said. "Roy is draining the energy from his girlfriends. Like when Keeli collapsed. We were afraid you were next."

Marny made a disbelieving noise in her throat.

"Really," Jennet said. "That time, at Roy's, he was trying it on you. Don't you remember? That's why I got you out of there so fast."

Marny sat up straight. Her gaze moved from Jennet to Tam. "You guys think you're telling the truth, don't you?"

"We are!" Jennet said.

Tam leaned forward. "Let's try this. You've played Feyland, right?"

"Yeah, and hated it." Marny folded her arms. "What's the game got to do with this?"

"Feyland's more than a game," Jennet said. "Remember the fight we had with the chimera?"

Marny made a face. "I've tried to forget every wasted moment in that sim."

"Well, don't. The chimera had two heads. One spit fire, the other poison."

"I remember." The big girl waved her hand impatiently. "Get to the point."

"Some poison dripped on your arm in-game, during the fight."

"So?"

"So, roll up your sleeve."

"You two are severely insane." Marny shook her head. "I had an allergic reaction to something at Roy's. Jennet's making way too much out of this."

"Just do it," Tam said. "Please. It's not like we're asking you to take your clothes off in the middle of the cafeteria."

"Fine. But I still think you're drinking the crazy water." She pushed up the sleeve of her purple sweatshirt and held out her arm. "There. A couple hives, that's all."

Jennet studied her friend's arm for a long moment. The line of five round marks still looked red and painful.

"Come on," Tam said. "That's not hives, it's burns."

"Wait a sec." Marny lifted her marred arm. "I remember, all right. I spilled my mocha on myself, at Roy's."

Jennet shook her head. "No—but he wanted you to think so. Marny, *look* at your arm. Do you actually think spilling a mocha on yourself—one you'd already been drinking—would leave marks like that?"

Marny's brows drew together under the straight black fringe of her bangs. Slowly, she pulled her sleeve back down.

"I'm gonna have to think about this."

"Fair enough," Tam said. "It took me a while to get used to the idea, too."

Jennet nodded. She remembered her own world-tilting shock when she finally realized that what happened in Feyland was *real*.

"You have to stay away from Roy." Jennet glanced to the front of the cafeteria, where he was still distracted by the blond girl.

"Maybe." Marny folded her arms, keeping the marked one close to her body.

"Actually," Tam said, a thoughtful note in his voice, "It might not be a bad thing if Marny keeps hanging with Lassiter. I'd like to keep him a little confused, at least until we figure out what to do."

"Well, you two can keep plotting the fate of the world over here." Marny got to her feet. "I'm going to finish my lunch. Not that it's delicious or anything."

Without saying goodbye, she strode back to Roy's table. The smile she gave him seemed genuine.

Great. Jennet tried to push down the despair uncurling inside her. She glanced at Tam, seeing an echo of her own mood in his expression.

"That was less than flawless," she said. "Now what?"

He raked a hand through his hair, letting it fall messily back over his eyes. "I think, for Marny, we just wait. And the game... can we break into VirtuMax? Can we use your dad's work pass to get into company headquarters?"

"And do what? Even if we hack the systems, or firebomb the place, that won't stop Feyland from eventually being released." She dug her fingernails into the pad of her thumb. "No—the answer has to be in-game. Somewhere."

CHAPTER THIRTY-ONE

Tam didn't want to head home after school—half in fear of seeing Mom teetering on the edge, half because of the restlessness running under his skin.

He and Jennet watched as Marny boarded the school bus, alone. At least she was safe. Lassiter went off with his newest spark—the blond girl. There was nothing they could do about that, though Jennet suggested tackling her and holding her down while they smeared ointment on her eyes.

He'd been tempted, but no. At this point they didn't have enough proof the ointment worked. And even if it did, where did that leave them? Lassiter still had a whole school to pick his victims from.

Tam wanted to spend more time with Jennet—like a plant yearning for the sun—but she had to go. Since Tam had gone into that coma, Jennet's dad had scheduled her for regular health checkups, just in case. Not that the docs ever found anything wrong, but she couldn't skip an appointment without getting in trouble—and they had enough trouble right now.

Not thinking too much about where he was going, Tam ended up at Zeg's. The owner took one look at him, gave him a wave, and left him alone.

It was easy to lose a few hours playing Madkartz, racing fiendishly convoluted tracks that absorbed his attention until, at last, he surfaced. Played out—for now. He set aside the sim helmet and wandered into the front room. Not many customers in the place this afternoon. *This evening*, he amended, with a glance outside at the darkening sky.

"Want something?" Zeg asked from behind the counter.

"Nah, I need to get home."

"Hold up. Marny messaged, looking for you, and I told her you were here. She's on her way."

"She is?" That could be bad, or good. Tam slid onto one of the stools fronting the counter and started messing with the paper napkin holder.

"Here." Zeg put a cup of hot tea in front of him, something steaming and minty.

"Thanks." He grabbed the honey and stirred a big dollop in, since this was probably dinner.

"Anything to keep you from reprogramming my napkin holders." Zeg smiled from inside his bushy beard, then looked over as the front door swung open. "There's my girl."

He came out from behind the counter to give Marny a hug. A bear hug, of course.

"Hi, Uncle Zeg," Marny said when she emerged from his embrace. "Thanks for..." She tipped her head at Tam.

"Let me get you some tea. It's frosty out there tonight."

"That would be great."

She pulled off her fuzzy mittens, then her coat. Without really looking at Tam, she took the stool next to him. Before the silence between them strained into something more serious, Zeg slid his niece a mug of tea.

"There you are. Now I better go check the kitchen. Get talking." He gave them a wink, then headed through the swinging door.

"So subtle," Marny said, rolling her eyes.

"Part of his charm. So—what's up? I need to get home."

Marny twisted her mouth to the side, as if she'd bitten a lemon. "I owe you and Fancy-girl an apology. I guess you guys were right."

Tam sat up a little straighter. "Apologizing to me doesn't get you out of talking to Jennet."

"I know. But I didn't want to wait." Her gaze dropped to her mug of tea. She played with the handle, rotating the mug back and forth. Back and forth. "I didn't want to believe you. When I said Roy made me feel special—well, I didn't want to have to lose that. If I kept one eye shut, I could at least pretend."

"Pretending's never as good as the real thing." He should know.

"It was never even real." Marny sounded more vulnerable than he'd ever heard her.

"Hey. Just because Lassiter was playing you, doesn't

mean you're not something special. It's too bad nobody else in this town is awake enough to see it."

She gave a snort, sounding more like her old self. "What, you're suggesting I need to go to the city in order for anyone to notice me? Or should I leave the country altogether?"

"You're the strongest person I know. I mean it. Too strong for Crestview High, that's for sure. But Marny, you know that."

"Yeah." She sighed and set her chin in her hand. "But I'm tired of having to fight for every inch. Why can't it be sparkly and easy for once?"

"Because sparkly and easy isn't for people like us." Tam took a gulp of his tea, trying to wash down the bitter words.

She cocked one eyebrow. "Do you really think easy is for *anybody*? I mean, from the outside, things might look great—but our own problems cut us the most."

His felt razor-sharp, that was for sure. But was it any better for Jennet? He had some idea of her problems, but, like Marny said, only from the outside. Even Lassiter probably had issues. Becoming the Bright King's tool— there had to be reasons.

"There you go," Tam said. "All the answers again. Quit being so smart."

"Smartass, you mean." Marny looked at him, the beginnings of a genuine smile in her eyes.

"That goes without saying."

She grinned at him. "So, got any more of that stuff

Jennet put on my eye? Going around like this is making me dizzy."

"It's faerie ointment—and Jennet's got the jar. I'm sure she'd be happy to smear you up first thing tomorrow."

"Ok." She sipped her tea. "I get that there's some freaky sort of... something going on here. But really, Tam—faeries? Glittery pink winged things?"

He shook his head. "Not those kind of faeries. We're talking dangerous, mysterious, nasty creatures. I'll show you."

He bent, pulled *Tales of Folk and Faerie* out of his backpack, and set it on the counter between them. One of these days he was going to have to remember to give it back to Jennet.

He paged through, pausing at the picture of Wicked Peg, the water hag, complete with green pond-weed hair and pointy teeth. A few more pages brought him to the Wild Hunt. A shiver went through him, remembering how it felt to be pursued by those red-eyed hounds and menacing riders.

"Hold up." Marny set her hand on the illustration. "This hunt—it has someone blowing a horn, and dogs and things. Right?"

"Yeah." Not to mention a terrifying dark figure with huge antlers on his head—the huntsman that led the pack.

Her brows drew together. "About a month ago, around Halloween, there was some creepy stuff going on, late at night. Don't tell me you didn't hear it, too—though it was during the time you'd, um, gone missing for a few days. Anyway, I asked Jennet about it, and she was pretty evasive."

Tam wrapped his hands tightly around his mug of tea. "That was the Wild Hunt."

The eerie sounds had echoed over the Exe, waking him from a fitful sleep. At first he'd been sure the hunt was after him—but when they moved off, he knew they were seeking Jennet. That had been a rough night.

Marny tapped the page with her finger. "So, somehow the things in here are coming to life?"

"Not exactly. Feyland is based on the book and, well, it's like a gateway. It's connected to the Realm of Faerie, and the realm is breaking through, affecting real life."

He expected Marny to slam the book closed and shove it back at him, reacting with the same disbelief he had when Jennet first tried to explain. But to her credit, Marny pursed her lips and drew *Tales of Folk and Faerie* closer, flipping slowly through the pages.

"Who's this?" she asked, tilting the page so he could see.

The midnight gaze of the Dark Queen stared back at him—stars snared in her hair, her dress wisps of cloud and moonlight. Tam's breath caught in his throat. For a moment he smelled roses, tasted burnt sugar on his tongue. A terrible yearning swamped him, followed by the icy touch of fear. He was done with the Dark Queen.

Wasn't he?

"Hello—Tam?" Marny waved her hand in front of his eyes.

He yanked his gaze from the book. "Yeah, sorry. Um, that's the Dark Queen."

"Hm." She gave him a considering look, but didn't push it. She was good at knowing when to back off. "Feyland truly is affecting the real world? My arm, and whatever's with Roy? And… the stuff going on with you and Jennet last month, right? That, may I say, almost killed you."

"Yeah, basically." He scrubbed his fingers through his hair.

"So—what are we going to do?"

He studied her a moment. It would be good to have Marny on the team—but she didn't like to sim, and she still didn't understand everything that was going on. Not that he did, but at least he and Jennet had more to go on.

He looked out the windows. Night had fallen, the pale orange streetlights doing little to push back the dense darkness. "I need to get home. We can fix up your eye and talk more tomorrow."

"Ok."

He grabbed Jennet's book and tucked it in his pack, then slid off the stool and headed for the door.

"Hey, Tam."

"Yeah?" He turned, to see Marny's concerned expression.

"Be careful."

"I always am."

As careful as he could be, living in the Exe. Not to mention fighting off evil faeries that wanted to take over the world.

Still, he paid extra attention making his way home. The back of his neck prickled, like something was watching him, but no fey creatures rushed at him out of the night.

The yellow light coming from their windows cheered him more than he wanted to admit, and he took the stairs two at a time. Inside, it was reasonably warm, and smelled of frying synthi-meat. The Bug leaped on him, and Mom smiled from the kitchen. Everything was all right.

So why did he have the feeling serious trouble was just waiting to break loose?

CHAPTER THIRTY-TWO

"Your father has arrived home," HANA said, interrupting Jennet's homework. *"He requires your presence in the living room."*

Great. "Tell him I'll be down in a minute."

After a short pause, HANA said, *"I have notified him."*

When Jennet reached the living room, her dad was sitting on the couch. He looked tired as usual, his eyebrows pulled into a nearly perpetual frown. Getting moved off of Feyland hadn't been good for him. Neither had swimming against the company tide. It seemed the company-mandated psych sessions weren't doing much to help.

He glanced at her. "Come in and sit down, Jen. We need to talk."

She perched on her chair like it was the edge of a cliff. "What's going on?"

"It has come to my attention that you and Tam have been using the Full-D systems. Which you know are off limits."

She swallowed and clenched her fingers together. "Dad, we had to. You have no idea what's at stake! Feyland can affect the real world—we can't let the game be released."

"So by breaking the rules and using the Full-D, you're saving the world?" He shook his head. "I'm afraid Tam's not welcome here any more."

"What?" Panic squeezed her chest. "But… he has to come over."

If she and Tam couldn't go in-game, how could they possibly find a solution? They'd saved Marny—but what about everybody else?

"I can't trust you." Her dad pinched the bridge of his nose. "If Tam comes over again, there will be serious consequences."

"When Feyland is released, there will be serious consequences for every person who plays it! Dad, you have to believe me. Please… just come in-game."

He gave her a tired look. "At least it looks like our hardware is fixed—since neither you nor Tam required hospitalization after playing."

"I told you, it's not the system, it's the Realm of Faerie—"

"This is the modern world, not some fairytale."

"But—"

He held up one hand. "Jennet, listen to me. The company is scheduling the beta-testing for Feyland. And I've volunteered to be a tester for the game."

"You have?" She blinked at him. Suddenly the tables were turned, and she didn't like it one bit. "But… what if you get hurt?"

"I won't—because I'm starting to believe Dr.

Lassiter is right. A couple of the early prototypes had neural interface issues, but the company has worked everything out. And if there *are* problems, I'll be right there, willing to speak up."

Worry settled in the pit of her stomach, like she'd swallowed tar. She couldn't talk Dad out of playing—especially not when she'd just been begging him to. And maybe, just maybe, he'd see she was right. She let out her breath.

"When does beta-testing start?" she asked.

"In another week. Now, do I have your promise that Tam won't come over again?"

If she didn't agree, he'd probably do something even more drastic, like forbid her to see Tam at all. Or ship her back to Prep, her old school, as a boarding student.

"All right." The words tasted sour in her mouth.

A solution seemed as far away as the moon, but she and Tam had to figure out some way to keep playing. They had to break the Bright King's power and shut off the connection between Feyland and the Realm of Faerie. Permanently.

Jolted from a deep sleep, Jennet opened her eyes, but it was too dark to see anything. What had woken her? She turned to look at the glowing numerals on her clock—but it wasn't there.

In fact, she wasn't even lying in her bed, but on

something velvety and way too soft. Fear washed over her, kicking her heartbeat up and winding her breath tight.

Relax. Breathe. It's just a bad dream. Any second now, she'd wake up. She kept her eyes shut, trying to ignore the faint chiming in her ears. *Wake up. Wake up.*

Warm air surrounded her, scented with flowers. Then brightness, red against her closed eyelids. A high, bright laugh, quickly smothered.

Maybe if she pretended to be asleep, whatever-it-was would just go away.

"Fair Jennet, why do you feign sleep, when our king awaits?" The voice was familiar—the sweet tones of the Bright King's handmaiden.

Dread squeezed through her—she couldn't deny the knowledge any longer. She was in the Bright Court. But how?

She took a deep breath and opened her eyes. As she'd feared, there was the luminous pearl high overhead, the fantastical gemmed trees. And the dais where the Bright King sat, watching her. His silvery gaze was fathomless, and a faint smile etched his handsome, severe face. Fear shivered through her bones.

Pushing away the silken coverlet, she sat up. A quick check confirmed she was wearing the tank-top and flannel pj pants she went to sleep in.

She was in Feyland. For real, this time. A cold wave of dread washed over her.

"Welcome again to my court, Fair Jennet," the king

said. "You grace us with your mortal beauty."

"How did I get here?" And how could she get out? She was afraid of the answer.

"As you used that which you took from my realm, so I summoned you." He nodded to his handmaiden, who held up a dainty golden box.

The twin of that box was currently sitting on her bathroom counter. She swallowed, and tried to project a confidence she didn't feel.

"Well, I appreciate the invite, but I can't stay long."

Laughter shimmered over the gathered fey-folk, and the pixies flew in mirthful spirals. She had the hollow feeling she didn't have much choice in the matter. If only Tam were there, he would know what to do. She wrapped her arms around herself and tried to think.

The king had used his magic to bypass the interface of the game altogether—his power was growing way too strong. How was she going to get back? Despite the warm air, she felt chilled to the core.

"You will stay as long as I wish it. Am I not the ruler here? Come, Fair Jennet, and sit beside me."

When he beckoned to her, her body rose, pulled to standing against her will.

"Hey!" she cried, "stop it."

She tried to sit back down again, but it hurt—like ramming her head on a concrete wall. After a second, she gave up, tears of pain blurring her vision. The king smiled in satisfaction as he watched her walk to the dais and settle upon the golden grasses.

Ok, calm down. She took a shaky breath. Her body wasn't under her control, but at least her mind was. And her mouth. Still, it wouldn't do any good to insult the Bright King or rail against him. She had to play this smart, and that included not insulting her host. Yet, anyway. She didn't even have any weapons, so challenging him to a duel was out. It would have to be a battle of wits.

So, what did she know that could help her? Anything about escaping the Realm of Faerie?

The fey-folk loved stories, if she remembered it right from her book. And somehow, Roy managed to freely come and go from the Bright Court—if only in his avatar form. Maybe Roy's adventures would hold a clue to her freedom, if she could get the king to talk.

"Will you tell me a tale, your majesty?" she asked.

The king raised his thin brows. "A tale?"

"Yes. Have other mortals visited your court? I mean, recently?"

At that, he threw his head back and laughed, a crystalline sound that set the bejeweled trees clinking.

"A tale of a mortal in my court? Methinks you do not mean Burd Ellen, who visited nary a handful of moons ago—yet centuries in your fragile, mortal time."

"Never heard of her."

Although... the name tickled her memory. Something she'd read in her old book, a scrap of story or ballad. She pressed her lips together, trying to chase down the wisp of recognition. No luck—it was gone.

"Fair Jennet, I know it is the tale of the Royal one you seek. His reflection is in your eyes, though it is Bold Tamlin who holds your heart."

She stiffened, as much as her body would let her. The king saw way too much. "Tell me about Roy."

"Very well." The king steepled his fingers together. "It was first a disturbance at the edge of my Realm. I sent one of my guards to investigate, and he returned with the description of a proud young mortal questing too near my lands. I sent the white stag out, to lure him closer. When the stag failed, the dryads aided me, closing the forest behind so that the path here was the only open way. And thus, the Royal one came to my court."

She wanted to ask him how long ago, but any answer the king gave was useless in terms of human time. At a guess, a few months. Last summer, maybe, around the time she had gone to the Dark Court. It made a sort of twisted, symmetrical sense.

"He claimed to be a prince among humans," the king continued, "and I took him at his word."

Right. She blew a puff of air out her nostrils. Trust Roy to always claim the spotlight. Not that she was going to blow the whistle on him right now.

"Okay," she said. "Did he make some kind of bargain with you?"

That was how it went in the stories—and you had to be very careful when dealing with the faeries. She frowned, wishing she could cross her arms. Seemed like she and Tam hadn't been cautious enough, trading her hair for the faerie grass. Not as if they'd had a choice.

"Indeed, he did strike a bargain." The king smiled, painfully bright, like sunlight reflected off a mirror. "In return for his assistance, I bestowed on him a small bit of faerie magic."

"The power of glamour."

The Bright King gave her a thoughtful look. "Indeed. I understand now why you desired the grass from my throne. But no matter. The Royal one has proven difficult, of late. Perhaps we shall see what he has to say for himself."

"Wait," she said, her stomach knotting. "If you mean to bring Roy here, it's really not necessary."

Not what she'd had in mind at all. Things were already way too messy without adding Roy Lassiter to the mix.

"Ah, but it is, Fair Jennet. Just as you carry the echo of the Dark Queen within you, the Royal one is marked by my magic, and he has a reckoning to give. Now, silence."

The king raised his hands. Brilliance began to coalesce between his palms, shining brighter than the pearl suspended overhead. The king's control of her body meant she couldn't even turn her head away from the glare. It was so intense, she had to close her eyes.

The clearing grew quiet, the dryad's plaintive harping dying away. Even the pixies stilled, their silvery chiming hushed by the greater magic of the king. There was a flash, scarlet behind Jennet's eyelids, and then dimness.

"Hey! Whoa, what's going on?" It was Roy, sounding sleepy and confused.

Jennet opened her eyes, to see him sitting on the velvet couch where she had first arrived. He was wearing a white t-shirt and plain boxers.

"Greetings, Royal one," the king said. "I have summoned you to my court."

"But it's, like, the middle of the night." Roy scrubbed his face with his hands, then looked up. His eyes widened when he caught sight of Jennet. "Jen, you're here? This is some tweaked dream, for sure."

She frowned at him. "Not a dream, Roy. Sorry to say."

"What?" He stood up and kicked the couch. "Ow."

Grabbing his bare foot, he sat back down. Behind him, the pixies shimmered with mirth, and the faerie maidens laughed. At the edge of the clearing, the harper struck up a lively tune.

Roy looked over at her. "I don't get it. Why are you even here?"

"An unwise bargain between me and the king," she said.

He made a face. "Yeah, these guys are tricky to deal with. Sorry you got sucked in. I should have told you Feyland was, uh… different."

"I already knew, Roy."

"You did?" He frowned. "Then why didn't you tell me?"

"Because—"

"Enough of your mortal bickering," the king said, an edge of fire in his voice. "I am not best pleased, Royal one. Three times now you have failed to uphold the bargain we struck."

"Your majesty, I'm sorry, but life happens, you know? I'll do better next time."

"There will be no next time. The agreement we made is now at an end." The Bright King stood, suddenly fearsome in his contained fury.

Roy paled. "But, what about my powers? I still have to—"

"No more." The king held up his hand. A moment later, a glass sphere containing flickering violet fire appeared in his palm. "This is only half-full, Royal one. You have failed me."

Jennet bit her lip, trapping her gasp of surprise. The sphere was nearly identical to the one the Dark Queen had used to imprison Jennet's mortal essence. The king passed his hand over the glass, and the flames leaped up, out of the glass and into his body. For a moment, he was outlined in a freakish violet glow.

"Hey," Roy said, reaching for the sphere. "I can get more, I swear. Give it back. Just one more chance?"

"No." The king's voice was cold. "Your chances are spent, mortal. Our bargain is finished."

The words hung in the air, then shattered. The sound of breaking glass—the end of a promise made in the realm. Jennet flinched. When she looked at the king again, his hands were empty.

"Um. Ok." Roy hunched his shoulders. "I guess you can send me back now. And her." He jerked his head at Jennet.

"It is never that simple. I am still owed the bright flame of humanity, Royal one. You and Fair Jennet will bide with me for some time longer, until that debt is paid. Now—sleep."

He waved his hand, and Jennet felt her body begin to fold down into the soft grasses of the dais. No! She had to warn Tam. She had to fight the soothing darkness twining around her senses, the sweet lethargy stealing up her limbs. She had to…had to…

CHAPTER THIRTY-THREE

Tam flinched inside his sleeping bag. Something was pinching him.

"Bug," he mumbled, "go back to bed and leave me alone."

"Bold Tamlin," a high voice piped, "you must wake. Trouble is afoot in the Realm of Faerie."

Puck! Tam sat upright, the dozy warmth of sleep doused by icy realization. If Puck were here, something was wrong. Provided it really was the sprite, and not some weird dream-fragment. Tam rubbed his eyes. Anxiety clenched his gut when he saw Puck hovering, cross-legged, beside his sleeping bag.

"What is it?" Tam whispered. "And keep your voice down, or you'll wake my family."

He glanced over at the blanket-covered lump of the Bug, asleep on the couch. The kid was still snoring.

"Fair Jennet requires aid," Puck whispered. "The king has brought her to his court—and does not intend to let her go."

"What? How?" Cold fear sliced through him. "Was she in-game? What time is it?"

The clock in the kitchen shed a greenish glow, and

he squinted at the numbers. *1:43.* Awfully late for Jennet to be simming.

"She did not enter Feyland by the usual route," the sprite said. "The king took her from her bed."

Crap. This was beyond severe.

"How do I get her back?" Keeping one eye on Puck, he started pulling on his clothes.

The sprite cocked his head, his eyes glinting. "That is for you to determine, Tamlin. I merely bring warning. Good luck—and farewell."

"Wait!" Tam hissed, reaching for the sprite.

Too late. There was only empty air where Puck had been, and the faint echo of chiming bells. *Damn, damn, damn.*

"Tam?" The Bug turned over. "I heard a thing."

"Shh, go back to sleep. I'm just going to the bathroom."

He grabbed his pack and retreated to the bathroom. It was dim and cramped—but private. Tam grabbed the taped-together flashlight from under the sink and clicked it on, ignoring the scuttle of bugs away from the light.

When he'd made his bargain with the Dark Queen, Jennet had saved him by using the words of an old ballad. It was time for him to return the favor—and the only instructions he had for dealing with the Realm of Faerie were in her book.

The back section of *Tales of Folk and Faerie* held ballads and scraps of tales that were hundreds of years old. He paged through, his heart giving a jolt at the one titled *Tam Lin*. No—that story had already played out. He needed something different, something about a girl taken by the faeries.

The Golden Ball—no. *The Fish and the Ring*—not at all. He was running out of pages. Forcing himself to go slowly, he went back and scanned the text as well as the titles.

Midway through the section, the words *Open from within, let me in, let me in*, jumped out at him with a shock of recognition. One of the rhymes he and Jennet had said to open the door under the hill. This had to be it.

He went to the top of the page and read the title. *Childe Rowland*—a tale he'd just skimmed over before. The weak flashlight beam wavered across the page. Taking a deep breath, Tam began to read.

For once, the stars were out from behind the clouds, and a thin moon illuminated the frost-covered city. It had taken him almost an hour to get up to the gates of The View. Tam breathed into his hands in an effort to un-numb them. His gloves were half holes, and didn't do much against the cold.

The gates were closed and locked. No doubt set with an alarm. The high walls encircling the development were studded with razor-sharp spikes. He retreated to a nearby clump of evergreen bushes and huddled down, trying to think.

First, he had to get into The View. Then break into Jennet's and get to her sim-system, without alerting the house network. Power-up, enter Feyland, and follow the directions the old tale had laid out. Sure.

So many things could go wrong. He felt sick.

Headlights pierced the darkness, and Tam ducked behind the foliage, hoping his brown coat would help camouflage him. A truck pulled up to the gates, *Crestview Sanitation* written in faded letters on the side. Of course. The maintenance crews would come in at night, so as not to disturb the residents with the sight of their trash being taken away. This was his chance.

He only had a few seconds—the gates were swinging open, the truck's engine revving. Tam sprinted from his hiding place and leaped for the back of the truck. His chilled fingers scrabbled for purchase. *Come on!* He reached up, desperately searching for a handhold.

Right before the truck pulled away, his fingers closed over a metal crossbar. Feet dangling, heart pounding, he gritted his teeth and held on. The vehicle sped under the plas-metal arch of The View. Tam held his breath, but no alarms sounded, no guards leaped out to rip him from the truck and slap him in cuffs.

The truck was going too fast for him to let go now, though his shoulders burned from the strain. He had to get off, and soon. Wasn't there a stop sign up ahead?

Yeah—but apparently it didn't apply to midnight maintenance vehicles. The truck blew past without even slowing, the sign just a passing blur of red and white.

Then they veered around a corner. Tam slammed hard against the edge of the vehicle. His fingers lost their grip, and for a crystalline moment, he was suspended in the air. Flying. *Oh, crap.*

The ground came up to meet him, and he rolled, trying to break the speed of his fall. He came to a stop halfway on the sidewalk. Breathless, he lay there, staring at the orange halo of the streetlamp above him.

Get up. He had to get up, even if something was broken.

With a groan, he levered himself to standing. No stabbing pain, nothing too serious. He ached all over, though, and his side was going to be one big bruise. He was lucky he'd ended up in somebody's yard and not wrapped around the streetlamp. His tumble from the truck hadn't dislodged his access badge, either. Little miracles.

A quick glance at the skyline confirmed his direction. With the city-glow of Crestview on his left, he limped along the street, keeping to the shadows. He'd be able to get to Jennet's. A lifetime of dodging down alleyways in the Exe had honed his ability to navigate to his destination, no matter how twisty the route.

It took him about ten minutes, and a backtrack from a cul-de-sac with wakeful dogs, to get to the Carter's mansion. Their fountain was on, even in the middle of the night. He didn't trust the water for drinking, but pulled off his gloves and splashed a couple icy handfuls on his face to shock away the tiredness. Behind him, three stories of privilege waited, tight as a fortress. How the hell was he going to break in?

The water before him swirled, and for a moment he thought he saw a pale face below the surface. Then the liquid flowed upward, sheening off the body of a beautiful fey woman. He blinked, not as surprised as he should have been to see a faerie in the Carter's fountain.

"Bold Tamlin," she said, her speech like the burble of a creek over stones.

"Uh, greetings, water sprite. Do you live here, in this fountain?"

She laughed, showing sharp teeth. "I am the Nixie, and I dwell in all moving water. Bard Thomas sent me to aid you. Come closer."

She didn't look trustworthy—but he didn't have a lot of other options at the moment. And she knew Thomas.

Tam stepped to the edge of the fountain. The Nixie flowed up to him, cupping his face in her cool hands.

"Give me a kiss, and I will give you the code," she said. Her eyes were deep pools—but he was too wary to fall in.

"Was that part of Thomas's instructions?"

She scowled and her hands curled against his cheeks, her pointed nails pricking his skin. "Meddling mortal."

"I'll take that as a no. How about you just give me the code, whatever it is, and we'll call it good."

Her expression grew even more petulant, but she dropped her hands. Water dripped down his chin, tickling, until he wiped it away with his sleeve.

"Very well," she said with a pout. "I am bid to tell you this. *0173397*. Goodbye, foolish human. You had the Nixie in your hands, but let her go."

With a splash, she plunged back down under the water. It foamed and rippled, then finally cleared. There was just a quiet basin with a few inches of water—no fey creatures lurking in the bottom. The fountain played on, oblivious. Tam swallowed. He'd bet that, with Jennet in the Bright King's court, the boundaries between the realms were stretching thin. Another reason to get her out of there as soon as possible. Urgency beat through him, banishing the cold.

Under his breath, he repeated the numbers the Nixie had given him, until they were solid. He didn't think much of Thomas's messenger, or her methods, but the bard had to work with the dark fey of the Unseelie. He probably had to use what he could get.

0173397. If he were lucky, it was a manual entry code. He turned and faced the Carter's mansion. The imposing front doors stared back at him—but there was another way in. Nerves jumping, he cut through the side yard and up the plain walkway that led to the back door.

As he'd half-recalled, there was a covered box mounted on the wall. His breath filled the air in shaky white puffs as he flattened himself along the wall. Hands almost numb, he slid open the cover to reveal a keypad. With one stiff finger he tapped out the numbers, then held absolutely still—just a shadow among other shadows. *Please, open.*

After a heart-clenching second, he heard the click of the interior lock releasing. He gave a gentle push, and the door swung open into the soft, warm dark. Tam slipped inside and pressed the door closed behind him, moving as noiselessly as possible. As long as HANA didn't open her big mouth, he should be ok. He didn't think she would, though—she'd never addressed him directly.

But would she wake up Jennet's dad or the housekeeper? Or was she on her downtime—if house networks even had such a thing. Either way, he had to keep going. He clicked on the flashlight, the dim yellow beam making the house seem like a foreign country he'd never set foot in before. Quietly, he crept up the staircase, then padded along the corridor.

The door to Jennet's bathroom was slightly ajar, and he could see the golden box reflected in the mirror. It was glowing. Swallowing hard, he hurried past.

He took a right at the main hall, then down to the end—the game room. He kept himself from sprinting the final few feet. Slow and easy.

Tam silently closed the door behind him and locked it. The flashlight beam glinted off the Full-D systems, which looked menacing without the lights on. The jammer box hummed nearby. He flipped the switch, sending the blocking signals into the air. There—that would help with HANA, too. Letting out a deep breath, he slid into the chair and geared up.

One knight in shining armor, on the way.

CHAPTER THIRTY-FOUR

The golden light of Feyland swirled around him, and Tam held the image of the Bright Court in his mind. *Take me there*, he thought fiercely. The usual queasiness faded, and he felt solid ground under his feet. Had he done it? He opened his eyes.

Relief washed through him. He was standing in the middle of the faerie ring that led to the Bright Court. He never thought he'd be so happy to see those poisonous white-flecked mushrooms again. With one hand resting on his sword, he jumped over the ring and hurried down the path.

No twiggy guards blocking his way this time, no bright pixies flashing through the trees—which was just fine by him. As soon as the forest thinned out, he started jogging, pushing his pace. It was day here—it was probably always daytime, just as the Dark Court was in perpetual midnight.

Before long, he reached the fence line that marked the first field. He climbed quickly over the stile, then stopped in surprise. The herd of flame-eyed horses stood before him, waiting. With a whinny, the leader tossed his head and bent, indicating that Tam should mount.

"Nice," Tam said, swinging up and taking a firm grip on the rough, silver mane. "This is going to help a lot—I appreciate it."

The horse's muscles bunched as he leapt into movement. They were going so fast, the grasses and flowers blurred past like an old-fashioned painting. When they reached the silver-latched gate, the steed didn't hesitate. Tam had only a second to brace himself when it was clear they weren't going to stop. Four hooves left the earth as the horse jumped up and over the gate. For a moment, Tam swore they were flying.

The horse landed lightly, then resumed his wild pace. A moment later, they galloped past the black cows. The spritely cow-herd waved from her perch on the largest animal's back, and the bull lifted its head briefly, coal-bright eyes glowing.

As they approached the gold-latched gate, Tam hung on tight. Sure enough, his mount leaped that gate as well, white petals scattering as they landed in the orchard. The horse pounded between the rows of trees. Tam leaned low over his mount's neck to keep the branches from scraping him off.

Speckled chickens scattered, squawking, as Tam and the silver horse tore through. The hen-wife shook her fist, and the horse neighed, the sound suspiciously like laughter. Then they were past, and a round green hill rose into the sky—but the ride wasn't over yet.

The horse leaped, ascending the first terrace, the second, the third. At the very top of the hill, the door to the Bright Court stood open. Tam tried to untangle his fingers from the horse's mane so he could dismount, but his hands were stuck fast. Guess he wasn't getting off until his mount wanted him to.

Indeed, the silver horse didn't slow, but pounded through the door, straight into the warm misty corridors beneath the hill. It wasn't until they reached the ornate golden doors leading to the heart of the king's court that Tam's mount slowed. The horse came to a halt and bobbed his head, and Tam found that this time he could let go. He slid off, and a moment later, the white-haired man stood before him.

"Make haste," the horse-man said. "Thy lady lies within."

"I don't know how I can repay you," Tam said.

The man smiled, his eyes flashing silver. "Restore the balance, mortal. Farewell."

Before Tam could ask what he'd meant, the man transformed back into a horse. White flames glimmering about his feet, he pivoted and galloped away, leaving Tam to face the Bright Court—alone.

The golden doors slowly swung open, the brightness beyond making him narrow his eyes. Alright then. Time to get Jennet out of there.

The gemmed trees shimmered as he passed, the emeralds and rubies winking, bright shards of green and red. Hand to his sword, Tam walked light-footed over the velvet mosses. Not that there was any hope his coming was a secret.

Harp music drifted through the glittering forest, and he caught the flash of pixies up ahead. Almost there. His stomach flipped in fear.

This was worse than facing the Dark Queen. At least he and Jennet had fought that battle together. This time, everything was on him.

The light brightened, the radiance of the pearl illuminating the clearing. Just as before, there was the bright dais with its damn golden grass. He'd known that trading Jennet's hair had been a mistake.

The throne was empty. He darted a quick glance around. Was this a trap? Nothing leaped out at him, and he forced himself to keep walking, despite the prickling on the back of his neck.

To either side of the throne were the silken velvet couches. And lying on one of them—Jennet.

He missed a step, then ran forward into the eerie emptiness of the Bright Court. Jennet was pale and beautiful, and looked oddly out of place in her modern clothing. Her eyes were closed, and he couldn't tell if she was breathing.

Tam fell to his knees beside the couch.

Please, just be asleep. He laid his hand on her cheek. Her skin was warm, and the horrible fear clawing its way through him backed down a little. She wasn't dead.

"Jennet, wake up," he said, stroking her hair. She didn't move, didn't give any sign that she'd heard him.

He shook her shoulder, called her name, tried to lift her up. None of it worked. She was in some kind of magical sleep.

Heart pounding, he glanced around the clearing. The golden tray with the food the king had offered them caught his eye. Could he dash the milk in Jennet's face? What could he do to wake her up?

An old vid he'd seen as a kid flashed through his mind. There had been a princess, enchanted into sleep, and a prince who had fought to save her. He'd woken the sleeping princess with... ah, yeah. A kiss.

Slowly, Tam bent over her still form, and brushed his lips against hers. *Come on, Jennet, wake up.* She stirred, then seemed to fall back into dark dreaming.

Again he kissed her, this time pressing his mouth more firmly over hers, printing the shape of her lips on his. She murmured, and he pulled back, barely breathing. *Wake up.*

No—she grew still and quiet again. Hot grief tried to well through him, but he forced it down. He was going to wake her. No way the Bright King was winning this one.

Tam gathered her in his arms and, holding her hard against him, pressed his lips to hers once more. Urgent and breathless, gave her a desperate kiss. *I love you, Jennet. I love you.* The words he could never say, ringing through him.

Her arms came around his shoulders, her lips moved under his, and it was like a firework detonated inside him. Loud and bright and stunning, swamping his senses, shining into his soul.

It was hard, breaking the kiss. He wanted it to go on and on—but they had to get out of Feyland.

Her eyelids fluttered open and she gave him a smile that nearly broke his heart.

"Tam. I knew you'd come."

"Don't scare me like that." He buried his face in her hair, breathing in the scent of her.

"What about Roy?" She turned her head, scanning the silent court.

"Lassiter? What do you mean?" Had Puck somehow alerted him, too? Had he come to try and save Jennet? The thought scraped uncomfortably.

"The king brought him here," Jennet said. "You didn't see Roy anywhere?"

"No—but I was only looking for you." He reluctantly let her go.

She sat up. "Check the couch on the other side of the throne."

He stood and scanned the court. Sure enough, another body lay on the second couch, partially obscured by silken covers. He walked over and flipped the golden silk back. Great, it *was* Roy Lassiter.

Knowing it wouldn't work, he grabbed Lassiter's shoulder and shook him, hard. The guy didn't move.

"I found him," Tam called. "Sound asleep—just like you were when I first got here. He's not waking up, either."

No way was he kissing the guy. Or letting Jennet do it, for that matter.

A sudden gust of wind blew through the court, setting the jeweled trees clinking. The faint sound of chimes echoed within the gemmed forest, then a low rumble, like thunder. Tam hurried to Jennet's side. She gave him a quick, scared glance, and he pulled his sword from its sheath. His shield appeared, strapped to his left arm. Ready for combat.

"Mortal!" The word reverberated through the air.

The Bright King strode into the clearing. His faerie handmaidens trailed behind him, and the cold fire of the pixies darted overhead. Instead of his robes, he was clad in golden armor and wearing a high, twisting helm. He held an enormous sword, made of silver so bright it made Tam's eyes water. He swallowed and gripped his weapon more tightly. This was it—the end-game fight.

"My wrath is upon thee," the king cried, swinging his blade in a furious attack.

Tam lifted his sword, just in time. Metal clanged on metal, with a shock he felt to the soles of his feet. With a quick twist, he disengaged and danced to the side, moving away from where Jennet stood.

The king's eyes glowed, nearly as bright as the sun. He rushed forward again, pressing Tam back to the edge of the clearing. If Tam didn't get on his game right *now*, this was going to be a very short fight.

The fey-folk of the Bright Court ringed the clearing—sprites and dryads, the twiggy-fingered guards, and gnomish figures. Tam took them in with a quick glance, but didn't see the one he'd hoped for. If Puck were here, he probably couldn't do anything to help, anyway. This was Tam's battle. *Come on, concentrate.*

Something shiny whizzed toward the king, bouncing with a clatter off his golden armor. Another missile winged the edge of his helmet, and the king spun, sword held high. Sick with fear, Tam watched as Jennet ducked behind the throne. She'd found the serving tray and was flinging the contents at the king.

The goblet was next. White liquid flew in an arc, spattering the ground. This was his chance. Tam darted forward. He slammed his shield against his opponent's sword arm, then thrust at the king's chest. The king staggered, and a small, fierce flame lit within Tam. Yes— he could do this.

A spoon whirled through the air to ping against the king's shoulder. It was a small distraction, but enough to give Tam another opening. He beat again at his opponent, connecting with a solid thwack.

The king let out an angry shout and swung at Tam, his sword singing. Tam dodged back, but not fast enough. The blow hit the side of his shield and sent him spinning around from the force of it. *Dammit!*

Now it was the king's turn to press the attack. Breath rasping in his throat, Tam moved backwards around the clearing. It was nearly impossible to get a swing in at his opponent, not while most of his energy was spent fending off the king's heavy blows.

Movement glinted in the corner of his eye. Jennet, her long hair flying, leapt from the dais, the golden platter held high.

No! She was too vulnerable as her human self, not an avatar. She could die in here!

Tam grabbed his sword in both hands and, uncaring that it left him wide open to the king's attack, lifted his blade high overhead. The Bright King smiled, sharp as metal, and pulled his own weapon back, readying the killing blow.

Clang! The golden tray slammed across the back of the king's helm. His eyes widened and his sword dipped. Tam felt a sudden, quick pain in his thigh. *Ignore it—strike now!* Clenching his jaw, he aimed for the king's neck and brought his sword down with all his strength.

Time stilled. For a moment, Tam was utterly certain that he was about to be impaled on the king's blade. Game over.

Then his own sword connected with a meaty thunk. The Bright King let out a cry and fell to his knees, the impact shaking the gemmed trees. The watching fey-folk gasped, and then a shocked silence spread out from the clearing, like ripples in a perfect lake.

Jennet was poised behind the king, holding the now-dented tray. Blood trickled from a cut on her finger, but otherwise she looked unharmed. Tam glanced down, half-expecting to see his armor peeled back like a can opener, but other than a jagged slice on his thigh, he was whole.

"Mortals," the king said, his voice deep and powerful, "you have gained an unexpected victory. I concede the battle."

Relief shivered through Tam. *They had won.* He could scarcely believe it.

Jennet set down the tray and circled around to stand beside Tam. "Your majesty, do you agree to release all the mortals currently held in your court—including him?" She nodded to the couch where Lassiter still lay in an enchanted sleep.

The Bright King rose gracefully to his feet. Whatever injury Tam had given him, it didn't show at all.

"Very well," the king said. "I will free your companion."

"And send us all three safely back to the mortal world," Tam added. It never hurt to be too specific when dealing with the faeries.

The king waved to his chief handmaiden. "Peaseblossom, fetch the elixir of undoing."

She bowed, graceful as a plume of grass bent by the wind, then went to the dais. A chest appeared beside the throne, ornately bedecked with gems. The faerie maid lifted the lid, and more brightness spilled into the clearing, as though a bit of the sun were kept inside. She drew out a vial of blood-red liquid and carried it back to the king.

The cut in Tam's thigh burned—but they had to finish this and get out of there. He risked a quick glance at his leg. Despite the dark slice in his armor, there was no blood. Hard to tell if the injury was bad or not. He'd find out as soon as he left game.

The Bright King strode to the couch where Lassiter lay. He unstoppered the vial and tipped it. Three drops fell onto Lassiter's face, and he opened his eyes.

"What? Hey!" He jumped up, then wobbled on his feet. "Jen, you ok?" His gaze went to Tam. "You too, Exie? What is this, some kind of tweaked party?"

"Enough," the king said, his tone cold. "I shall send you three back to the mortal realm. Henceforth, all dealings between us are ended. The way to the Bright Court will be closed to you."

"But... wait a sec," Lassiter said, his voice desperate.

"Shut up, Roy." Jennet took his hand and dragged him over to where Tam stood. "You're lucky to be getting out alive."

"Heed Fair Jennet," the king said, with a disdainful look at Lassiter.

"Your majesty. Ever will I remember your court. And you." Jennet put one foot behind her and curtsied. Despite her pj's and tangled hair, she looked like a princess from a long-ago tale.

The Bright King must have thought so, too. There was a flash of something like regret in his eyes.

"Farewell, mortals." The words were for all of them, but his gaze never left Jennet. "Perhaps we will meet again—in vision or dream."

Lassiter opened his mouth, and Tam jabbed him in the ribs. The sooner they were out of the Bright Court, the better.

The king lifted his hand and traced a pattern through

the air. Flame followed the movement, inscribing bright runes that burned against Tam's vision. He closed his eyes, and felt Jennet take his hand and hold on, hard.

Then the world tipped and so did his stomach. The pain in his thigh flared, mingling with the sick feeling of exiting the game. They were leaving the Bright Court of Feyland.

He hoped—forever.

CHAPTER THIRTY-FIVE

Tam stumbled out of the sim chair. At least he could bear weight on his leg—the injury wasn't that bad, though pain jabbed through him. He took a second to power down the Full-D and turn off the jamming switch. No point in advertising he'd been there.

He thumbed his flashlight on and went to the wall. There was a cupboard with med supplies somewhere near the corner—he needed to at least slap a bandage on before he left. It wouldn't do to leave bloodspots behind him. Blank wall met his questing fingertips. Maybe the cupboard was a little more to the right.

The corner of the end-table emerged from the dark, banging him right below the knee. He swallowed back a yell and tried to catch himself, but it was too late. With a sick sense of inevitability, he crashed forward, knocking over the lamp and piles of books on the table.

It wasn't a loud collision—but the lights suddenly flared to full brightness. A second later, a screeching alarm split the air. He jumped, his heartbeat spiking hard.

"WARNING!" the house network called. He heard the sound echoing down the hall, projected from every speaker in the place. *"Intruder detected in the gaming room. The*

authorities have been notified, and the subject contained."

Crap. He felt like the alarm was shrieking inside him, just under his skin. He levered himself up and scrambled to the doors. With trembling hands, he wrenched at the knobs. They were locked. Of course.

He glanced wildly around. Could he hide behind the couch?

The doors flew open, and he jumped sideways, trying to get to cover.

"Tam!" It was Jennet. She hurried to his side and slid one arm around him. "Why didn't you tell me you were hurt?"

"Later," he rasped, trying to make himself heard over the shrilling alarm. "I need to get out of here. Now."

Before they got to the door, Jennet's dad rushed into the room, belting on a thick plaid bathrobe.

"What the hell is going on here? HANA!" he yelled, "turn off that alarm."

Silence fell. Tam took a deep breath, trying to push down the fear drumming through him.

"Jennet." Her dad turned to her, his expression grim. "What's Tam doing here?"

"Freeze!" a voice shouted from the hall. "Keep your hands where I can see them."

Oh no. The View's security had arrived. Two men in combat gear appeared at the door, guns out and pointed at Tam. Scenarios flashed through his mind, all of them ending with him in jail. The only thing keeping the panic at bay was Jennet's arm around him, warm and solid.

"Wait, wait, wait," an accented voice said. It was Marie, the house manager, no doubt elated to find that Tam had tripped the alarms. "The Carters are in there! We must not have a hostage situation. This boy from the Exe is very dangerous. Shoot him, if you must."

"No!" Jennet moved in front of Tam. "This is my boyfriend—he was just, um…"

One of the security guards gestured with his weapon, and Tam flinched.

"Move away from the suspect, miss," the man said. "We don't want anyone injured."

"Stop it," Jennet's dad said. "Everyone calm down. This is all a misunderstanding."

"Hey," Tam said. "I'm unarmed, ok? Just—quit waving your guns around, and I'll come quietly." He hoped they'd at least bandage his leg before they threw him in a cell.

"Arrest the boy, now," Marie hissed at the nearest security guard.

"Marie—you are not needed here." Mr. Carter sent the house manager a stern look. "Go reassure the rest of the staff that nothing untoward has happened."

She screwed up her face, as though she'd like to say a lot more.

"Marie."

She blew a huff of air out her nose, then gave a single, short nod. "If you insist, Mr. Carter."

As she turned to leave, she pinned Tam with a

narrow-eyed gaze, as intense and burning as a laser. He had no doubt she would have loved for things to get ugly for him.

Though there was no guarantee they still wouldn't. The guards were jumpy as hell.

"Dad—" Jennet began.

He waved her to silence, then addressed the uniformed men. "Thank you for your prompt response. I'm sorry that my daughter's boyfriend made the poor choice to try and sneak in to visit her—but it's not a criminal act, as you can see."

The guards glanced at one another. The one on the left lowered his weapon.

"Are you sure, sir?" The second man gave Tam a wary look. "I mean, if he's from the Exe, we should take him in for questioning."

"Just because he's from there doesn't make his every breath illegal," Jennet said. "I cannot believe you people! In fact—"

"Jen." Her dad raised his brows in warning, and she subsided. He nodded to the guards. "We can handle everything from here, gentlemen."

"Okay," the wary guard said. "But we still need to fill out a report and take your statement."

He stared at Tam for a second more, then holstered his gun. Tam felt the constriction around his lungs ease. Relief chased through him, and surprise that Jennet's dad had even marginally taken his side. It would have been so easy to get rid of his daughter's sketchy boyfriend.

Mr. Carter went to the door. "I'll accompany you gentlemen downstairs, and we can take care of the paperwork. As for you, young lady," he turned and fixed Jennet with a serious look, "We have a number of things to discuss. Both of you, wait here for me."

"Yes, Dad," she said. Tam just nodded.

She stayed in front of Tam until the men had gone, then whirled. "You sit down right now, Tam Linn. Because if you fall over, I'm not dragging you to the couch."

Except she probably would. Tam gave her a weak smile.

"My leg's not too bad," he said, sitting. Though he had to admit, it felt better not to be standing on it.

Jennet went to the cupboard he'd been searching for—a little lower down than he'd thought—and came back with antibi spray and plas-skin.

"What is it with you always hurting your leg?" she said. "Ok, get out of your jeans and we'll fix you up."

"Uh…" No way did he want Jennet's dad coming back in the room to find him with his pants off. "Can't you just cut them? My jeans are already ruined."

She dropped her gaze to the slice in the fabric. "Yeah, ok. Let me grab the scissors."

He was so tired, his eyelids felt like lead. He rested his head on the back of the couch. What was it, four in the morning? At least he wasn't in jail. Maybe he could still get home before Mom woke up.

He felt Jennet tugging at his pants leg, heard the snip

of scissors, but he was too spent to lift his head.

"Your leg looks okay," Jennet said. "We've brought worse out of game, for sure."

He made himself sit up. It wasn't fair to make her deal with his injury, no matter how exhausted he felt. He glanced down at the gash in his thigh. It started throbbing again, as if by looking, it suddenly became real. He probed at the edges.

"Don't touch it until you wash your hands," Jennet said, pushing his hands away. "Sheesh, Tam, basic hygiene. Here—I'll do it."

"Alright."

She grabbed the can of antibi spray. He couldn't help flinching as the cold spray stung his wound. Jennet bent and liberally applied the plas-skin, then taped a big gauze pad over his thigh.

"There," she said. "You'll be good as new in a couple days."

"Thanks. Got any painkillers in that med kit?"

She dug around, then handed him two white pills. They were bitter on his tongue, but he swallowed them dry. She set the kit down and settled next to him on the couch. The warmth of her against his side felt better than any meds, and he slipped his arm around her shoulders, pulling her closer.

"Aren't you going to ask how I got here, and onto your Full-D system?" he said.

"I don't need to. You always find a way, Tam." The smile she gave him was like the sun coming out from behind a cloud. "Thanks for rescuing me—but how did you know?

"Puck woke me. It was a surprise to see Lassiter in there, though."

"Yeah, for me, too."

He frowned. "Do you really think the Bright King is finished with him—that their bargain is over?"

"The faeries don't joke around with that kind of stuff." She pushed the short strand of hair out of her face. "And it solves one of our problems, anyway. The king won't be pulling any more power from the mortal world."

Tam felt a chill. "At least, not until the game is released. Then nobody will be safe."

What were they going to do? They'd managed to defeat the rulers of both the Bright and Dark Courts—but the mortal world was still in severe danger.

Jennet's dad walked back into the room. He halted in front of them and folded his arms.

"I'd like an explanation, Mr. Linn," he said. "Obviously, you weren't just here to see Jennet. You were gaming on the Full-D system, weren't you?"

Tam gave the equipment in the middle of the room a guilty glance. "Yeah, I was. But Jennet didn't know about it—or even know I was here, until the end."

"The end of what?" Her dad nodded to Tam's leg. "And how did you hurt yourself?"

"Tam had to come in-game, Dad," Jennet said. "I was trapped in Feyland—kind of like what happened to him, before. He was wounded there, fighting to free me."

Mr. Carter's eyebrows climbed. "Do you need medical attention?"

"I'm ok," Tam said. "Jennet fixed me up—it wasn't that serious."

"I'll tell you both what *is* serious. Jennet, did you neglect to tell Tam he wasn't allowed to visit any more?"

"What?" Tam turned to her. "Since when?"

"It was just this evening," she said. "I didn't get a chance to tell him, Dad."

Her dad's expression hardened. "So he was breaking and entering all on his own? I don't think that was a very wise choice. Neither does Crestview Security. They'd still like to bring Tam in for questioning."

"But, Dad—"

"However, in return for his promise that he stay away from you, I'm willing to hold off the security boys."

Tam leaned back into the cushions, trying to look harmless. "Mr. Carter, you don't really think I came here to steal stuff, do you?"

"I don't know what to think." Jennet's dad pinched the bridge of his nose, looking suddenly tired. "I *do* know that whatever you were up to, it wasn't within the bounds of what we'd call appropriate behavior."

While Tam wanted to argue that rescuing Jennet was incredibly appropriate, he knew when he'd lost. Back-talking now would only make things worse.

"It isn't Tam's fault!" Jennet's voice was rough with emotion. "Without him, I wouldn't even be here."

"I'm sorry, but there have to be consequences. Now, please get off the couch." He glanced at her, no sympathy on his face.

Jennet leaned into Tam a moment more. He squeezed her close, then made himself let go. Slowly, she stood, leaving a cold, empty place beside him.

"Tam isn't welcome in your life," her dad said. "You can agree to abide by that—or I can take the security guards up on their offer to haul him in and press charges."

Jennet swallowed, the sparkle of tears in her eyes. The look she gave Tam was full of strangled emotion.

Mr. Carter fixed his gaze on Tam. "Tam Linn—I expect you to respect this decision. My daughter is off-limits."

It was ironic. Jennet's dad thought he might be a criminal, but still expected him to be bound by his word. Of course, there was also the threat of being turned in to the authorities hanging over him. Tam swallowed.

"Alright," he said.

He gripped the arm of the couch and stood, only wincing a little. At least the pain meds were taking effect. It was going to be a long walk back to the Exe.

Mr. Carter gave him a long, level look. Then, with a slight shake of his head, he addressed the house.

"HANA, tell George I'm sorry to wake him, but his services are needed."

"Right away, sir." After a few seconds, the house continued, *"He will be waiting with the car in five minutes."*

"Back to bed, Jennet," her dad said. "We'll talk more about this in the morning."

She turned and flung her arms around Tam, holding tight. He held her close and tried to memorize everything—the smell of her hair, the warmth of her body where it pressed against him, how she fit right next to his heart.

"Now." Her dad's voice was hard.

Jennet clung to Tam a moment more, then slowly let go. He made his arms open, though yearning was ripping right through him. This had happened because he'd saved her, and there was nothing they could do.

Nothing.

CHAPTER THIRTY-SIX

Jennet spent most of Ancient History class trying not to think about Tam sitting in the back row. It was no good. She couldn't just shut off her awareness of him, any more than the moon could stop rotating around the earth.

Every time she glanced over her shoulder, she found he was looking at her, too. Finally Ms. Lewis noticed and asked her to stop fidgeting. Jennet let out a low breath.

No matter what Dad said, no matter the consequences, she and Tam *couldn't* stop seeing each other. There was way too much at stake. The Bright King would twist human desires to his own ends. The Dark Queen would wreak havoc on the mortal world. She shivered, an icy chill settling in her bones.

How could she and Tam possibly stop them?

At lunch, she squared her shoulders and walked back to their usual table. She didn't think Dad would have spies at school, but it was a chance she'd have to take.

Marny gave her a solemn look from her place at the table—clearly she knew the basics.

"Hey," she said. "You better plan on sitting here, Fancy-girl. Or are *all* your friends off limits?"

Jennet set her tray down with a dull thunk. "I guess you heard I'm not supposed to see Tam."

"Last I checked, he's not here. Sit down." Marny took a bite of her sandwich. "Besides, you know we have to talk about what's going on. All three of us. At the same time. Now, sit."

Pressing her lips together, Jennet slid onto the bench across from Marny. She glimpsed Tam from the corner of her eye, coming toward the table. He paused, and Marny gave him a scowl that could curdle milk.

"Stop tweaking about this," she said, beckoning to him.

Tam stood there for a second, not meeting her eyes, then put his tray beside Marny's.

"Ok," the big girl said. "I hear Tam was caught at your house last night, Jennet. That was careless of you guys."

"It's not what you think," Tam said. "I wasn't even in her room."

"He had to come over," Jennet added. "Because of the game—he needed to get on the Full-D system in order to come into Feyland and get me out. Did he tell you that?"

Marny nodded, her bobbed black hair swinging around her shoulders. "And Roy was there, too?"

"Yeah," Tam said.

"Then where is he—still stuck in Feyland?"

"I haven't seen him today," Jennet said. "I don't think the Bright King injured him, but—"

"No such luck," Tam said. "He just walked into the cafeteria. And he's heading over here."

Jennet glanced up, relieved to see Roy safely back in the real world—though he didn't look happy about it. His clothes were rumpled, his hair messy and unstyled, and there were dark shadows beneath his eyes. The frown on his face deepened as he stalked up to the end of their table.

"Well, well." He folded his arms. "It's team Feyland. Planning to ruin any more lives today?"

Marny looked him up and down. "You look like hell, Roy, but ruined? I wouldn't take it that far."

"Oh, I'm ruined all right." Without asking, Roy sat down next to Jennet. She scooted away, putting several more inches between them.

He leaned forward, his words coming low and bitter. "Whatever you did at the Bright Court, you wrecked everything. I've spent the morning in detention, trying to explain why I've barely handed in any schoolwork. Everyone's looking at me like I've turned into a toad. I got in such severe trouble with my mom, she's taking my grav-car away. And it's all your fault." His hot, angry gaze slid over Jennet, then came to rest on Tam. "Especially you, Exie."

"Stop it." Jennet wanted to punch Roy, she was so mad. "*You* were the one who made the bargain with the Bright King. Did you really think it wouldn't come back to bite you?"

"Not like this." He pinned her with his furious

brown eyes. "I had the most flawless deal going, ever."

"Yeah," Marny said, "At other people's expense. How's Keeli doing, by the way? Did you ever bother to visit your *girlfriend* when she was in the hospital?" Her mouth curled with distaste. "I can't believe I thought you were anything special, Roy Lassiter. You're so ordinary it hurts."

"Shut it!" His cry made the nearby students look over at their table. Hunching his shoulders, he glared at Marny. "Like you should talk about being ordinary, fat girl."

She bared her teeth at him in the semblance of a smile. "You said it yourself—I'm different. I'm the biggest girl in this school, and I own it. What do you own, rich boy? And I'm not talking about your fancy toys."

She'd cut right to the heart of him—Jennet could see it in his eyes. His anger was swamped for a second by a scared, desolate look.

Roy was as lost as any of them—probably even more so. At least she, Tam, and Marny had a clue about who they were.

"I know you're angry with us," Jennet said, "but what you were doing was wrong, Roy. Wrong at a really deep level. Can't you see that? Getting tangled up in Feyland never brings any good. Trust me—I know." Her experience with the Dark Court had been more serious than Roy could imagine.

Roy stood abruptly, not meeting any of their eyes.

"Just leave me alone. Stay out of my way—and out of my life."

"Gladly," Tam said.

Jennet didn't say anything as Roy stalked away. The girls who used to flock to him stepped aside as he passed, and the other students rubbed their eyes, staring after him in a confused way. Without the faerie glamour, Roy Lassiter was back to being just a regular guy.

"Good riddance," Marny said, stabbing her fork into the pickle on her tray. "I'd be happy to never talk to him again."

Jennet watched as Roy ducked out of the cafeteria, all his cocky assurance gone. Brief sympathy twinged through her. She knew how it felt to be the new kid at school, and one of the rich outsiders, at that.

"Maybe," she said.

She had a feeling they weren't done with Roy Lassiter.

Jennet was dreaming—or was she? She stood in a meadow spangled with white flowers, the sky a clear blue dome above. The soft air of Feyland wrapped around her, scented with mint and lavender. She'd been here before. With Tam.

As if the thought summoned him, he appeared next to her. His brown hair was sleep-tousled, and instead of silver armor, he wore a black t-shirt and low-slung gray sweats. Her heart jolted with happiness. Sitting with him at lunch wasn't enough—it just made her ache inside even more.

"Jennet." He smiled and stepped forward, opening his arms.

She went into his embrace like a diver too-long submerged, breaking at last into the sweet, essential air. It was almost painful, the intensity of joy flowing through her. She hugged him hard, feeling the wiry muscles, the lean strength of him.

This was a dream—she wasn't responsible for her actions here. She tipped her face up to his. Without hesitation, he kissed her. This was more than the simple, soft kisses they had exchanged before. Fire sparked her nerves as their mouths molded desperately together.

She wanted to climb inside his skin and stay there with him, forever.

"Ahem." Someone coughed, discreetly, behind her.

It had to be Thomas. He was always a part of this dream, too.

Slowly, Jennet pulled back, though her lips begged to stay touching Tam's. She stared into his clear green eyes for a long moment, then turned to face her old friend. Tam slipped his arms around her, and she leaned against him with a sigh.

"Hello, Thomas," Tam said, his voice vibrating her back. He didn't sound surprised to see the bard, either.

Thomas made them a bow, his eyes sparkling. "Greetings, Tam and Jennet. Once more you are victorious within the Realm. And I am pleased to see you have at last reached an understanding."

Tam looked down at her with a crooked smile. "If only the rest of the world understood, we'd be fine."

"Oh, they will." Thomas's expression sobered. "There are more battles ahead, my friends—trials that will tax you to your very limits. Trust one another, and trust those who rally to your side."

Jennet swallowed, her happiness fading. "You have to tell us, Thomas—how can we keep Feyland from being released?"

He let out a deep breath. "You cannot, any more than you can hold back the water when the dam is fatally cracked."

"Then what can we do?" Tam's arms tightened around her. "The mortal world's about to be in serious trouble."

"The way will be revealed," Thomas said. "When it opens, you must take the path without hesitation, even if fear rises up to choke you."

Frustration blazed in her chest. "That's so not enough. Thomas, you have to help us. Tell us how—"

"Already I stretch the boundaries of what is allowed." The bard gave her a sorrowful look. "Do not ask more."

"Can't you at least tell us where we need to go?" Tam asked.

His eyes weary, Thomas shook his head.

"Aha!" a high voice cried. "He cannot—but I can."

"Puck!" Jennet scanned the meadow until she caught sight of the sprite leaping over the white flowers. He made a complete flip, then bowed jauntily at their feet.

"Are you supposed to be here?" Tam asked.

"I come and go throughout the Realms as I please," Puck said.

"Aye, causing mischief in your wake." Thomas gave the sprite a half-smile.

"Tis simply to give you more to sing about, Bard. You should be glad of it. But Bold Tamlin, you speak true—trouble is not far from your mortal world. There is only one place you may turn to for aid. A place deeper than the Realm of Faerie. A place where even *I* tread lightly."

Jennet's throat went dry, but she had to ask. "What place is that?"

Puck gave them a look—more serious than she had ever seen. "The Twilight Kingdom."

His words hung in the air, and the light dimmed as though clouds had covered the sun. Jennet was grateful for Tam's warm, solid presence at her back.

"How do we get there?" Tam asked.

"As I told you," Thomas said, "You will know the way when it opens before you."

"Why do you have to be so secretive?" Jennet wanted to shake him.

"He must," Puck said. "The allegiance he has sworn binds him. Now hurry, this place-between is fading. Kiss one another once more, 'ere the moment is over."

"Farewell," Thomas said, holding up his hand. "Stay true."

Then he was gone, and Puck as well, the sprite's laughter still chiming in the air. Jennet turned in Tam's arms. His lips were warm on hers, but fading, fading…

She was alone, on the edge of waking. A cold wind bent the meadow-grasses and the light took on a purplish hue.

Jennet opened her eyes in the dimness of her own bedroom.

Everything was quiet, with the early-morning stillness that descended in the hour before dawn. The memory of Tam's kiss kept her warm, though the dark shadow of the future was rising quickly before them.

A future that led to a place she'd never heard of …

The Twilight Kingdom.

ACKNOWLEDGEMENTS:

Thank you to the many people who made this book better: the encouragement and feedback of my terrific CP, Peggy, fabulous proof and beta-readers Sean (aka Captain Grammar Pants), Chassily, Marissa, Theresa McHarney, and Brynn. Extra-big hugs to my patient and supportive in-house editor, Lawson, and keen-eyed reader Ginger.

For the absolutely gorgeous cover, huge thanks to Kim Killion at Hot Damn Designs. And for the inspiration to move forward, ongoing gratitude to all the indie and self-publishing advocates out there.

Resources used include: Katharine M. Briggs, *An encyclopedia of fairies: Hobgoblins, brownies, bogies, and other supernatural creatures*, and *Faeries* by Froud, Larkin, and Lee

Jennet and Tam's adventures in the Bright Court were partially inspired by the fairy tale of Childe Rowland. Special thanks to The Baldwin Project for their fine version of the text. http://www.mainlesson.com

Thank you for reading FEYLAND: THE BRIGHT COURT!

Please help other readers find this book:

1. Lend it to a friend who might like it.

2. Leave a review on Amazon, Goodreads, or any other site of your choice. Even a line or two makes a difference, and is greatly appreciated!

3. Sign up for Anthea's new releases e-mail and quarterly newsletter at antheasharp@hotmail.com to find out about the next book as soon as it's available.

FEYLAND: THE DARK REALM

First in the Feyland trilogy – Available now!

FEYLAND: THE TWILIGHT KINGDOM

The series concludes – Late Fall 2012

ABOUT THE AUTHOR:

Growing up, Anthea Sharp spent most of her summers raiding the library shelves and reading, especially fantasy. She now makes her home in the Pacific Northwest, where she writes, plays the fiddle, and spends time with her small-but-good family. Contact her at antheasharp@hotmail.com or visit her website – www.antheasharp.com.

Made in the USA
Lexington, KY
15 April 2014